Prai  r
Mystery Series

"Angela introduces a charming amateur sleuth, fun and well read. She so lovingly describes the town of Copper Bluff that readers can feel the breeze and smell the autumn leaves. Cozy enthusiasts who like Joanne Dobson and Sarah R. Shaber will dive into this new series."
—Viccy Kemp, *Library Journal*

"A deftly crafted novel of unexpected twists and surprising turns, *An Act of Murder* clearly establishes author Mary Angela as an impressively skilled and original storyteller. Certain to be an enduringly popular addition to community library Mystery/Suspense collections, *An Act of Murder* will leave dedicated mystery buffs looking eagerly toward the next Professor Emmeline Prather adventure!"
—Margaret Lane, *The Midwest Book Review*

"Emmeline's shrewd questioning of students and professors uncovers hidden motives and secrets in this clever academic mystery."
—*Publishers Weekly*

"Angela has a nifty talent for description, and although it was still full summer when I read this book, her painting of the South Dakota wind had me shivering [...] A delightful holiday read."
—Betty Webb, *Mystery Scene Magazine*

"Cozy mystery fans will love the small town scene and protagonist—spirited, clever, and very human professor Emmeline (Em) Prather."
—Charlene D'Avanzo, *New York Journal of Books*

"This was a tightly woven whodunit that captured my attention as I had to know what happened next. The pacing was on par with how the story was being told keeping me riveted to the pages as one by one, the suspect pool dwindles and Em is closer to the revealing the killer's identity."
—Dru Ann Love, *Dru's Book Musings*

"Another carefully woven plot by Mary Angela with a tip of the hat to Agatha Christie."
—Christine Gentes, *Map Your Mystery*

"This series is becoming more of a favorite with each book I read."
—Marie McNary, *A Cozy Experience*

"*A Very Merry Murder* is a classically crafted and masterfully methodical mystery with carefully placed subtle clues. It is a gem of a read with its Agatha Christie feel."
—*Book Club Librarian*

"I was thrilled to have found *A Very Merry Murder* by Mary Angela. This is a perfect cozy mystery to curl up with on a cold winter's night. The storyline is a page turner from the first chapter to the last and the reader will be pleasantly surprised with climactic suspense."
—Cathleen Stout, *Reader Views*

"*Passport to Murder* is an engrossing story that will pull the reader in from the first page."
—*Long and Short Reviews*, 5 stars, Book of the Month winner

"If you haven't found a chance to read this series, now is the time. You will be enjoying a new friend, strong community, and mysteries that are exciting and fun."
—*Bibliophile Reviews*

Coming Up Murder

A Professor Prather Mystery

MARY ANGELA

CAMEL
PRESS

Kenmore, Washington

Epicenter Press
6524 NE 181st St.
Suite 2
Kenmore, WA 98028

For more information go to: www.epicenterpress.com
www.camelpress.com
www.maryangelabooks.com

Cover design by Dawn Anderson

ISBN:978-1-94189-078-3 (Trade Paper)
ISBN: 978-1-94189-091-2 (eBook)

Library of Congress Control Number: 2019945114
Produced in the United States of America

To my daughters, Madeline and Maisie,

with hugs and kisses

Acknowledgments

To my dad, a great teacher, reader, and friend. It seems like just yesterday we were reading the Amelia Peabody series together. I miss you.

To my mom, what else can I say but thank you. Nobody could ask for a better mom, sounding board, editor, or friend.

To my husband, Quintin, and our daughters, Madeline and Maisie, thank you for making our home the world's greatest place to work—and the busiest! You fill my days with love.

To my family and friends who've attended events, bought books, and shared them with others, you're the best. I mean it. Thank you.

To the scientists at Sanford Health Imagenetics, especially Allison Hutchinson, thank you for taking the time to answer my questions about genetic testing. People like you make research fun. Any errors are my own.

To Catherine Treadgold, thanks once again for your editorial acumen. It's been a pleasure working with you.

To Phil Garret at Camel Press, thank you for publishing my work, and to Jennifer McCord, thank you for your advice and guidance. It's been a wonderful adventure.

Finally, thanks to all the readers who've found this series and said nice things about it. It means a lot to know I'm not alone in my love for these characters. No matter where I go, Copper Bluff will always remain close to my heart.

Chapter One

"Love is in the air …" I sang as I walked to campus in my cheetah sandals. It was late April, and the night before, Lenny and I had bought a used record at This and That, the thrift shop downtown. The song was "Acapulco," and we'd listened to it over a glass of red wine. I smiled to myself. We did things like that now, and Neil Diamond was right. It *was* nice.

Outside Harmony Music Museum, a burgundy banner announced the arrival of Shakespeare's First Folio, the historic publication that contained almost half of Shakespeare's plays. The hosting museum had to meet stringent requirements for air and light quality, as well as security. Since Harmony housed sensitive instruments, it was the natural choice. For security purposes, no one had been told exactly when the folio would arrive, but now that it had, lots of events were taking place, like today's sonnet writing contest in the Herbert Hoover Library.

I glanced at my watch as I crossed the street. Maybe I had time to pop in and take a look before my first class. I imagined a room full of scribbling students and reluctant professors jammed into the desks on the second floor, stirring up dust storms with the strokes of their pens. Claudia Swift, a poet and professor of creative writing, had demanded volunteers at our last English faculty meeting. I'd sidestepped the obligation with a timely trip to the restroom. Lenny wasn't as lucky. He and three other English professors, including the infamously lazy Allen Dunsbar, were compelled to sign up before leaving the meeting. I cut across the quad. Seeing Allen write a sonnet was definitely worth the detour.

I paused briefly at Shakespeare's Garden, which was closed for construction. Although the garden wouldn't reopen until Friday, I could smell the hard work our Shakespeare authority, Reed Williams, had put in. For almost a year he'd been growing flowers in our campus conservatory, flowers such as honeysuckle, primroses, and violets that featured prominently in Shakespeare's works. Recently transplanted, the bushes and flowers would revive the overrun garden, dedicated by the class of 1923, and so would the new benches and statue. I tried to peek around the barrier, but it was no use. I wouldn't see a thing until Friday.

The campus was beautiful and green, full of life after frequent March rainfall, and I was glad the weather was cooperating with the grand reopening. Mid-April in Copper Bluff, South Dakota, could be cool. Actually, it could be downright chilly. But the weather had been unseasonably warm, and the sun invited students to linger on benches, play Frisbee, and catch up with friends. The lunch hour had passed and with it, their enthusiasm. With a month left of classes, they were reluctant to hurry anywhere. By May, though, they would quicken their step, eager to leave for the summer. Then the campus would change. The buildings would sit empty, the halls would grow still, and professors would be able to catch up on the work they'd put away for nine months.

For once in my career, I didn't have work to do, and it felt good. I'd finished *Words of Their Own* and submitted the manuscript to several scholarly presses three months ago. Now I just had to wait for somebody to publish it. It was an easy thing to do, wait, except when it wasn't. Waiting had given me an excuse for my late-hour walks to campus. Other nights, insomnia was my excuse. But the truth was I enjoyed roaming the campus unobserved. It was the best place on earth for a girl who liked books, liked music, liked to hear people talk. Though I would turn thirty this summer, I felt like a kid who'd gotten away with something wonderful.

A group of students rushed out of the library, and I waited for them to pass before I entered. Among much older buildings, the 1970s library was distinct and reminded me of home. A little dated, a little musty, but comfortable and tidy. I climbed the stairs to the second floor, where the sonnet-writing contest was taking place in an oversized study room. Outside was a locked box where participants could submit their sonnets. I peeked through the slot. Quite a few pieces of paper were inside already. Poets didn't have to participate in the write-in to submit their work, but Claudia had drawn a good crowd anyway. *It must be her subtle art of strong arming*, I thought as I glanced through the doorway. Allen Dunsbar was inside, looking perplexed. It was his go-to look. His gray hair, scruffy beard, and prominent chin enhanced the effect. Maybe he *was* perplexed. After all, he hadn't attended an English event since my arrival on campus, and I was finishing my third year. Maybe he was wondering how long he had to sit there before Claudia let him leave.

Lenny glanced up from his paper. I'd been spotted. I smiled, and he smiled back, his cute dimple appearing as he folded his paper in half. A good-sized man, six feet with broad shoulders, Lenny looked uncomfortable in the small desk. He grabbed his navy barn jacket—the color matched his eyes—from the back of his chair and gave Claudia a salute as he left the room. Then he dropped his sonnet in the submission box.

"Are you checking up on me?" he said, brushing my cheek with his lips.

Though we'd been dating since Christmas, the kiss sent a shiver up my spine. "Yes."

"I like it," said Lenny.

I chuckled. "How did the sonnet go?"

"Fantastic." He led the way to the stairs.

"Really?"

"What?" he said. "You don't trust my rhyming ability?"

I remained silent.

"You'll see," said Lenny. "You're helping Claudia judge the entries, right?"

"Right," I said. "The contest closes at ten tonight. We're judging them tomorrow." Though I was no poet either, I helped edit *Copper Bluff Review*, the small journal published on campus, and Claudia wanted me to go through the entries with her. It was a job that should have been given to Allen Dunsbar, but I was certain Claudia hadn't asked him. She'd performed one miracle by getting him to show up at the event. There was no way she could make it two.

Lenny paused on the landing. "If the contest goes all day, I don't know why she had a write-in in the first place."

"She's trying to build a sense of community," I said. "Great things happen when people with pencils line up in desks. You should know that. You're a teacher."

He kept walking. "Writing's more of a solitary activity, if you ask me."

"I don't think anyone is asking you," I said with my sweetest smile.

"That's going to cost you," said Lenny. He put his arm around me. "You're paying for coffee."

Coffee with Lenny sounded lovely, but I had class. I reminded him.

"Ah yes, your murder club," said Lenny. "How could I forget?"

"It's not a club, it's a class," I said. "And we study romances, too." This was my second time teaching Crimes and Passion: Women Writers of the 21ˢᵗ Century, and Jim Giles, our department chair, said it could become a permanent offering if enrollment kept pace. So far it looked good.

"A rain check for tonight then," said Lenny. "Should we get takeout?" His dark eyebrows rose slightly. I loved how they contrasted with his blond, spiky hair.

Dinner together on a plain old Wednesday. How great was that? "Perfect. I'll call you later."

"If you don't, I know where you live," joked Lenny.

I waved goodbye and started for class. He was referring to my bad habits, including forgetting my phone, not charging my phone, and ignoring my phone. Witnessing the next generation's obsession with technology renewed my faith in the good old landline. I was probably the only person under thirty who had one.

Halfway to Harriman Hall, the building that housed my class and the English Department, I felt my pocket vibrate and reached for my cell. Lenny must be teasing me. But I stopped dead on the path when I saw the caller ID. Los Angeles, California! Surrounded by two stately maple trees, several old buildings, and acres of farmland, I couldn't think of any place more exotic. I accepted the call.

"Is this Emmeline Prather?" asked a woman on the other end of the line.

"Emme*line*, like Caroline, but yes," I said. "This is she."

"My name is Maria Sanchez. I'm the associate publisher at Dewberry Press."

It was one of the small presses that had requested my complete manuscript a month ago. "Hi." I rolled my eyes. I sounded like an idiot.

"Uh, hello," she said. "We're interested in your manuscript, *Words of Their Own*. Is it still available?"

Was it still available? Incredibly. "Yes, it is."

"As you know, we primarily publish fiction and poetry, but occasionally a book of nonfiction captures our interest," said

Maria. "We'd like to add more titles like yours to our list. Could I email you a contract to look over?"

Someone's backpack bumped me, hitting my arm, hard. I gripped my phone like the precious thing it was now—my connection to Los Angeles, California, and sparkling opportunities two thousand miles away. "Yes, of course. I'd be happy to consider it."

Consider it? Who was I kidding? Maria Sanchez at Dewberry Press was a smart, kind, and patient woman. I could tell that from the thirty seconds we'd spent on the phone. Unless she required one of my organs along with the signature, I'd be signing the contract.

"Wonderful," said Maria. "I look forward to your response."

I remembered to thank her before ending the call. For a moment, I stood gazing at Harriman Hall like a lover. Dear Harriman Hall. Even the asbestos didn't dim its shine. Nothing could. Boyfriend, career, spring? Check, check, and check. Life was good.

Chapter Two

—

AFTER MY CLASS, I headed for the English Department on the second floor. I wanted to tell Giles about the call from Dewberry Press and receive proper congratulations. It was almost five o'clock, but knowing Giles and his Midwestern work ethic, he would be at the office well into the dinner hour. The stairs made happy creaky sounds as I bounded them two at a time. With the heavy literature books in my backpack, it normally wasn't an easy thing to do. Today, though, I felt lighter than air.

"*Emmeline*," said a voice, stopping me in my pursuit of a hearty handshake. It was Barb, our department secretary. Her face was as pale as the moon, nothing unusual. She always looked slightly spooky.

"Yes, Barb?"

"You still haven't sent me the syllabus for your 100-level class," said Barb. "You know I need them for my records."

Yes, I knew she needed them for her records, but it was the same syllabus I used every semester. I didn't understand why she couldn't re-file the one from the fall. Records looked like the last thing on her mind. Her office was in complete disarray.

Boxes, copy paper, coffee cans. "I'll send it today," I promised and continued walking down the hallway.

Giles and I had a connecting office located at the end of the hall. His was a nice corner room with two walls of windows. Mine was a small space with a decent bookshelf and small alcove. I couldn't complain. Being this close to Giles meant I could hear everything, but I never repeated it. Despite my colleagues' outwardly composed appearances, their lives were full of drama. Grades, schedules, students, promotions, domestic partners. It was enough to make my head spin, but Giles handled all the crises with aplomb. He was the calm in a sea of troubles.

His door was open, so I knocked. Two men were seated inside. I frowned. My good news would have to wait. "I'll come back," I said.

"No, come in, Emmeline," said Giles. "I want you to meet our visitors." In his well-worn jacket, he reminded me of so many of the professors who had taught me in college: intelligent, genteel, and slightly shabby. His type shrugged off materialism as something ugly and slightly embarrassing. I glanced at my cheetah-print sandals. At least I'd bought them on sale.

"This is Felix Lewis—I'm sure you recognize his name from the program—and Andy Wells, his mentee at Denver. Gentlemen, this is Emmeline Prather."

I didn't recognize the name but assumed Giles was referring to the schedule for the upcoming Shakespeare conference. I, too, was presenting on murder in Shakespeare's plays.

"Good afternoon," said Felix, standing to shake my hand.

As soon as I heard his accent, I remembered who he was. Felix Lewis was the Englishman headlining the symposium. He was giving the opening lecture on *Henry VIII*. His hand was gentle, like his manners, but his brown eyes were sharp. On fence posts outside of Copper Bluff, I'd seen hawks with the same eyes. "It's nice to meet you," I said. "I'm excited for your lecture."

"Reed Williams and I are mates," said Felix. "I was happy to accept his invitation." Though his hair was silver, he couldn't have been older than fifty-five. He'd grayed prematurely, as some people do, in a way that made him distinguished and handsome.

"And you're presenting also?" I said, turning to Andy. He didn't bother to stand or shake my hand. He gave me a dismissive once over.

"A chapter from my book *Shakespeare Today*," said Andy. "Macmillan is publishing it this fall."

I waited for the rest of his CV. He was the type who would recite his résumé in one fell swoop if you let him. Young and smartly dressed, he made our own hip Thomas Cook look old-fashioned. When he didn't continue, I decided to share my own good news after congratulating him. "I just got word from Dewberry Press. That's what I came to tell you, Giles. They've accepted my book for publication."

"Congratulations," said Giles. "That's wonderful news."

"Dewberry Press …. Is that a niche publisher?" asked Andy.

I couldn't exactly say, since I wasn't sure what a niche publisher was. From the way he pronounced *niche*, though, it didn't sound good. "A small press," I said.

"Where are they located?" Andy kept on.

Why did that matter? It was a publisher. That was the good news. "Los Angeles."

He relaxed in his chair. I was no longer a threat, not that I ever had been. He was receiving his PhD from a big-name school and had a book coming out from a big-five publisher. Copper Bluff offered different advantages Andy Wells wouldn't have understood. Giles was beaming, and I felt proud. I was one of the younger faculty members, and to have anything at all published was an accomplishment.

"I don't have any details yet, but they're sending me a contract to look over," I said.

"Keep me posted," said Giles.

I nodded. "By the way, you'll be happy to know Claudia had good results with the write-in. I was over there this afternoon, and the room was packed."

Giles explained the sonnet-writing contest to Felix and Andy.

"How quaint," said Andy.

This guy was starting to get on my nerves.

"It sounds like jolly good fun," said Felix. "I'd like to try my hand at a sonnet again. What do you say, Andy?"

"There's still time," said Giles. "The deadline for submissions isn't until ten."

Andy laughed. "Oh sure. Why not? We're here, aren't we?"

I scowled at the little brass buttons on his navy jacket. But Andy's arrogance went unacknowledged by Giles, who had invested a good deal in the month of activities. From the write-in, to the conference, to the garden, Giles had procured the money despite our college's budget constraints. The First Folio's security alone was a consideration. They had been lucky to find the ideal spot in the Harmony Music Museum. To make it all come together, he and Reed Williams had done a lot of legwork.

"It was nice to meet you, Felix," I said, intentionally slighting Andy. "I'm sure I'll see you soon."

"You, also," said Felix.

"Goodbye," said Giles.

I glanced at my office, deciding against stopping. It was after five, Lenny was waiting, and I had good news to report. I skipped down the stairs. Wouldn't he be excited! He knew how much the book meant to me and how hard I'd worked on it. From medieval letter writers to authors of modern-day romances, each individual I discussed expressed herself in unique ways. In my mind, I had given a voice to the voiceless—women who weren't considered serious writers but should be.

I didn't slow my pace until I reached Oxford Street, where

apple blossoms perfumed the air with sweetness only spring could bring. I inhaled deeply. After months of harsh winds and snowstorms, the smell was intoxicating—which gave me a thought. Maybe I should pick up a bottle of champagne at Variety Liquors? A proper celebration called for champagne, and Lenny and I were fond of late-night cocktails.

I was choosing between white or pink when a noise startled me. I turned to the white two-story on my right. Now for rent, the stately house had seen better days. The porch had been remodeled with cheap siding that made it curve like a bell, and the green-plaid couch sitting kitty-corner didn't help its appearance. It was as flat and dirty as a floor rug.

The noise came from Tanner Sparks, who had slammed the front door. A graduate student in the English Department, he had a lot going for him. While I didn't have him in any of my classes, my colleagues raved about his scholarship and acting skills. He was starring in *Hamlet*, which opened tomorrow. Though I wouldn't attend the play until this weekend, I knew he'd do well. Having seen him play Willy Lowman in *Death of a Salesman,* I knew he was a phenomenal actor. Until I saw it for myself, I could never have imagined the good-looking student as an aging salesman.

"That girl is psycho," he muttered, coming down the stairs.

I kept my head down. I didn't want him to know I'd overheard the personal comment.

"Oh hey, Dr. Prather," Tanner said.

I looked up. "Sorry, Tanner. I didn't see you. All set for tomorrow?"

"I hope so," he said. "I'm on my way to the theater now."

He was being modest. I knew how confident he was, and rightly so. He was giving me one of his suave smiles right now that made me forget I was years older than he was. "I'm sure you'll be great."

"Are you going?" he asked.

"This weekend," I said. "I need to get tickets."

He started for campus. "I'll see you tomorrow at the Shakespeare conference?"

"For sure," I said. "I'm looking forward to your panel."

"Thanks," he said over his shoulder, quickening his pace.

I was still standing in front of the house, a mournful shell of its glorious past. The upstairs windows reminded me of two eyes, the fringed shades beating back and forth in the half-open window as if blinking at me. With a little TLC, it might be restored to its original splendor, or someone could at least wash the brown dust off the white siding. But it was a rental, and student renters had different priorities: studying, partying, fighting. Somewhere inside, I heard a door slam. As I started walking, I told myself it was probably the wind. It wreaked havoc on the Great Plains. I looked back—just in time to see someone shut the shade.

Chapter Three

—

THURSDAY MORNING, I awoke to a loud meow in the face. With the warming weather, my cat, Dickinson, was spending more time on the porch, and she was ready to start the day even if I wasn't. When I didn't immediately respond to her request, she patted me lightly with her paw. I rolled out of bed with a groan, slid into the new Eiffel Tower slippers Lenny had bought me for Christmas, and followed Dickinson to the door. She was ten steps ahead of me. Since my porch was screened, I left the door open as I made coffee.

It was just as well I was up early. Today was the Shakespeare symposium, and like Tanner, I was presenting. Others from the department were also presenting, and I didn't want to miss their panels. The event would draw a good crowd from surrounding schools and communities. Everyone wanted to see Shakespeare's First Folio, and today the Harmony Music Museum wasn't charging admission. The exhibit was part of the larger Shakespeare Festival on campus. Felix Lewis's keynote lecture would end the symposium on Saturday night, and several scholarly panels on the great bard were scheduled from now until then. I wondered when Andy's panel was.

I poured my first cup of coffee and walked to the porch. I was willing to bet he would come off just as pompous in his presentation as he had in conversation. I sat down crisscross in the comfy rocking chair. Considering the number of panels, Andy had some competition if he was going for the smartest-man-in-the-room award.

A perfectly curled gray head came into sight, then a pink smile. It was Mrs. Gunderson, taking her dog, Darling, for a walk. Dickinson crouched low in the wide windowsill, ready to pounce. I stood and walked out to greet Mrs. Gunderson.

"Good morning, Mrs. Gunderson." *Her name is Gertrude,* I reminded myself. After living next to her for three years, I'd finally learned her first name but never used it. She was a widow in her seventies, so everyone called her by her married name.

"Good morning," she said. "Were you and Leonard out late?"

Instinctively, I touched my hair. It must have looked a mess. "Yes, we were celebrating. I found out yesterday my book has been accepted for publication."

"That's good news, dear," said Mrs. Gunderson. Darling was kicking up his back paws near my tree. "I know how much you think of your books."

"They're going to give me an *advance*," I said.

"I'm sure I don't know what that means, but I'm glad to see you're getting out more. At your age, the more dates, the better." She scooped up Darling's deposit. "Leonard isn't going to wait around forever."

"What about you, Mrs. Gunderson?" I asked, sidestepping questions about my relationship with Lenny. "Do you ever think about remarrying?"

She stood ramrod straight. "Absolutely not."

"Why?" I lifted my coffee cup, trying not to smile, but her indignant expression made it hard.

"Some things are meant to be done only once, and marriage

is one of those things." She marched on toward Main Street, signaling that our conversation was over.

There were many reasons Harmony Music Museum was the perfect location to exhibit Shakespeare's First Folio. One was it housed fifteen thousand instruments from the sixteenth and seventeenth centuries, the same instruments Shakespeare's own players would have used. Normally, there was an entrance fee, a small price to pay to see one of the best collections of instruments in the nation. But today, the entry fee was waved, and all the festivities were free and open to the public. As I walked up the steep ivory-colored steps, I realized what a great opportunity the festival offered for scholars and townsfolk alike.

A volunteer pointed the way to Shakespeare's First Folio. The large room, which normally housed instruments, now held one of the most expensive books in the world. One copy had sold for three million dollars. I inched up to the display. I could be clumsy at the most inopportune times.

Though many of Shakespeare's plays were published in his lifetime, many were not. Theater companies purchased the handwritten scripts directly, which meant plays like *Macbeth* and *The Tempest* would have been lost if friends in Shakespeare's company hadn't had the plays printed in a collection after his death. According to one account, only 235 copies of the First Folio existed. The Folger Shakespeare Library in Washington, D.C., owned 82 of them, and at this very moment I was looking down at our copy through a protective glass case. It took my breath away.

" 'To be or not to be. That is the question.' "

I turned to see Lenny behind me. "You've done your research." The book was open to Hamlet's famous soliloquy. It was cradled in a special holder, which according to the note, was built to take stress off the spine.

"Nope," said Lenny. "I got here thirty minutes ago."

I returned to the book, studying the intricate type. "I didn't know you were so excited about the conference. You should have submitted a proposal for a panel."

"No way," said Lenny. "I'm an American lit teacher through and through. They couldn't pay me to read Shakespeare."

"Shhh!" I said, pulling him aside. "A comment like that could get you killed in here."

He smiled. "I'm confident you'd solve my murder."

We walked over to one of the wall panels provided by the Folger. It explained why we still read Shakespeare. I didn't want to hear Lenny's answer. He agreed with the philosophy of Ralph Waldo Emerson, who once famously said: "The English dramatic poets have Shakespearized now for two hundred years." It was time for a new kind of literature—Lenny would say *American* literature.

"Have you met Felix Lewis or Andy Wells?" I asked.

"Yes, they're extraordinary chaps," Lenny said in his best British accent. "And a wee bit uppity, too."

"Your accent is dreadful, but you're right about Andy," I said. "The kid is a jerk."

Lenny raised a dark eyebrow. "I don't know if you're old enough to call him a kid."

"Well, I just did," I said, digging for the program the volunteer had given me. It had already found its way to the bottom of my book bag. "His panel starts at nine … on the second floor. Let's go see if he's as smart as he pretends to be."

"Okay," said Lenny. "They have free coffee up there."

We walked toward the marble staircase. "I'm impressed. Usually, this museum doesn't allow food or drink. They must be making an exception for the conference."

"They probably realized we couldn't stay awake through the panels without it."

I gave him a sharp look. "I'm presenting."

He put his arm around me. "I know. And you're going to be great."

A sign on the door announced the name of the panel. After grabbing coffees, we walked in. Four chairs stood behind a table at the front of the room, where a display of classical mandolins provided a gorgeous backdrop for the speakers. Andy sat at the table, as did Tanner Sparks and two other students. Thomas Cook, the moderator, was already at the podium.

We scooted in near Reed and Giles. Felix was on the other side of Giles, and I gave him a wave before taking my seat. Reed was a tall man with a large nose. His legs looked too long for the chair, and I felt bad for the way he was folded up in the seat. Giles was talking to Felix about Andy's paper. Felix was Andy's committee chair just as Reed was Tanner's committee chair. They both looked excited to hear their scholars present. I was excited, too. I'd seen Tanner act, but I'd never heard him present. Plus, I was curious about Andy's chapter. Was his scholarship worthy of a contract with a big-name publisher? It remained to be seen.

Wearing a classic navy suit, Thomas Cook began the introductions, his smart East Coast accent used to good effect. He was an English professor and the moderator of the panel, which meant he didn't have much to do except look cool. It was the perfect role for him. Academic panels allowed each presenter about fifteen minutes, depending on panel allotment. The moderator introduced and closed the discussion and asked for questions from the audience. He also intervened if something went wrong. *For instance, if Andy chokes on his donut and requires the Heimlich, he will need help from the moderator*, I thought to myself.

"What are you smiling about?" whispered Lenny. "Thomas's new jacket?"

"I'll tell you later," I whispered back.

Much to my delight, Andy went first. He was a good speaker, but his chapter wasn't anything I hadn't heard before. We read Shakespeare because we still care about the universal themes in the work: jealousy, love, hate, revenge. It was interesting but hardly Macmillan-worthy. Smugly satisfied, I leaned back, now more inclined to enjoy the rest of the presentations. Tanner was up next. He began with Stratford-upon-Avon, Shakespeare's birthplace. *Here we go again*, I thought. Another rote topic. But the next words out of his mouth made me sit up and take notice.

"The tome downstairs wasn't written by a boy with a grammar-school education," said Tanner. His eyes sparkled, and I wondered what he was up to. "It was written by the aristocrat and Earl of Oxford, Edward de Vere."

A wave of discomfort rippled through the room. Giles visibly shuddered. Lenny laughed. I'd heard this theory before, of course, just never in a roomful of English-literature scholars. Despite the visibly clenching fists, Tanner continued to expound the argument of his fellow Oxfordians, called such because they believed the Earl of Oxford, who received degrees at both Oxford and Cambridge and was a poet, wrote the plays attributed to Shakespeare. They didn't believe a person from a modest background like Shakespeare's could have written the works. The works had to have been written by someone who was well educated, well traveled, and moneyed. In other words, an author who had access to the material he was writing about. That argument led the first Oxfordian, J. Thomas Looney, who himself taught Shakespeare, to Edward de Vere. De Vere met all the requirements, and similarities had been found between his poems and one of Shakespeare's longer poems. The major problem with the theory was the date of de Vere's death—1604. A third of Shakespeare's plays were written after that. Oxfordians suggested they weren't written then but merely edited, because the real Shakespeare was dead.

The mystery intrigued me, and I listened closer. Tanner was telling a story I hadn't heard before, which didn't mean it was new. I wasn't a Shakespeare scholar—far from it. Prior to preparing for my presentation, I hadn't read Shakespeare for several years. Tanner stood in front of the podium, making good use of the length of the room to make his point. His performance was mesmerizing, and I wondered how much of its appeal came from his acting skills and how much from his scholarship. I didn't care. I just listened. I was a sucker for a good story.

"And while being honored that day at court, Edward de Vere was toasted with the words, 'Thy countenance shakes a spear.' " Tanner raised a hand holding an imaginary glass of champagne. He waited several seconds before continuing. "A nod to his skills at jousting? Perhaps. A recognition of his coat of arms, which included a lion with a shield? Maybe. Whatever the case, the name stuck, and the Earl of Oxford would write his many plays under a combination of that name—that pseudonym—Shakespeare."

Felix had heard enough. Red-faced, he whispered to Reed, "I can't believe you're going to allow him to spew this sophomoric garbage. What kind of hoax is this? We're here to celebrate Shakespeare, not make a mockery of his authorship."

Reed, already uncomfortable in his too-small chair, looked more so. "The student has a right to his opinion."

"Opinion isn't scholarship, Reed," huffed Felix. "You know that as well as I do."

Now that Tanner's presentation was finished, Thomas asked for questions from the audience. It was his duty as moderator; still, I kind of wished he hadn't. Tanner Sparks was a student—albeit a grad student. I didn't want him fed to the wolves in the audience.

I raised my hand.

"Professor Prather, go ahead," said Thomas.

"I don't have a question," I said. "I just want to commend Tanner for his academic courage. It couldn't have been easy to assert such a thesis in a roomful of Shakespeare scholars. Good job."

"*Courage*," growled Andy, who was seated at the table of

presenters. Leaning forward, he looked ready to pounce. "I'd call it stupidity."

Lenny's hand shot up like a rocket. He didn't bother waiting for Thomas to call on him. "Don't kid yourself. Tanner made some good points."

"It's all right, Professor Jenkins," said Tanner. He glanced at Andy, seated behind him at the table. "He's just mad that I've blown the theories in his upcoming book out of the water."

"Rubbish!" Felix called out from the audience. "I've heard the same claims before from men older and wiser than you. Andy's book is the work of a true academician, not a conspiracy hack."

"You haven't heard his most controversial claim," added Reed.

"I'm listening," said Felix.

"The Earl of Oxford faked his own death," announced Tanner, "and I'm going to prove it with his DNA."

Chapter Four

—

IF THE EARL of Oxford had faked his own death, he was alive when Shakespeare's later plays were written. The revelation, if true, would change the field of English literature forever. I was interested in how Tanner had obtained his DNA, and so was the rest of the audience. Unfortunately, Thomas Cook put a stop to the conversation, saying he had to move on to the next presenter to finish at the top of the hour. What he said was true. The last two scholars would have to rush their presentations. It wouldn't be fair to ask them to prepare weeks in advance only to cut their time short the day of the panel. I understood the dilemma.

Lenny nudged my leg. He wanted to go, and so did I. We needed to discuss what'd just happened, and I had to present in less than thirty minutes. We'd have to leave now if we wanted time to talk. When the next panelist turned on the projector, we slipped out of the row.

We found a roomful of keyboard instruments and ducked inside. The impressive display included an ivory organ that reached the ceiling and an ornate harpsichord. Lenny leaned against a pianoforte, a beautiful relic from the eighteenth century.

"Did you hear that Felix guy?" said Lenny. "I thought he would implode when Tanner said Shakespeare wasn't the author of the plays."

"Andy didn't hold back either," I said. "Do you think Tanner's claim really blows Andy's book out of the water, like he said?"

"Not directly," said Lenny. "But think about it. Andy's book is about the relevancy of Shakespeare in our time. How relevant is the Earl of Oxford—an aristocrat and titled gentleman?" He shook his head. "I'm no Shakespeare fan, but I'd prefer to think of him as the playwright with the grammar school education who made it big."

"Me, too," I said. "Everybody identifies with that story. I'd be curious to know what evidence Tanner has. If true, it would change the entire scope of the conversation."

"And the direction of Shakespeare scholar's lives."

"You really think it'd change lives?" I asked. "You'd go that far?"

"I would," said Lenny.

"Can you imagine?" I plucked a cat hair off my jacket. "Shakespeare not being written by Shakespeare?"

"Yeah, I can," said Lenny. "They've been feeding us lies for years. This is probably another one."

I stifled a laugh. Lenny was an avid conspiracy theorist. He'd like it if Tanner's research turned out to be true, but I was less enthusiastic. Scholars like Reed would be heartbroken, and who could blame them? It would be like Lenny finding out that Walt Whitman's works were actually written by a titled gentleman.

Lenny crossed his arms, still leaning on the delicate pianoforte. "You think I'm going all Mel Gibson in *Conspiracy Theory*, but he turned out to be right, didn't he?"

I didn't see how a movie from the 1990s supported his case. "Don't lean on that piano. It looks fragile."

He pretended to fall, moving his arms erratically.

"Stop it." I reached for him.

That's all it took for him to pull me into an embrace, an unexpected moment of bliss. We stood kissing for a full minute before I realized what we were doing—and where. I pulled back reluctantly, telling him I had to freshen up before my presentation, which meant reapplying the lipstick he'd kissed off.

"I'll meet you there," he said.

I gave him a little wave. The feel of his arms holding me lingered long after I left the room.

After a stop at the restroom, I went downstairs to set up my slideshow, a compendium of the murders in Shakespeare's plays. It was outside my wheelhouse, if French literature was still my wheelhouse, but Reed had reviewed my research. He said it was *refreshing*. I just hoped it would stand up to other scholars' work. Denton Smart, the second-year medical student sitting beside me, was almost a doctor, in the medical sense. He knew not only Shakespeare but also how to perform surgery. It was hard to compete with that degree of expertise.

I began my presentation with *Hamlet* because it was opening night of the school's own production, and death and murder were important themes in the play. During the course of five acts, a whopping nine people die, not to mention the jester, who's dead before the play begins. It would take me a while to discuss all of them. Eventually, though, I moved on to *Julius Caesar* and *Othello*. As I was speaking, I observed Tanner Sparks slipping into one of the last rows, next to Lenny. I was glad he hadn't been tarred and feathered after his revelation. He was as charming as ever, whispering something to Lenny that made him smile.

I refocused on my last slide: the murder of Desdemona. Othello, her husband, becomes convinced she has been unfaithful after he obtains ostensible proof of her cheating. Here I brought up a picture of the fateful handkerchief. Othello kills her before discovering that his friend Iago has been feeding him lies, including the one about the handkerchief. After learning the truth, he kills himself. No mystery surrounds the murder—Othello smothers Desdemona with a pillow—but citing one of Shakespeare's best-known tragedies was a nice way to end my presentation.

"Thank you, Professor Prather," said Alexander Schwartz, theater director and moderator of the panel. "That was … interesting." Shaped like a barrel, he was a visionary and a perfectionist. He was the director of *Hamlet,* and I was excited to see his version. "Any questions for Professor Prather before we move on to our next panelist?"

Several people had joined the audience late and stood at the entrance or lingered near the back of the room. Andy was one of them. I really hoped he didn't ask me a question. I was still mad at him for calling Tanner stupid. I wasn't sure my response would be calm.

"I have a question," said Lenny.

I breathed a sigh of relief. "Yes?"

"For an English professor, you know a lot about murder," said Lenny. He gave me a cheeky smile. "Have you ever thought about going into law enforcement?"

"That's a good question," I said, returning the smile. His dimple got me every time. "Had I not spent so much time and money on my PhD, I might think about switching professions. It's a little too late to invest in another direction."

That got a few chuckles.

"Yes, in the blue shirt," said Alexander to a girl with long, dark hair.

"Seriously, though, you've been involved in a few homicide cases," said the girl. "What makes someone commit murder? Do they just erupt, like Othello? Or are some people incapable of killing, despite being highly motivated?"

It was a great question, one I'd already considered. Was anyone capable of murder, say, if someone they loved was threatened? I'd seen a lot of ordinary people act rashly when driven by extraordinary circumstances. "If you examine the motives behind the murders in Shakespeare's plays, you'll see the reasons are deeply human. It's why we feel the tragedy of them. Othello, for instance, is fiercely jealous, an emotion we can all relate to. So, to answer your question, I think Shakespeare understood human nature all too well. Most people aren't born to kill, and circumstances do make a difference. The same motives still compel them: jealousy, love, hate, the lust for power, the need to control. Are some people incapable of murder, no matter what? Who can say?"

"Any other questions for Professor Prather?" asked Alexander. He waited a few seconds before introducing the next speaker, Denton Smart, a short man with rimless glasses. Though I didn't know him, I was interested in his presentation, which concerned poisons in Shakespeare's plays and the effects produced in the characters.

Denton started with *Romeo and Juliet*, discussing what substance might have put Juliet into a sleep that resembled death. Knowing something about plants, I followed along easily. Many scholars believed Juliet's coma was caused by deadly nightshade, aka belladonna, which meant "beautiful lady" in Italian. I agreed. The plant could cause not only death-like symptoms but death itself. Denton moved on to the queen's poisoned goblet in *Hamlet*, speculating on its contents, and again I could follow his evidence. But when he discussed Regan's symptoms in *King Lear*, he lost me and half his audience with too much medical terminology. I noticed Lenny's head bobbing during the last five minutes. I, like Lenny, had tuned out. I was wondering about an email from my publisher and calculating the difference between time zones when Alexander asked for questions.

"Nice presentation," said Tanner, who seemed engaged and even excited. "I like how you used the characters' symptoms to recreate timelines. Do you do that a lot in the medical field?"

"We do," said Denton. He gave a lengthier response, but I found myself focusing on his glasses instead of his explanation. While he talked about the body's reaction to certain elements, he fidgeted with his spectacles. Were they new? Were they misaligned? Was he sweating? It was beginning to irritate me. It took a great effort to focus on what he was saying.

"As you and I know," Denton said, "modern medicine can determine cause of death, and more importantly in this case, *time* of death." Denton paused. "Through DNA research, Tanner and I hope to prove Shakespeare was actually the pen name of the Earl of Oxford."

Pleased with Denton's revelation, Tanner stretched his legs, preening a little. While what followed didn't amount to the ruckus of the previous panel, it was bad enough, and I had a feeling Tanner liked the attention. I could tell by the way his eyes sparkled with excitement. Denton, on the other hand, looked less comfortable. He swallowed hard, gathered up his papers from the podium, and walked back to the table without waiting for more questions.

Alexander, our moderator, wasn't going to let Denton off the hook that easily. "I have to say, Denton, while shocking, your assertion can hardly be taken seriously. We have two men, two graves, and thus two writers. One, our beloved Shakespeare, and two, the mediocre Earl of Oxford. Modern medicine can't refute simple math."

"Two men but *one* author." Tanner answered for Denton, flashing a smile at Alexander. "For years, much has been made of the curse on the fake Shakespeare's grave at Stratford-upon-Avon. It was put there to keep us from learning the truth. Recently a scholar suggested Shakespeare's 'grave' points us to Poets' Corner in Westminster Abbey, where the Earl of Oxford lies. He wasn't moved there—as his cousin suggested—but was interred there at the real time of his death, well after 1604."

Alexander's mouth formed a lowercase *o*. "I'd love to hear more of this fascinating *tale*, Mr. Sparks, and if anyone appreciates your storytelling abilities, it is I, but we need to get to the last panelist. Maybe after the conference."

"Any time, Professor," said Tanner. He and Alexander shared a comradery from Tanner's work in the theater, but Alexander wouldn't let even his favorite actor make a claim like that without providing further explanation.

Our final panelist approached the podium, but I was still thinking about Tanner and his revelation. He intended to prove Edward de Vere was alive after 1604 with a DNA sample. Though DNA evidence from so long ago wouldn't be irrefutable, it might answer the question surrounding his date of death. But I knew nothing of Poets' corner in Westminster Abbey or how two graves could point to one man. Tanner's research was well outside my area of interest. It was becoming an area an interest, however, after this morning's presentations. Truth be told, this was the most excitement I'd ever witnessed during an academic conference.

After the panel, Lenny stuck around long enough to congratulate me. He had to teach class, and I'd promised Claudia Swift I would help her judge the entries from yesterday's sonnet-writing contest. But we decided to get together later so we could discuss the debate consuming the Shakespeare Conference. Judging from the look of the crowd surrounding Tanner and Denton, the two men's research was on everybody's mind. As a teacher, I was happy for them. They were engaged in the kind of academic debate I always encouraged. As a member of the English Department, I was less enthusiastic, especially when I considered the feelings of scholars like Reed Williams. Outside these walls, people trampled on others' beliefs without much care or forethought. Academia was a safe haven of sorts. People said we lived in a make-believe world. Maybe that was true. But maybe modern life needed an escape hatch.

Leaving Harmony Music Museum, I paused at a bench in the quad to check my email. While students moved, herdlike, in and out of buildings, I waited for my inbox to update. I glanced at Harriman Hall, where Claudia was waiting for me. I tapped my finger on the screen, hoping to propel it into action. It must have worked, because an email from Dewberry Press arrived, complete with attachment. I opened it and scanned the text. I needed to sign the attached contract, send a headshot, and write a short bio. Once the contract was in place, work on the book could begin. My editor's name was Owen Parrish. *Owen Parrish,* I repeated. *Perish the thought of him finding any significant errors.* I brushed away the fear. I'd read the manuscript five times before submitting it. How could a mistake escape my notice?

The email closed by asking me to return the signed contract as soon as possible. A quick scan didn't reveal anything that would prevent that from happening. Due dates, editorial dates, publication dates—I had no problem getting work done on time. Growing up in the Midwest, I couldn't fathom not meeting a deadline. I put away my phone and stood. It was a done deal as far as I was concerned.

It wasn't until I entered the second floor of Harriman Hall that I remembered the English Department potluck. The smell of casseroles and chocolate chip cookies hit me—along with a wave of guilt. I'd forgotten all about the event, which was our department's way of celebrating the Shakespeare Festival. I was supposed to bring a dish to the Writing Center. It was the reason Claudia and I were meeting here in the first place. We could eat lunch while reading the entries.

Claudia was walking toward me, breezing down the hallway with her long purple scarf flowing behind her. Her fine brown hair was turned into a French twist, a pencil sticking out of the side of her head. She made everything look easy—raising kids, writing poems, sparring with her husband, Gene. I admired her for that. Claudia might be drama-prone, but she was a good friend, and I always looked forward to spending time with her.

"Thank you for the chips, though you signed up for a salad," said Claudia, reaching for my arm and turning me toward the Writing Center. "Lenny dropped them off this morning, along with his … beenies and weenies." She stuck out her tongue.

Hooray for Lenny! I loved the way he remembered that I was good at forgetting things. "You're welcome, and really, his beenies and weenies aren't that bad. He puts a special spice in there, you know."

She let out a breath. "Love must make you blind *and* ruin your palate. The beans are dreadful."

Maybe it did. I was also growing fond of his chili.

We entered the Writing Center, where a long table was filled with hot dishes, salads, and tableware. It was early, and many people from the department were still at Harmony Music Museum, so Claudia and I collected our plates right away.

"I heard something interesting at the festival this morning," I said, taking a spoonful of Lenny's dish. "Tanner Sparks said Shakespeare was really the Earl of Oxford, and Denton Smart said DNA tests could prove the earl was alive to write the late plays. Several scholars were miffed." I put the lid on the Crock-Pot and reached for the chips.

Claudia was dishing up vegetarian lo mein. "I don't believe a word of it, but I'll admit Tanner's pretty convincing. I chalk it up to years of acting classes."

"You've heard it, then?" I grabbed a brownie—chocolate chocolate chip.

"Of course," said Claudia. "I'm on Tanner's dissertation committee." She glanced at my brownie. "What happened to eating healthier?"

"That was January," I said, taking a cookie bar. "This is April."

"What a difference a few months make," muttered Claudia, leading the way to her office. Unlike mine, her office was large enough for a small round conference table, which is where we sat. She had two bookshelves filled with poetry collections and pictures of her kids, Sylvia and Benjamin. There was also a nice picture of her and Gene in Italy, where they'd renewed their vows after a few uncertain months of fighting. As far as I knew, they were still in each other's good graces, though no one could say for how long.

"And I have more news," I said, placing a napkin on my lap. "I received the contract from Dewberry." I'd told Claudia yesterday about their offer to publish. "I need to sign it and send it back ASAP."

Claudia took a sip of her iced tea. "Let's have Gene take a look at it first. You don't want to sign anything too quickly."

Gene was a lawyer and famously busy. I didn't want to wait on his opinion. "I think it's all pretty standard. I didn't find anything unusual in it."

"Still, he should take a look," said Claudia. "We don't know what's standard and non-standard in the publishing world."

"*You* do," I said. "You've published poetry."

"In academic journals," said Claudia. "I think this is different."

"I *hope* it's different," I said. "I'd like to get paid in money for once instead of contributors' copies." When academics sent articles to scholarly journals, they were rewarded with several free copies of said journal and the gratification of knowing they were moving toward tenure. Although I didn't expect my book to be a best seller, I did hope it would earn me a few dollars, maybe enough to buy a new TV. Mine was a clunky relic from graduate school and didn't even have a flat screen.

Claudia finished her last bite of lo mein and threw her plate in the trash. "If you're finished getting your sugar fix, let's start reading the sonnets."

I washed down my brownie with a glug of coffee. "How many submissions?"

"Forty-two."

Forty-two? I might need a refill before reading all the iambic pentameter in forty-two sonnets. I tossed my plate and napkin in the trash, and Claudia handed me a stack of poems. She said we would create three piles: "yes," "no," and "maybe." Before making any final decisions, we would reread the yeses and maybes together.

I put a lot of poems into the maybe category before choosing any yeses. It was hard to know what poems stood out until I'd read several. I stopped at Allen Dunsbar's entry, scanning the lines twice. Iambic pentameter was a pattern of an unstressed syllable followed by a stressed syllable. Dunsbar's poem didn't adhere to the form. "Allen's poem isn't written in iambic pentameter. Are you granting any leeway on style?"

"Absolutely not," said Claudia. As a poet herself, Claudia was firm on the point. "We're celebrating Shakespeare, and he wrote his sonnets in iambic pentameter. Period."

I slipped Dunsbar's poem into the "no" pile and picked up the next submission. I smiled. "It's Lenny's." I scanned a few lines. "It's for me." Lenny had written a love poem, describing a friendship that had blossomed into love. I blushed as I silently read the final couplet. "This is definitely a 'yes.' "

Claudia rearranged her French twist. "Do you think you might be partial?"

"No. Yes. Read it." I handed her the paper.

She read it and put it in the "yes" pile.

I picked up another poem.

She shoved a pencil through the silky strands of brown hair. "I'm glad you followed my advice for once. I could see your happiness long before you could."

It was so like Claudia to take credit for the match. But I didn't argue. She was right. I was happy, and so was Lenny. No matter how we'd gotten here, we were together.

A few lines into the next poem, I could feel the smile leaving my face. As if seeing a spider, I recoiled from the paper.

"What is it?" asked Claudia.

The sonnet was written in all caps, perhaps to disguise the identity of the writer. No name appeared, and no wonder.

It was a warning of events to come. The final couplet made my arms turn to sandbags. I read it aloud: "THE TIME HAS COME FOR YOU TO MEET YOUR FOE / A MAN WILL DIE AND BRING TO NONE GREAT WOE."

Chapter Five

———

CLAUDIA LOOKED UP from the poem she was reading, her eyes wide. She snatched the paper from me, turning it over in her hands.

"There's no name on it," I said, answering her unspoken question.

"If this is somebody's idea of a prank, I don't think it's funny," said Claudia. "It's childish." She spoke loudly, as if the prankster were in the hallway, listening.

"What if it's not a prank?" I said. "What if it's a warning?"

Claudia picked up the paper and brought it close to her face. "It's not. It can't be. For one, the person knows Shakespeare. He or she references Hamlet in the second stanza. And two, the theme of the poem is death. Maybe the student wanted to end on a dramatic note."

Drama was one thing; murder was another. Unless planning to kill someone, how could the writer predict a death? And what was meant by "foe"? It was as if the lines were directed at me, I told Claudia.

She waved off the idea. "Students use second-person all the time. You know that. Besides, no one knows you're helping to judge the contest. If the lines are intended for anyone, it's me."

The office was silent for a moment. I could hear dishes from the potluck clinking down the hallway. It looked as if Claudia's thoughts were going somewhere dark.

She sucked in a breath. "God, do I have any foes?"

Oh, so now the threat was plausible because the lines were intended for her. "I can't think of any. Your students love you." And they did. Though not the best poet in the world, Claudia was one of the best teachers. She took genuine interest in her students' work and helped them develop into writers.

"I bet Gene has foes aplenty," said Claudia, tapping her pen on the table. "Just leave it to him to get me killed."

I had to bite my lip to keep from smiling. Not that I didn't sympathize; I did. Gene's wandering eye had caused a lot of fights, but their relationship had been better since they renewed their vows in Italy. At the first sign of personal difficulty, though, she blamed Gene. But the contents of the sonnet did not point to Gene. The person who wrote the poem was familiar with Shakespeare and knew the campus well. Gene stayed as far away from the university as possible.

"Like you said, it's probably a prankster, a student trying to rattle your nerves," I said. "To be honest, it's a good poem. The student definitely knows how to write a sonnet. I think we should put it in the 'maybe' category—after we contact the police."

"The police!" said Claudia. "I can't turn in one of my students for writing a dark poem. It's out of the question."

"We can't ignore a threat," I said. "It's our duty to report it." For once, I was the sensible one in the room. It was a new feeling.

"This is *creative* writing. It isn't real. It's fiction. And I didn't stipulate that the sonnet had to be sunshine and rainbows."

Claudia had definite opinions on creative writing. I understood not censoring the students, but I didn't believe in letting them kill anyone either. I snatched the paper and stood.

"Let's take it up with Giles. He'll know what to do."

She had no choice but to follow me down the hall. Giles was just picking up his first forkful of macaroni and cheese when I stuck my head in his office. "We have a problem."

He put down his fork.

"Not a problem," said Claudia. "A question."

I handed him the poem. "This was submitted for the sonnet-writing contest. I think it's a warning. I think we need to contact the police."

"And I think it's a disturbing poem but hardly deserving of censure—or alerting the police," said Claudia.

"No one's going to be arrested," I said, "but we have to notify the authorities." I liked the way *authorities* sounded. I'd heard the same word on the mystery channel last night.

Giles refolded the poem and stuck it in a cubbyhole on his desk. "Emmeline is right. We have to notify somebody, but I think campus security will suffice."

"You approve of censoring writers?" Claudia huffed. "Frankly, I'm shocked."

"I approve of warning security of possible threats," said Giles. "In today's world, you can't be too careful."

"I know Officer Beamer would approve," I said.

"Let's not get Officer Beamer involved just yet," said Giles. "If he keeps getting summoned to our department, I'm afraid I'll have to award him an honorary degree."

The idea of Officer Beamer in a cap and gown made me smile.

"Well I'm glad *you're* happy with the outcome," said Claudia. "I, for one, think it's a big mistake to involve security in the sacred writing process. This is the one place the imagination should be allowed to roam free." She turned on her heel and left.

Giles lifted his eyebrows, deepening the three horizontal groves on his forehead. We were just two more in a long line of people searching for ways to handle departmental issues.

"You'd better follow her before she organizes a sit-in."

I nodded. "Thank you, Giles. I appreciate your support."

He picked up his fork. "You're welcome—now go."

I hustled down the hall after Claudia and met Lenny on the way. "That was a fast class. Why are you done so early?"

He unlocked his office door. "They didn't read the material, and I'm hungry. I wasn't about to sit around and babysit them for the next thirty minutes."

"There's plenty of food in the Writing Center," I said. "Thank you, by the way, for bringing the chips. I forgot all about the potluck."

He smiled and started toward the Writing Center. "I knew you would, with your panel and all."

"Claudia and I are in her office. Join us when you're done. We're going over the sonnets from the contest." I reached for his arm. "I came across the most delightful one from you."

"I meant every word of it, Em," he said. "You've turned me into a babbling love poet."

"There are worse things," I told him. I stopped at Claudia's door.

We shared a smile before he continued on toward the Writing Center and I entered Claudia's office. "Lenny's great, isn't he?"

Claudia looked up from the poems, clearly peeved. "Yes."

I plopped down in the chair beside her and returned to the stack. "Don't be mad, Claudia. I have the students' best interests at heart."

"I hope that's what this is," she said, tapping her pencil.

"What is that supposed to mean?"

As she leaned back in her chair, the light caught the copper highlights in her brown hair. "You have a bad habit of seeing a mystery in everything."

"That's not true," I said. "I've had my fair share of mysteries, but they fall into my lap; I don't go looking for them." I pointed to the stack of poems. "This one happened to come via submission box."

"Tell me I made it to the winners' circle," said Lenny as he entered the office.

"You did," I said, picking up a chip.

"Em! You can't tell him that," said Claudia.

Lenny winked at me.

"You two are even more insufferable now that you're dating," said Claudia. "You know that?"

Lenny joined us at the table. His broad shoulders made the area seem smaller. "We're a team now. Bona fide."

We fist bumped.

"Well, the other member of your team just made a grave error," said Claudia.

"Em doesn't make errors," said Lenny, scooping up a spoonful of potato salad. "She corrects them. Are you acquainted with her red pen?"

In a rush, Claudia told him about the sonnet, the final couplet, and Giles's interpretation of it. Lenny was eating much more slowly by the time she finished speaking.

"I think Giles made the right call," said Lenny, after taking a sip of soda. "It sounds like whoever wrote the poem is up to no good. Maybe he's not planning murder, but he is scaring people. That's not right."

"Or she," I said.

"Or she," he repeated. "I know you believe in equal opportunity for murderers."

I chuckled.

Claudia's jaw was clenched. Lenny's wasn't the sympathetic ear she was hoping for. "Let's get back to it, then. I have kids to pick up."

Lenny stood. "Dinner tonight?"

"Yes." I nodded. "I want to show you my contract from Dewberry Press."

"I'll pick you up," he said.

"I'll be waiting," I said.

As he left the office, Claudia grumbled, "How will I ever get through the spring?"

Chapter Six

Due to our harsh and lingering winters, spring wasn't as beautiful in the Midwest as it was in some areas of the country. Many trees were still mostly bare, and it took perennials longer to blossom. What we had going for us was grass, brilliantly green from the abundant March rains. We also had farms, and tilling made the air smell fresh and earthy.

With any luck, though, Shakespeare's Garden would be in full bloom today for the grand reopening. Dedicated in 1923, the garden had gone to seed and was a mass of tangled weeds, tarnished statues, and rusty benches. The English Department had spent a good deal of money on the renovation, and Reed Williams had spent a good deal of time preparing for the reopening. This morning's itinerary would include the unveiling of the garden, the reading of the winning sonnet entry (unfortunately, not Lenny's), and the dedication of a new Shakespeare bust.

I rushed to put on my ankle boots, shooing Dickinson away from my bootlaces. I'd been up since six this morning and was eager to leave. The several cups of coffee I'd drunk hadn't helped my high anxiety levels. After Lenny and I discussed my book contract over dinner, it was impossible to think about anything else for the rest of the night. I tossed and turned for hours before I finally got up, signed the contract, and scanned and emailed the thing back just to get it off my mind. I'd only slept a few hours when I awoke to Dickinson's meows. She was feeling the restlessness of spring, too. When this semester was over, I really needed to think about taking a vacation, one that let you bring your cat.

As I left my little yellow bungalow, I heard Mrs. Gunderson—Gertrude, I reminded myself—call out my name.

"I noticed you didn't sleep last night." She was struggling with a weed near her front stoop. "Your light was on. I hope you aren't having difficulties with Leonard."

I walked over and gave the weed a yank. "Nope, Lenny's fine. It was my insomnia. I can't seem to shake it for very long."

"It's all those books you read," she said, dusting off her hands. "They put terrible ideas in your head."

"Then what were *you* doing up?" I said sweetly, but Mrs. Gunderson was smart. She gave me a look that said she wasn't going to let me outsmart her.

"Crocheting."

She said it as if she'd been crowning the king of England.

"Have a good day," I said, tossing the weed in the street as I continued walking to campus. The morning was as quiet as on a Saturday or Sunday, but that was just because it wasn't yet eight, and few classes were held that early. The garden ceremony didn't begin until nine, but I thought a walk might help revive me. Besides, it was Friday, and the ladies at St. Agnes were making cookies for the school kids. I took a short detour so I could pass by the church—a faded orange brick, like the bluff of town. I was disappointed to find the back door locked. That was unusual. Returning to the sidewalk, I hoped nothing was wrong. It was unlike them to be absent on a Friday.

All the way to school, I was off kilter, tripping once over a rock and then again on the curb. I glanced down to see if my laces were the culprit, helped along by Dickinson, but they were perfectly tied. I hustled to cross the street to campus, glad for the protection of the towering old buildings. Nothing could get to me here, even the strong wind.

From a distance, I could see that the barricade around Shakespeare's Garden was gone. I breathed a little sigh of relief. One thing was going right this morning. Reed Williams would be happy to see the garden was event ready. The sun was out, too, willing away the wind. As the day progressed, it would grow warmer, encouraging visitors to stay awhile. I was glad. I wanted people to marvel over how much work had been put into the garden. Reed had been planning this event for over a year. Finally, he would reap the harvest of his hard work.

As I approached, I noticed Reed in the garden. He was staring down at something on the bench. Maybe an inscription had been mangled. Woe to those who misquote Shakespeare. Then I spotted a person on the bench, a man. How unseemly that on our pretty little campus, someone had passed out in Shakespeare's Garden! Reed was trying to wake him, and I hurried to help. Reed was touching his arm, but I wouldn't be afraid to give the student a shake if I had to. People would start arriving any moment.

Until I saw the student—Tanner Sparks. His face was distorted, unnatural, the skin ashen. It could only be the sleep of death.

Reed looked up from the body. "I found him like this. He's not breathing, and I … can't … find a pulse."

"Have you called an ambulance?" I was already pulling out my phone.

"I … no. I just got here." Reed was dazed and having trouble putting together simple sentences. "I was going to try CPR, but his face was cold."

I punched in 911. "They're on their way," I said, ending the call. Tanner's face was slack, his frozen features so unlike those of the spirited student I knew. Alive, he'd been one of our most animated actors and passionate scholars. He loved the attention he got from causing a scene. This was one scene, however, he wouldn't have wanted to star in.

I glanced around the garden, looking for clues to his death. Had he tripped? Fallen? Everything was in perfect order for the event. Not even a stray branch from the wind. I checked his body for a wound. No blood stained his clothes—jeans and a T-shirt. Then I saw it: a substance emerging from his ear and forming a liquid trail to his neck. I pointed. "What's that?"

Reed squinted, his large nose protruding even farther. "It appears to be … I don't know." A tall man, he bent over for a closer look.

"Don't touch it," I said. "It might be important."

He straightened, and I noticed how his shirtsleeves didn't reach the wrists of his long arms. He looked at me, the garden, and then back at Tanner. "It *is* important."

For the first time since I arrived, he was able to pull himself together. He was the rational Shakespeare scholar from down the hall once more. "What do you mean?" I asked.

He gestured to the garden, which featured an impressive array of pink, red, blue, and purple flowers. "Don't you recognize the scene?"

The garden, the bench, the liquid in the ear. Something did seem familiar.

" 'Upon my secure hour thy uncle stole / With juice of cursed hebenon in a vial / And in the porches of my ears did pour,' " quoted Reed.

Hamlet—of course! I remembered at once. In the play, the ghost of Hamlet's father tells his son that he did not die of a snake bite in the garden. Hamlet's uncle, eager to usurp the throne, poisoned him. "But what exactly is hebenon?" I asked Reed.

"As far as we know, Shakespeare was referring to henbane, a poisonous flower, but it could have been hemlock or a nightshade," said Reed. "Hebenon doesn't actually exist."

"I imagine henbane wasn't on your list of flowers—"

"No," Reed said decisively and maybe with a touch of anger.

The ambulance and police sirens pierced the eerie silence that had fallen over the garden. A small town, Copper Bluff didn't have many emergencies, and the EMTs and police tripped over each other getting into the garden. One man lagged behind, and I knew from the square shape of his shoulders and old-fashioned cap that it was Officer Beamer. I liked to imagine we were friends but knew this wasn't exactly the case. He was cordial to me, and I admired his dedication. Could one call that friendship? I wasn't certain; his furrowed brow suggested otherwise.

The EMTs were busy with Tanner, so I met Officer Beamer halfway through the quad. He kept plodding toward the scene, and I followed along, retracing my steps as I talked. "Officer Beamer, it's good to see you. Of course it would be even better under different circumstances. One of our English students, Tanner Sparks, appears to be dead. Something very suspicious is coming out of his ear. It could be what killed him."

We had reached the garden gate, and Beamer stopped. He pointed to a circular bench in the quad. "Sit. I'll get to you later."

He shut the gate to Shakespeare's Garden, leaving me open-mouthed. I stomped over to the bench. He didn't have to be rude. Reed Williams was still in the garden. Why shut me out? The seat was cold, and I pulled my sweater under my rear. It wasn't so bad. I had a good view of the scene and could see what was happening from here. I pulled out my phone and texted Lenny.

Could you meet me? I'm in Shakespeare's Garden.

Is everything coming up roses? he texted.

No, I said. *Coming up murder.*

LENNY ARRIVED TEN minutes later. Dressed in a red sweatshirt with a university logo and jeans, he looked like a grad student.

He also wore tennis shoes and was practically running toward the garden. I called out to him before he reached the gate, and he veered quickly in my direction.

He stood, catching his breath in front of me. "Who is it?"

"Tanner Sparks," I said. "He's dead."

"*Our* Tanner Sparks?"

"The very same. Reed found him in the garden. I arrived just afterwards."

"Was it really murder?" Lenny glanced toward the garden. Crime scene investigators were taking pictures. "They must think so."

"We won't know for sure until after the autopsy," I said. "He was lying on the bench when Reed found him. A liquid was coming from his ear."

Lenny turned back toward me. "Like in *Hamlet*?"

"Yes," I said, surprised by how quickly he had put it together.

He sat down, embracing me with his warm arm. "You're cold. Are you okay?"

"I'm fine," I said. "It's the wind." But I was upset. Though I didn't have Tanner as a student, I did know him from the department. I couldn't believe a young man so full of life could be dead. I took a deep breath and pointed at Beamer. "He wants to talk afterward."

"I bet," said Lenny. "It might be awhile, though." Students were gathering around the garden. They were keeping a safe distance, but many had their phones out. Sophie Barnes, my former student and a detective on the Copper Bluff Police Force, was telling them to stay back, but it was no use. They were coming out of their dorms in droves now to investigate the commotion.

In the midst of the chaos, a girl broke through the crowd, her blonde bun bobbing back and forth. Heedless of Sophie's warning, she was quickly nearing the garden as if intending to walk right in. An officer stopped her but not before she was near enough to see Tanner's lifeless body.

"No, you don't understand," she pleaded. "That's Tanner Sparks. He's my boyfriend."

Now I recognized her. Her name was Mia, and she lived with her friends in the white two-story house down the street from me. She must have been the one Tanner called "psycho." I studied her more closely. She didn't look psycho; she looked like any girl on campus, except less awake. Her clothes—a half-shirt and sweatpants—told me she must have received a call from one of her friends in the crowd surrounding the garden.

"I know her," I told Lenny. "She and her friends live down the block from me. I heard Tanner call her *psycho* when he was leaving the house the other day."

Lenny followed my gaze. "Maybe he meant it affectionately. She looks pretty upset to me."

"How can you call someone *psycho* in an affectionate way?" I said. "Never mind. Here comes Giles."

Giles, wearing his signature tan blazer with elbow patches, was walking and talking with Felix and Andy, the scholars visiting our campus. Engaged in conversation, he didn't seem to notice anything amiss until he saw the police officers. Then he stopped in the middle of the quad and stared. Scratching his head, he turned to Felix. That's when he saw Lenny and me. We stood to meet him.

"What's going on?" Giles's voice was measured. Even in a crisis, he remained calm. "Why are the police here? I didn't get a campus alert."

"It's Tanner Sparks," I said. "Reed found him on the park bench this morning. Dead."

Giles blinked, not speaking. He was taking the news harder than I expected. Usually the one to comfort others, he stared silently into the garden.

"Don't worry, there's no active threat," said Lenny. "Tanner must have died sometime last night."

At Giles's elbow, Felix and Andy were speaking in voices too low to hear. Felix was wearing a well-tailored suit and tie. Andy was wearing a Ralph Lauren sport coat that made his black hair look almost blue. Both were overdressed for a garden party, I thought, and looked out of place on our small college campus.

Felix raised his voice to include the rest of us. "Tanner Sparks. That's the student who said Shakespeare isn't Shakespeare?" He sighed. "Poor fellow. Maybe he had too much to drink. A lot of alcohol poisoning on campuses these days."

Andy shook his head. "I don't think so. Tanner didn't drink anything but Mountain Dew. Bottles of it."

"You knew him?" I asked. He sure hadn't acted like it when he criticized his presentation.

"We were undergrads together at Iowa," said Andy. When nobody said anything, he added, "What? I grew up there."

Lenny and I exchanged a look. Each of us always knew what the other was thinking. The well-dressed windbag was in his own backyard.

Chapter Seven

I WOULDN'T HAVE guessed Andy was from the Midwest, and from Lenny's skeptical expression, he didn't believe it either. People from the Midwest had a sensibility about them that Andy didn't share. Maybe I was stereotyping, but coming from Michigan and now living in South Dakota, I had experience to draw from. People here were friendly and down-to-earth. Andy was neither.

A breeze blew through our makeshift circle. "I didn't realize you knew Tanner," I said. "I'm sorry for your loss."

"We went to college together," said Andy. "We weren't friends."

"Still, it must be a blow," said Felix. He gave Andy a solid pat on the shoulder. Andy squinted in his direction. The sun was coming over Winsor Hall now, spotlighting the crime scene.

"He applied to Denver," Andy said to Felix. "He didn't get in. Maybe you heard of him."

"No," said Felix. "Not until yesterday. I would've remembered a student with a dissertation proposal refuting Shakespeare's identity."

Yes, he would have, so why didn't he? I pondered the

question while I watched Sophie Barnes close the garden gate. Maybe they were done questioning Reed.

Giles sighed. "I can hardly believe it." He looked at me and Lenny. "You saw him yesterday. He was the picture of health—like any student on campus. Some … accident must have befallen him."

"Perhaps," I said to comfort him. His voice was laden with grief, and I knew what it was like to lose a student. As chair of the English Department, Giles had closer contact with Tanner than I over the years, as a teacher or mentor or both.

"Of course it was an accident, a terrible accident," said Felix. "Come on, Jim. Let's take a walk. Andy, you too."

Giles turned to me as if asking permission.

"That's okay," I said. "You go. I'll stay and talk to Sophie Barnes. It looks as if she's finishing up."

Lenny and I watched them walk away.

"I'm starting to really dislike him," said Lenny.

"I assume you mean Andy," I said. "Can you believe he's from Iowa? He acted like Copper Bluff was in the middle of nowhere."

"Coming from the Midwest is nothing to be ashamed of," said Lenny. "The guy's a jerk."

"Agreed," I said. "Do you think he had anything to do with Tanner's death?"

"Here we go."

"I observed his lifeless body in the garden," I said. "Someone staged that scene on purpose, and you yourself said Tanner's bombshell would impact a lot of academics. Maybe Andy felt as if his work was being threatened. He's so dang proud of his New York publisher."

"You have a point," said Lenny. "He wouldn't want to go back to his hometown hanging his head in shame if his book tanked, or worse yet, was pulled from publication."

"But who would kill someone over a book?"

Lenny motioned to the crowd in the quad. "About seventy-five percent of the people here."

"Here comes Sophie," I said. "I mean, Detective Barnes. Let's see if she has any information."

Detective Barnes was short, with brown hair always worn in a tidy updo, off her collar. Today she had it in a slick bun. She looked older and wiser than the student from my first year on campus. Back then, she'd had a fondness for literature and almost changed her major to English. Thankfully, she continued on her original course: a degree in criminal justice.

"Hello, Professor."

She'd never heeded my plea not to call me professor. She claimed it was a habit she couldn't break.

"I'm so glad you're here," I said. "Tanner Sparks was a student in the English Department. What happened?"

She glanced over her shoulder, then back at us. "Beamer sent me over here to get your statements, not relay news. Were you also first on the scene, Professor Jenkins?"

Lenny shook his head. "No, I just got here."

"Then I'll just need to speak to Professor Prather."

"Sophie! Can't you tell us anything?"

She lowered her voice. "Look, Beamer told me to mind the books on this one. He warned me about getting too 'friendly' with my old professors, and he meant you."

"Oh," I said. "I understand." She had been my student. I wanted the best for her, even if that meant finding out the answers to my questions another way.

"I didn't mean it like that. You know how much I look up to you." Sophie took a step closer. "Between us, it appears Tanner died by some kind of poisoning, maybe even alcohol. There are no stab wounds or entry wounds of any kind. We won't know for sure until the coroner examines him."

"The liquid in his ear, right?" I said. "Did you see it?"

"Yes," she said, almost in a whisper. "They swabbed it for testing." Her voice returned to normal. "If you'll excuse us, Professor Jenkins, I need to ask Professor Prather a few questions."

"Sure," said Lenny. "I'll be right over here." He walked to a nearby bike rack and leaned against it.

Sophie flipped open her notebook. "I like my notebook app, but Beamer prefers pencil and paper."

"Technology fails. Pencils and paper rarely do."

Sophie smiled, looking like the young student I remembered. "I forgot. You don't like technology either. You never used it in your classes."

"I use it more now," I said, which was kind of true. We were required to keep grades updated online, at least for freshman and sophomore classes.

"What time did you arrive on campus this morning?" Her pencil was poised to record my answer.

"A little after eight," I said. "On Fridays, I like to stop by St. Agnes, but the door was locked. I knew it was a bad omen. They never lock the church. In fact, I think there's a rule. Maybe it's illegal—not cop illegal but Catholic illegal."

Sophie cleared her throat. "So you arrived a little after eight. What did you see?"

"I saw Professor Reed Williams in the garden. I also saw someone on the bench. I didn't know it was Tanner until I came closer. At first, I thought a student had passed out."

"And what was Professor Williams doing?"

I hated admitting Reed had his hands on Tanner. I worried he might be a suspect. "He was sort of … nudging Tanner to wake him up."

"What did you do when you got closer? Did you attempt to wake him?"

"Heavens no," I said. "I could see he was dead the moment I entered the garden. I called the police."

"Why do you think Reed didn't call the police?" asked Sophie with an undertone of suspicion. "As you said yourself, a dead body can hardly be mistaken for a live one."

"I … maybe he didn't have his cellphone with him. He was obviously in shock. He was the chair of Tanner's dissertation committee. I don't think he wanted to believe Tanner was dead." I took a breath. "I still can't believe it. Who would do such a thing?"

"We can't be sure it wasn't Tanner himself," said Sophie. "So far, I've seen no evidence of foul play. Professor Williams said last night was opening night at the theater. Maybe he and the cast celebrated by drinking too much."

I shook my head. "Talk to Andy Wells. He's here for the Shakespeare conference. He was an undergraduate with Tanner at Iowa. According to him, Tanner didn't drink."

She wrote down the name. "I will, but people change. Graduate school is a lot more pressure, or so I've heard. One of my friends quit after a year."

"Also talk to his girlfriend," I said. "She lives down the street from me, and I heard him call her *psycho*."

She shut the notebook. "Beamer warned me of this. He said you'd try to steer the investigation if I let you. He said I needed to be firm."

"I'm just repeating what I heard."

"I don't mind," said Sophie. "I like working with you. It's like having our own Miss Marple in town."

"Except younger and with better shoes." I gave her a wink. "Do you still keep up with your reading?"

"How do you think I know about Miss Marple?" She tucked her notebook under her arm. "Thanks to you, I'm probably the only person under thirty who reads Agatha Christie."

"Not true," I said. "I'm teaching a new Crimes and Passions course now. We read Christie every semester."

She chuckled. "Thanks, Professor. Don't forget your flowers when you go."

I turned back to the bench. I hadn't brought any flowers with me. But there on the curved cement bench was a small pot of red flowers. "These aren't mine ..." I said, but Sophie was several steps away from me. I looked for Lenny. He was still by the bike rack, conversing with another English faculty member, Jane Lemort. Actually, Jane was talking, and he was glancing over Jane's shoulder, probably trying to find a way out. She was our medieval scholar, and holding a conversation with her could be hard. If the talk didn't have something to do with medieval times or her important committee work, she had nothing to say. Little did Lenny know, I was about to rescue him.

I reached for the plant. It was a begonia. Every spring I bought yellow begonias to match my house. I touched the dark red flower, drawn to it like Sleeping Beauty to the spinning wheel. It was lovely, so why did I have a sinking feeling in my stomach?

"Did you bring me this?" I asked Lenny. "Hi, Jane."

"I certainly hope he didn't," said Jane. She wore a long A-line dress, black, adorned only with a string of black beads. The roots of her hair matched her dress, but the rest of her locks were blonde and pulled into a low ponytail.

"Why not?" I asked Jane.

Lenny answered at the same time. "I didn't."

"Every flower has a meaning, Emmeline, and this is a begonia."

"So?" I said. "I love begonias."

"Years ago—"

"Uh-oh," said Lenny. "Here it comes, a medieval history lesson."

"Ha ha, very funny," she said, not amused. "People used to know the meanings of flowers. I cringe when I go to funerals and see yellow carnations. They were once employed to reject a suitor."

"A hundred years ago, maybe," said Lenny.

"*Anyway*, what do begonias mean?" I prodded.

Jane smiled, holding onto the nugget of information like a piece of gold. "I would think you'd have come across it in your Crimes and Passions course."

"I haven't," I said through gritted teeth.

"They mean … beware."

Chapter Eight

After imparting this grim bit of flower trivia, Jane turned and left. A fellow committee member called to her from the pathway, and she wasn't about to miss an opportunity to socialize with genuine intelligentsia. Lenny and I were too young to be taken seriously. Then again, so was she, but her dour voice was more convincing. Plus, she was better than we were at inserting herself into academic life. She joined everything, organized everything, and championed everything that had anything to do with medieval times. I'd staked out a similar path for myself in graduate school—except in the field of French literature. I was a dedicated scholar who had little room for anything else other than books. Then I came to Copper Bluff, met Lenny, and got pulled into my first murder investigation. Plans fell by the wayside, and life took over, marching in another direction.

The surprise was I didn't regret any of it. Though I'd planned to get a job at an Ivy League school, become chair of my department and then dean of my college, I'd also planned on dating a sommelier who recited poetry. Lenny wasn't even close to that fantasy, but since we'd been dating, I was happier than I'd ever been, and my classes had benefited too. They had little to do with French literature, yet it had been my best year to date. I looked down at the begonia in my hand. Maybe that was about to change.

"Don't let what Jane said bother you," said Lenny, reading my mind. He was good at that. "You *love* begonias and had no idea of their meaning. Nobody does."

"Jane does," I said. "Maybe somebody else does too."

"Maybe they're not even meant for you. How about that?" Lenny took the pot and tossed it in the trash by the bike rack. "Now they're nobody's."

As we walked toward Harriman Hall, I couldn't shake the feeling they were intended for me. That somebody had left them there for me to find, as they had the poem, taunting or tricking me. But who would do that? A student on a bike whizzed by. Students were problematic. I'd given my fair share of failing grades to those who hadn't shown up, not turned in work, or missed requirements. But would a struggling student go to the trouble of writing poems and sending flowers? Most of the time, they couldn't be bothered to submit work. Why exert themselves now?

Lenny held open the door to Harriman Hall for me. I couldn't think of any grievances I had with faculty members. Sure, Jane could be difficult, but she wouldn't threaten me, and I couldn't think of anyone else with a reason to be annoyed with me, except maybe Giles, when I was behind on my grading.

I followed Lenny up the steps. The building was deserted, and I was glad we had a quiet place to talk. When we arrived at the English Department on the second floor, however, I heard Giles talking in his office, probably to Felix and Andy. He had left the garden with them. Lenny and I ducked into his office, where he'd recently upgraded his coffee pot to a Keurig. The machine was silver, shiny, and out of place among so much wood, including bookshelves, a desk, and a chair. Baseball memorabilia dotted the space and vintage Beatles' posters covered the open walls. Lenny was a Beatles fanatic and played the guitar well enough to procure gigs with the university and local bands. Although messy, the room was comfortable. Like my space, only bigger. I was jealous of all the room he had.

I sank into a chair as my cellphone dinged. I checked the screen. "It's a campus alert. They're canceling classes."

Lenny inserted a K-Cup. "What about the Shakespeare Festival?"

I scrolled through the message. "It says all extracurricular activities will continue as scheduled."

"Even *Hamlet*?"

"It says *all*," I repeated. "Scholars have flown in for the conference, and I'm sure they can't reschedule events they've already sold tickets for. Which reminds me, Tanner played the lead in *Hamlet*. Do you think his understudy could have killed him for his part?"

He handed me a Dodgers cup. "Really?"

"Think about it. The crime scene was perfectly staged: a garden, a body, poison oozing out of the dead person's ear. Someone in the theater must be responsible."

He turned back to the Keurig to make himself a cup. "Tanner's no king, and Copper Bluff isn't even close to Denmark."

I waved away the sticking points. "King Hamlet said his brother Claudius killed him to usurp the throne. Maybe someone is usurping Tanner's part."

"Or Tanner's girlfriend," said Lenny. "Claudius also married King Hamlet's widow."

I paused, the cup at my lips. "I hadn't thought of that. Tanner's girlfriend lives right down the street from me. It will be easy to ask around."

Lenny grabbed his cup and sat down in his desk chair. "Before you go asking anything, can we wait for the police to call it murder? It might have been a tragic accident."

"It's tragic, but it's no accident. There are too many coincidences: the sonnet, the garden, the flowers." I crossed my legs. "In my Crimes and Passions course, one of the givens is that the first twenty-four hours are the most crucial in an investigation."

"Then the police will be busy," said Lenny. "You've got your publishing contract to worry about. Did you send it to Gene like Claudia suggested?"

I shook my head, finishing a sip of coffee. "I couldn't sleep last night. I signed it and sent it back."

"What about the revisions clause? I thought you were worried about that."

"Not to brag, but on the phone the publisher seemed pleased with the work," I said. "She didn't mention any revisions."

"First, that was definitely bragging, and second, the publisher isn't the editor." Lenny took a drink of his coffee. "He could ask for all kinds of changes."

"It isn't a scholarly journal, Lenny. They publish mostly fiction. I'm sure any changes will be minimal."

Lenny raised his eyebrows but said nothing.

I stood and looked out the window. The crowd was clearing, but small groups of students and faculty still dotted the quad. Shakespeare's Garden was outlined in yellow tape. "See there? Crime scene tape. They don't use that unless it's a crime."

"Where did you read that?" said Lenny, standing and glancing over my shoulder. "*Murder on the Orient Express*?"

"Don't be silly." I spun around, meeting up with his broad chest. "That murder took place on a train ...." My words trailed off into the atmosphere, a space that didn't include a blond-haired, good-smelling guy with navy-blue eyes staring back at me.

He tucked a curl behind my ear, the one that always came loose from whatever accessory I pinned it into. "Let's get out of here," he said. "Classes are canceled, and I'm hungry."

"It would hardly be appropriate." My voice was a whisper. "To eat at a time like this."

Lenny was just about to argue in favor of its appropriateness when a knock interrupted him. He took a step back before saying, "Come in."

Andy opened the door. His collar was unbuttoned, giving him a more relaxed appearance. He still seemed uptight. "Jim Giles is looking for you, Emmeline. He told me to check for you here on my way out."

"Of course," I said, my words coming out as a squeak. I cleared my throat before adding, "Where are you headed?"

He smoothed an unruly spear of black hair. "Felix and I are going to breakfast before the first panel. You're welcome to join us."

"See?" Lenny whispered. "I told you it was appropriate."

I grabbed my jacket from the back of the chair. "You were on yesterday's panel with Tanner. You seemed … surprised when he came out with his theory about Shakespeare."

"Not really," he said. "Tanner had told me what he was presenting when I ran into him at your little library on Wednesday. I admit I was shocked to see so many sonnets in the submission box. How do you get students to participate?"

Two words: extra credit. But I didn't tell him that. The word *little* was stuck in my craw. "We have a thriving liberal arts culture." That much was true. Our art, drama, and literature events were well-attended. "I didn't realize you talked to Tanner at the library."

Andy checked his Apple watch. Maybe he was getting bored with our conversation. "Not for very long. He was on his way to the theater."

"Was Felix with you?" asked Lenny.

Andy gave Lenny a once over, perhaps judging his informal attire. "Jim Giles told us about the contest. Remember, Emmeline? Felix wanted us to participate."

"So why did Felix feign outrage at the panel?" asked Lenny. "You both knew what was coming, yet you called him out in front of his peers and colleagues."

Andy's brow furrowed. Like his hair, his eyebrows were thick and black. "What is this? Twenty questions?"

I tried to diffuse the situation. "I'm sorry, Andy. We don't mean to bombard you with questions. One of our star English students has just been found dead in Shakespeare's Garden. We're trying to wrap our brains around that."

"I apologize, too," said Andy. "Felix and I were at separate tables in the library, writing our sonnets. We were there maybe ten minutes when I saw Tanner. Recognizing my old classmate, I said hello. He was the same actor I knew, playing the part of a scholar who'd just hit academic gold. He told me enough to intrigue me. He didn't reveal his bombshell."

Tanner was the consummate actor, a man with many personas on hand to dazzle audiences at a moment's notice. Though I didn't know him personally, he always left me slightly mesmerized, and I had a feeling I wasn't the only one. It would make sense that he wanted to keep his big disclosure secret until the panel, his fifteen minutes of fame, as it were.

"And what did you think of his theory, once you heard it?" asked Lenny.

Andy looked from Lenny to me. "Personally? I thought it was kind of cool. Academically? I thought it was suicide, a surefire way not to get a job after graduation. That's why Felix was disgusted, not because of the theory itself. He was gobsmacked that Reed would approve the dissertation."

I gave him props for fitting *gobsmacked* into a conversation. I'd been trying for years. Still, it was hard to believe Felix had Tanner's best interest at heart when he called him out during his presentation. Reed Williams was a dedicated teacher. He wouldn't have chaired Tanner's dissertation committee if he'd thought Tanner's thesis was smoke and mirrors. Besides, plenty of scholars' dissertations never saw the light of day. Mine was still lying in the drawer, collecting dust, except for a few chapters I'd published in scholarly journals.

Andy patted the door frame. "I have to go. Felix is waiting for me. Don't forget about Giles."

"Thank you," I said. "See you later."

He gave Lenny a nod and left.

"I wonder what Giles wants?" I said. "I'll let you know."

"So, no breakfast?" said Lenny.

"I'm afraid not," I said.

"Then dessert." He brushed my lips with his.

"Lenny!" I said. "The door's open."

"I know," he said with a grin. "I just like seeing you blush."

I tossed him a look over my shoulder, irritated by the girlish response. He could already read my mind. Did he really need to read my emotions, too? I marched down the hall with the heat still in my cheeks. Trying to get my head back in the game, I gave it a little shake before I knocked on Giles's door.

"Come in," said Giles.

"Andy said you wanted to talk to me?"

"Yes, come in and shut the door."

This was new. Was I in trouble? I shut the door behind me and took a seat in the armless chair next to his desk. With all the windows, his office was probably the brightest room on the second floor right now, but his expression was dark, troubled. "Is something wrong?"

"Yes, there is," said Giles. "And you're just the person to help." He tapped his fingers together. "It's … personal."

This *was* new. I'd never seen Giles upset before, but upset was the way I'd describe him. More than upset. The furrowed brow, the narrowed eyes, the clenched jaw …. Though I could hardly believe it, Giles was angry. Gone were the three perpetual creases on his forehead and inquisitive tilt to his head. What I observed was pure ire. "I understand," I said, though I really didn't.

"I'm not talking as your boss now," said Giles. "I'm talking as your friend."

I nodded, touched that he thought of me as a friend. I

thought of him as a friend, but I was less reserved. I was too young to be anything but forthright.

"What I want to say is, I'm very upset about Tanner's death," said Giles. "He was my advisee for the past two years. To think that he won't graduate or teach or any of those things we'd talked about—it's inconceivable." He clenched his fists.

"I'm so sorry, Giles. I felt the same when Austin Oliver died, and I'd only known him a semester." My second year on campus, one of my students had died, and I'd helped solve his murder. "I can't imagine what you're going through."

"That's why I wanted to talk to you," said Giles. "I knew you'd understand needing to *do* something about it. The questions surrounding his death must not go unanswered. He was just a boy." Giles's voice cracked.

The depth of his emotion pierced my heart. It was hard to see him hurting this way.

"Felix and Andy ... what do they know of it?" He paused, perhaps recalling an unsatisfactory conversation. "But you, you understand."

"Of course I do," I said. "I want to help in any way I can."

"I know that you do," said Giles. "And I also know you have ways of getting information."

Was I hearing right? Was Giles asking me to investigate?

"You don't have to tell me those ways," Giles rushed to say. "But I trust you will put them to good use in Tanner's case?"

"Absolutely," I said.

Giles sighed, and his whole body seemed to relax. "Thank you, Emmeline. Justice should feel so lucky to have you on her side."

Chapter Nine

—

I CROSSED THE campus with a new determination in my step. Over the years, Giles had done me plenty of favors. He'd swapped my classrooms, given me a job editing the *Copper Bluff Review*, and added my Crimes and Passions course to the curriculum. Now he was upset and asking me, unofficially, to investigate Tanner's death. You'd better believe I was going to do my best. Lenny's voice popped into my head, reminding me it hadn't been declared a murder yet. I glanced at Shakespeare's Garden. There were still a few police officers milling about, but neither Beamer nor Sophie were in sight. I kept walking. No matter. I would talk to them soon enough about the cause of death.

Out of habit, I stood at the crosswalk, listening to the song of a spring robin. Not a single car passed. The campus was as quiet as during spring break. Like pebbles in a pond, students had scattered in different directions, retreating to their places of refuge. On my street, a few students gathered at the old two-story, and I crossed the road quickly to catch them before they ducked inside. I recognized Tanner's girlfriend, Mia, by her floppy blonde bun. She'd thrown on a light trench coat, which looked odd with her sweatpants, but I imagined fashion was the last thing on her mind. Two girls sat next to her on the steps, presumably her roommates. Like her, they were probably graduate students, as was Alice Hudson, who stood by her side. I recognized Alice from the English Department. She was studying Teaching English as a Second Language, a program that was currently missing a director. Though I didn't know her well, I'd talked to her a few times. She was smart, dedicated, and had an interesting scar on her cheek shaped like a star. She planned to teach English to students in China after graduation. I didn't realize she lived in the rental. I was glad to have a connection with the group.

"Hey, Alice," I called from the sidewalk. "How are you holding up?"

She attempted a smile. "Fine."

Alice also had a distinctive hair color, almost cranberry in the sunlight. It was one of the things that made her memorable. I'd love to try the color myself.

"I'm sorry for your loss." I directed the comment toward Mia, Tanner's girlfriend. "I'm Emmeline Prather, by the way. I teach in the English Department. I live down the street." I pointed in the direction of my yellow bungalow.

"Sorry," said Alice. "I should have introduced you."

"Thank you." Mia's voice was barely above a whisper.

"I saw Tanner at the conference yesterday," I continued. "It's hard to believe he's gone. He was so full of life."

The girls said nothing. Either they were too shocked to talk or didn't know what to say. "I'm kicking myself for not going to last night's opening of *Hamlet*. I suppose you were there?"

"All of us," said a blonde girl next to Mia. Even sitting down, the girl looked tall. Her shoulders were broad, and I guessed she played sports. I thought I recognized her as a volleyball player from the *Campus Views* newspaper.

"Are you ...." The name was on the tip of my tongue.

"Hailey Richardson," she said.

"Right, the volleyball player," I said. "How was the performance?"

"Amazing," said the other girl seated next to Mia. Her hair was pulled into a low, wheat-colored ponytail, blonde but more natural-looking than Mia's. She looked short sitting next to Hailey but might have played sports herself. She had on a shirt with our girls' softball team logo on it.

"I wish I could've seen it," I said.

"It was his best performance," said Hailey, "and I've seen lots of them."

"Do you work in the theater?" I asked.

"I graduate with my MFA in Directing this spring." Hailey pointed toward the softball player. "Mackenzie is in Music, and Mia is in Art. We all live in the Fine Arts Building, everyone except Alice." She gave Alice a grin. "She's usually in the Ed building."

So they had ample opportunity to observe Tanner's behavior. "Tanner seemed okay last night?" I asked. "He wasn't sick or …."

Mia shook her head. "He was fine—better than fine. Like Mackenzie said, he was phenomenal as Hamlet. Everybody thought so. We went to Harry's afterwards to celebrate. He ate a slider …." Her voice trailed off as she recalled the night.

"He loved those," said Mackenzie.

"The guy could eat anything and not gain a pound," said Hailey. The girls shared a small laugh.

"Did he drink anything?" I asked. "Alcohol?"

"The police asked me that too, but Tanner didn't drink," said Mia. "He smoked a little weed once in a while—"

"*Mia,*" Mackenzie whispered.

"What?" Mia said. "It's legal almost everywhere."

I held up my hand. "It's okay. I know a lot of students do it." Or they wrote about the legalization of marijuana in their papers for no reason. I tended to believe the former.

"He was high-strung," Mia explained. "Lots of artists are. He needed something to take the edge off, and like I said, he didn't drink."

A car drove by, and I waited for it to pass before I continued. "Was he edgy last night?" Without asking the question outright, I wanted to know if he'd toked.

The girls were reluctant to answer, shuffling about and exchanging quick glances. I felt a lie coming my way.

"It was opening night," Hailey said. "Everyone was edgy. *I* was nervous for the guy."

I took that to mean yes. The play went smoothly; he hadn't flubbed his lines. If opening night hadn't bothered him, what had? Had someone threatened to kill him?

A blast of wind cut through the group, and Mia shivered.

"We should get inside," said Alice. "The sun's going under."

The girls stood.

"If there's anything I can do, please don't hesitate to stop by," I said. "I'm just a block away."

"That's really nice of you, Professor Prather," said Alice. "Thanks for visiting."

As I continued toward my house, I created a hasty timeline in my head. On campus, plays began at seven and ended around ten. The group went out to Harry's after the performance. By eight o'clock this morning, Tanner was dead. I kicked a stray branch out of the way. Between ten p.m. and eight a.m., something went very wrong. I might be able to find out what happened at the pub from someone who worked there. Lenny and I would be going out for breakfast after all. I checked my watch. It was almost eleven. Okay, maybe lunch.

I waved at Dickinson, who was sitting on the windowsill, and pulled open my door. Once inside, I called Lenny, but he didn't answer. My stomach growled, so I grabbed a granola bar and my laptop computer. While waiting for Lenny to get back to me, I would look up our visiting scholars. I didn't know nearly enough about them, and the problems had begun, coincidentally perhaps, upon their arrival. I searched for the faculty page at their Denver university.

"Let's see how smart you really are, Felix Lewis," I said, watching the cursor spin.

Dickinson joined me, placing her orange butt squarely on my keypad. She loved my new laptop more than I did. I was starting to think it sent secret signals to her, for she came running every time I opened it. I worked around the giant impediment as delicately as I could, pulling her closer to my stomach.

"There he is," I said to Dickinson, clicking on Felix's picture.

Much of his biography was the same as what I'd read in the program for his closing lecture. Because he was the keynote speaker, our English Department had spared no paper. The brochure included a full-color photo. His faculty website listed the classes he taught: Shakespeare's Comedies, Shakespeare's Tragedies, Shakespeare in Film, Shakespeare Abroad, Shakespeare in the 21st Century.

"He's a Shakespeare god, Dickinson," I murmured as I scanned the text. "I bet his sonnet entry was topnotch. Claudia must have read it."

Finding nothing alarming, I leaned back in my chair and relaxed. He was just as smart and nonviolent as he looked. Silver hair, distinguished jacket, lapel pin with flower. *With flower!* I sat up, squinting at the screen. The sudden movement startled Dickinson, who leaped off my lap. I zoomed in on Felix's jacket. On the lapel was pinned a sprig of heather.

"Not so smart now, are you Felix?" I tapped the screen. "I see you have a weakness for flowers—as does our mystery man … or woman," I added. "I wonder if you know flowers as well as you know Shakespeare's plays?" Our own Shakespeare scholar, Reed Williams, knew plenty about flowers. It seemed any scholar specializing in the bard would have to have a rough understanding of them in regard to the plays. That gave me another idea. Maybe the actors and actresses had specialized knowledge as well. If this trail turned up nothing, I could always go to the theater.

I opened a new browser window, determined to find the meaning behind the heather sprig—without Jane Lemort's help. The language of flowers was not dead, but according to my search, alive and well. Several sites were dedicated to flower facts. So did Felix get it right? Was heather appropriate for the professional picture? Within a few minutes, I decided it was. Heather meant admiration and luck. Two qualities that couldn't be more essential to succeeding in academia. The information put Felix on my suspect list. If he was knowledgeable about flowers, he could be behind the begonias.

My cellphone rang just as I took a bite of my granola bar. At first I thought it was Lenny, returning my call, but it was a Los Angeles number. As I reached for the phone, I dropped it in the crack of my couch. Panicking, I grabbed the cushion and threw it on the floor, retrieving my phone from the crevice. "Hello? Hello, this is Emmeline."

"Emmeline, this is Owen Parrish, from Dewberry Press," said a nasal voice that made my name sound like a curse word.

"Hello, Owen," I croaked, running to the kitchen for a glass of water. A piece of granola had lodged in my throat, and I was on the verge of a coughing fit.

"I'm the fiction editor, so I was surprised when your project ended up in my lap. Then again, what doesn't?" he added more quietly.

I tried a chuckle, but it came out as a cough. His tone put me on the defensive.

"But you don't need to hear about our staffing problems," he said. "What you *do* need to hear is that I'd like you to get started right away on the rewrite."

Rewrite? No "Congratulations!" "Atta girl!" or "What a remarkable piece of scholarship, Ms. Prather"?

When I didn't respond right away, Owen continued, "I've made notes on the chapters that will need to be removed—"

"I'm sorry," I interrupted him. "Did you say *chapters* will need to be removed?"

"That's exactly what I said. The ending doesn't leave one with the upbeat feeling our readers expect. We don't publish obscure novels."

I tried to remain calm. Over the last ten years, I had gotten used to giving and receiving feedback on written work. If something needed to change, I could deal with it. "It's not obscure, and it's not a novel. What chapters need work?"

"What chapters *don't* need work might be the better question," said Owen. "The process is complicated, and I need you to be open to it one hundred percent."

I gauged myself at about twenty-five percent open. "Of course."

"Do you understand what I'm saying?"

Was I ten? Yes, I understood what he was saying. What I didn't understand was his adversarial attitude. We both had the same goal: to get my book out there so the masses could enjoy it. "I understand."

"Look for a document in your inbox this afternoon," said Owen. "Make sure you track all your changes so I can approve them."

"Track them where?"

Owen let out a long breath. "In Microsoft Word."

After that huff, I wasn't about to ask another question. I'd figure out how to track them when I opened my inbox.

"South Dakota," said Owen, pausing. "I bet it's cold there."

"It can be, but it's been unseasonably warm," I said, staring out my kitchen window. "Believe it or not, today's forecast—"

"I'll call you next week."

I guessed he wasn't into pleasantries. "Okay … thank you."

He hung up, and I glanced at my phone. Had that conversation really happened? For the first time in years, I was blinking back tears like a chastened child. I took a deep breath. I hadn't finished my granola bar; that was it. I was hungry and upset over Tanner's death. A student had been found dead on campus, and my department chair had asked me to figure out why. Of course I was upset. I wasn't superwoman. It was times like this that made me glad I had Lenny to talk to. I dialed his number again.

"I knew you'd change your mind," he said in lieu of a salutation. "I was just calling you back."

"Yes, do you want to go to Harry's for lunch?"

"What's the matter?" he asked.

"Nothing," I said.

"I can hear something's wrong in your voice."

"Let's talk at lunch," I said.

"Are you driving, or am I?"

It was beautiful out, a perfect day for a ride in my red '69 convertible Mustang. "I am."

"Good," he said. "I'll be outside."

Ten minutes later, I drove up to his olive-green house. His street was a collection of perfectly spaced houses from the 1970s. Though it was nothing like mine, I liked his neighborhood because of its outward orderliness. Each square of property was well cared for, including Lenny's. He was picking up stray branches in his yard when I pulled into his driveway. He stopped and smiled, then put the branches in a pile next to his house before getting into the car.

"Not putting the top down?" Lenny still wore his red sweatshirt and jeans. I wished I would have changed, too. I was too dressed up for the pub.

"Maybe later," I said. "The wind is chilly."

He hung his arm out the window. "I'm glad you called. I'm starving."

"I talked to Tanner's girlfriend, Mia," I said, turning onto Main Street. Soon the old-fashioned lampposts would be adorned with baskets of colorful flowers. The flags that read Welcome to Copper Bluff were already up. "She said they ate at the pub last night. I thought we could find out how late they were there, what they drank, etcetera."

"So the ulterior motive comes out," said Lenny. "Our sleuth never sleeps."

"I'm just saying, while we're there, we might as well ask a few questions."

"Work 'em in with the crinkly fries." Lenny gave me a grin. "Is that what you're saying?"

"Something like that." I pulled into an open spot in front of Main Street Grill, also known as Harry's or The Pub. It was a brick tavern with comfy booths, sticky tables, daily specials, and a bartender named Harry who made every trip worthwhile. I shut off the car, and we walked inside. I was glad to see a booth open near the front window. I liked to people-watch as I ate.

Lenny grabbed a laminated menu from the end of the table. "Nice. Today's special is fish and chips." He handed me the menu. "That's what I'm having."

I returned it to the end of the table. "Me too."

Lenny studied my face. "Something *is* going on. What is it?"

The waitress came, and I ordered two sodas and two lunch specials. When she left, I said, "Tanner was found dead a couple of hours ago. Isn't that enough?"

He unraveled a set of cutlery. "Not for you. What happened?"

"I talked to the editor at Dewberry Press," I said, smoothing my paper placemat. "Owen Parrish."

The waitress arrived with the beverages. "What'd he say?"

I stared at the bubbles in my soda. "He doesn't like me."

"What do you mean, he doesn't like you?" He sounded incensed.

"I mean, he doesn't like my work. He said it needs revision."

Lenny plopped a straw into his glass. "That's nothing. It's his job to revise things. He's an editor. You're an excellent writer."

"He said *chapters* need to be removed," I said.

"Chapters?" Lenny exclaimed. "What an idiot."

I was glad he didn't mention the revision clause. He could have easily said, "I told you so." It was nice to know he was on my side, even when he didn't know the other side.

"I'd like to see him remove one comma," he continued. "Has he seen your CV?"

"I don't know," I said. "He mentioned our weather, so I guess he has."

"Weather? The guy sounds like a lunatic."

I laughed out loud. Weather was a reasonable topic around here, not exactly lunacy. His support was nice, but I needed to switch gears. "Anyway, I talked to Mia, and she confirmed what Andy said earlier. Tanner didn't drink, but he did smoke pot."

"And you think that's what killed him?"

I shook my head. "According to every student essay ever written, no. No one's ever died of a marijuana overdose."

The fish and chips arrived, steamy hot. Lenny hit his chips with extra salt, and I dipped the battered fish in the homemade tartar sauce. "Mia said he was on edge. I thought maybe he had an argument with someone last night."

Lenny held up a chip. "About his Shakespeare theory."

"Possibly," I said. "It was a hot-button topic."

"I wonder where our visiting scholars were last night," said Lenny.

"Good question," I said. "Whoever murdered Tanner is a Shakespeare expert."

He munched his chip for a moment. "Expert?"

"The sonnet and staged death scene? I think so, and Felix and Andy both submitted entries."

"You think the same person who wrote the sonnet killed Tanner," he said.

"I do."

"But why alert someone to a crime you're going to commit?" asked Lenny. "That doesn't make sense. You might give yourself away."

"I know," I said, seeing the contradiction. "I suppose it's possible we have two Shakespeare authorities, one who wanted to warn us about the other."

"Like Felix and Andy."

It was a handy theory. I liked the idea of two out-of-towners, at odds over the way to handle Tanner's revelation. And Felix did have a real flower pinned to his lapel. I told Lenny.

"You looked him up on his faculty website?" He took a big bite of fish. "That's the woman I love."

It was the first time the word *love* had entered our conversations. I had to admit, I didn't imagine it happening over fish and chips at the pub. But there it was, sitting between us like the napkin holder, and I felt a ridiculous blush rise to my face. It was a figure of speech, a cliché, and here I was treating it like a declaration of affection. Stupid, stupid romances. I read too many, watched too many, and imagined too many far-fetched scenarios. No wonder my previous relationships ended in disaster.

Lenny reached for my hands across the table at the same time the waitress arrived with our check. He stopped midway. This was my last chance to ask her about Tanner. "Can I ask you a question?"

"Sure." Her nametag read "Linda," and her one-syllable responses let me know she was busy, which is why I hadn't asked her before. I'd hoped the rush would end before she brought the check. Now I had to think of a question that didn't require a yes or no answer. I did it all the time with my students.

"I'm wondering about a group of students who were here last night. Were you working?" Dang! That was a yes-or-no question.

She gave my outfit a once over. Maybe she'd think I was there on behalf of the college, which I kind of was. Giles wanted me to figure out what happened. "I was here until close." She tucked her order pad into her pocket. Maybe she was ready for a little break. "Who are you looking for?"

"A group from the theater," I said. "Tall guy, outgoing. His name was Tanner."

"Oh my god, *him*," said Linda. "He was here with a bunch of people. He was acting like an idiot."

"Was he drinking?" I asked.

"I think he'd had plenty before he came. His speech was slurred, and he was flirting up a storm. Then his girlfriend talks to his friend—'cause what's she gonna do, she's sitting there alone—and he blows up. Crazy."

His slurred speech was interesting, considering Mia and Andy said he didn't drink. Could pot slur your speech?

"Did they get into a fist fight?" asked Lenny.

"Nope," she said. "He left in a huff. I was glad to see him trip on the way out the door."

"His friend—do you remember his name or what he looked like?" I asked. She'd taken a step back from the table. Maybe she needed to return to her customers.

"No name, but he had glasses, nice-looking."

"Smart?" I asked, thinking of Denton.

That got a laugh. "I don't know. People aren't that smart when they come to the bar."

"Thank you," I said. "I appreciate it."

She walked away, leaving me wondering about Tanner, his slurred speech, and his fight with the man in glasses. It could have been Denton, but he didn't seem like the type who spent his evenings in the bar.

"I see the wheels turning in your head," said Lenny.

"The waitress said his speech was slurred, but Tanner didn't drink." I repositioned my straw. "Don't you find that odd?"

"Maybe he made an exception," said Lenny. "It *was* opening night."

I took a sip of my soda, considering the possibility.

"Someone could have bought him some shots, and he had to drink them," said Lenny. "I've been in situations like that."

"He did trip on his way out the door," I said. Plus, he was arguing with a friend. Some people become combative after a few drinks. "Did Tanner seem like the jealous type to you?"

"Not really," Lenny said. "But we wouldn't see that side of him. He was an actor, very … animated. He wore his emotions on his sleeve."

"That's true," I said. "He was an emotional guy. As an actor, he could also summon any emotion on the spot."

He finished his soda. "Guys like that—intense, I mean—they're always on the verge of exploding. Don't you think?"

I agreed. Maybe that's what Mia meant by "on edge."

Seeing Lenny was finished, I slipped into my blue spring jacket. Though the day was warm and the sun was shining, the wind was chilly enough for a coat. Lenny had no need for one with his sweatshirt. We grabbed for the check at the same time. (He liked to pay, and so did I.) A shock of static electricity happened between us, and I smiled.

He laced his fingers with mine. "Do you believe in magic?"

Had he said "spirits," "God," or "fate," I would not have hesitated to answer in the affirmative. But magic? That was another question entirely. That was the sleight of hand, the miraculous disappearance, the unexplained. Magic could happen with the flick of a wrist, a hat, or a glove. But then I remembered *David Copperfield*, the novel by Charles Dickens, and there was a kind of magic. With a flip of the page, I was in nineteenth-century England. Experiencing a different time, a different social class, and a different perspective—a man's. I would call that magic.

"Yes, I do." I made an extraordinary loop on the E of my name as I wrote out a check. The rest of the world operated on credit. In Copper Bluff, restaurants still accepted personal checks.

"It wasn't a test," said Lenny with a laugh.

"It's a difficult question, when you think about it," I said, ripping the check from the book.

"I don't think so," said Lenny. "I think you know it when you feel it."

I guessed we weren't talking about card tricks. He was staring at me with his dark-blue eyes, which made it hard to concentrate on why we were there: to gather information about the night before Tanner's death. Instead, my imagination went skipping ahead to scenarios in a regency romance novel. The words *Gretna Green* came to mind, and I shook my head. I was in the middle of the South Dakota prairie in the twenty-first century, pretty much as far away as I could get from that Scottish parish, the most popular wedding destination in the world, thanks to centuries of tradition and looser marriage laws.

"I know what you're thinking," said Lenny, still smiling.

"Oh, I highly doubt that," I said, sliding out of the booth. If he had, he'd run as fast as he could in the other direction. In the past, I would have too. If I wasn't careful, I'd ruin the best relationship I'd ever had. For years, I'd worried dating would wreck our friendship, but it was just the opposite. We were closer than ever.

"What if I was thinking the same thing?" he said, pulling open the door.

Unless he'd read the latest installment of *Scottish Bride*, he wasn't. I slid into my car. "You weren't."

"But if I was?" he pressed.

I gave him a glance and started the engine. "That *would* be magic."

Chapter Ten

＊

D ESPITE IT BEING a Friday—Friday nights were reserved
for Italian food and a classic movie—Lenny agreed
to attend tonight's production of *Hamlet*. Getting him to
commit involved arm twisting on my part. He said he'd rather
grade American Survey papers than sit through the entire
Shakespeare play. I promised him we would leave early if we
found out any useful information. What that information
entailed, I couldn't say. Giles *encouraged* all English faculty to
attend anyway. We had to put in an appearance. Reed Williams
had collaborated with Martha Church in the Art Department
to create an exhibition of authentic dress from the sixteenth
century. It would be on display before tonight's performance.
One hour before the show, attendees could view the historic
attire of commoners and royals alike. Actors performing in
Hamlet would be in costume, available to answer questions
about the time period. It would provide the perfect opportunity
to find out more about Tanner's fellow cast members.

After dropping off Lenny, I decided to see if the police had
uncovered anything about Tanner's death. I turned toward the
station. Beamer would want to know about the flowers—the

begonias that had been left for me on the bench—and the sonnet. Giles had informed campus security, but I doubted the information had been relayed to Beamer or even connected to Tanner's death. I wheeled into the parking lot. Probably not. A college campus was a world in and of itself, which was why Beamer needed me. We hadn't had a chance to talk this morning. Now we could compare notes.

"Hello," I said as I walked through the door. I recognized the officer at the small front desk. She was here when I left my DNA sample last Christmas, another story altogether. "I'm Emmeline Prather. Is Officer Beamer here?"

"Is this in regard to the student death this morning?" She picked up the phone.

"Yes," I said.

"I got it, Milly," said Beamer, walking through a hallway. "Come on, Ms. Prather. This way."

"Thank you," I said to Milly as I followed Beamer into his office. His room was at the end of the hall, larger than the others we passed, with no window. The white walls were plain but suitable for a man who didn't like things too complicated.

"To what do I owe this unexpected visit?" said Beamer as he fell into his cracked-leather office chair. It was well-worn, like all the furniture in the room. The rest of the building's decor was in far better shape. Whoever was in charge of remodeling hadn't been able to convince Beamer to part with his furniture. I imagined he was the type of man who only replaced something when it broke.

"I have some information for you, about the case," I said, taking the seat across from him. "We didn't have a chance to talk this morning."

"I told Officer Barnes to take your statement," he said.

"Oh, she did," I said. "But there was one thing I forgot to mention, and another strange thing that happened afterward."

He opened a notepad on his desk. "So two *things*."

"Right," I said, glancing around the room. "This office must be new."

"Yes."

"I thought I smelled paint." I indicated the walls. "I suppose you don't have your decorations up yet." When he didn't answer, I added, "Pictures, etcetera. They can make a space seem homier."

He rubbed his temples, and I noticed the tufts of gray hair behind his ears reached deeper into his hairline. It had to be the slew of cases he'd taken on lately. I was glad to be here for him. I wanted to help as much as I could.

"Could we get back to the two things?" he said.

"Of course." Beamer wasn't one for small talk. "A suspicious sonnet was submitted to our Shakespeare contest Wednesday. It warned of a tragedy. Jim Giles, our chair, called somebody about it, probably campus police. I don't know if you get those messages."

"And the second thing?"

I felt my brow furrow. "Don't you want to know what the poem said?"

He took a drink from his coffee cup. "I think I get the gist of *tragedy*."

Poor Officer Beamer. He really was in a mood. "The second thing was a pot of flowers, begonias. I was sitting on a bench, and when I got up to talk to Sophie—Officer Barnes, I mean— someone left me a pot of begonias."

"As a gift?"

I leaned in closer. "As a warning. My colleague, Jane Lemort, said begonias mean 'beware,' and although Jane's not very friendly, she's rarely wrong."

"So what do these two things have to do with Tanner Sparks?" Beamer's pencil teetered near the notebook, but so far, it hadn't touched the page.

"Somebody's messing with me." Truthfully, I was getting a little exasperated with Beamer. He was usually quicker than this. "They're trying to scare me away from the murder. We are calling it murder, now, aren't we?"

"*We're* not calling it anything, Ms. Prather," said Beamer. "You have nothing to do with this case whatsoever."

"But I do," I said. "Someone has placed me squarely in the middle of it, like it or not."

"Does that someone have blue eyes and curly hair?"

I opened my mouth, realized he was talking about me, and smiled. "I'm being serious, Officer Beamer. Even the crime scene was staged to look like a scene from *Hamlet*."

"Explain what you mean."

I described the connection to the play. This time he took notes.

"How much do you know about Shakespeare?" he asked.

"I'm an English professor, aren't I?" My answer was in no way a lie.

"I knew the body had been moved, but I didn't know why." He tapped his pencil on the notepad. "Now I do."

"How do you know the body had been moved?"

"Blanching. When a person dies, blood begins to pool right away, about thirty minutes after death. Skin in contact with a hard surface turns white, or blanches, which indicates the body position at time of death." Beamer paused. "In this case, the victim's blanching was on the wrong side."

"He didn't die on the bench," I said. "That's what you're saying."

"Probably not far from the bench, though," said Beamer. "The victim is decent-sized, and we didn't find any drag marks."

"He was moved to the bench to recreate the scene in the play," I said. "That's why the liquid was in his ear. Find out what the liquid is, and you'll find the cause of death."

LATER ON, AS I got ready to attend *Hamlet*, I considered the parallels between the play and Tanner's death. The clues pointed to someone in the theater, an actress or actor who enjoyed the spotlight. Lines from another Shakespeare play, *As You Like It*, drifted through my mind: "All the world's a stage, / And all the men and women merely players; / They have their exits and their entrances." Tanner Spark had been forced to exit much too soon. The cause of death was apparently copied from that of Hamlet's father. Could Tanner's iconoclastic theory about the bard's true identity have prompted the killer to give him a Shakespearean death? Tanner claimed he had proof that Edward de Vere faked his death, which meant de Vere could have been the author of the later Shakespeare plays. Was it possible that Tanner held the key to the Shakespeare mystery?

It seemed impossible, but I had a few ways to investigate. Reed Williams would have a draft of Tanner's dissertation. I could ask to see it. Denton Smart, the medical student helping Tanner with his research, would also know about it. When I thought about it, Denton might know more than Reed. He was in charge of the DNA. If anyone had physical evidence, it was Denton.

I checked my hair in the mirror. After a tussle and a spray, I slipped into my black ankle boots. They went with everything, including the blue and black skirt I'd selected. In the kitchen, I stared at my cupboards, wondering if I should eat something before the play. Because of my big lunch at Harry's, I wasn't hungry, but it was either now or after the play. Could I really wait that long?

My phone buzzed on the counter. Lenny had sent me a text. *Are you eating before the play?* I blinked. He really could read my mind. *Wondering the same thing*, I replied. *Let's hit up Vinny's afterwards. Pick you up in ten.* I sent him a thumbs-up and tucked the phone into my purse. I wanted to make sure I had it tonight at the theater.

I'd just finished feeding Dickinson when Lenny pulled up. I shrugged into my coat and grabbed my keys. Outside, Lenny and Mrs. Gunderson were having a conversation. As I locked the door, I heard Mrs. Gunderson ask Lenny if our relationship was *serious*. I paused, waiting for his answer.

"Dead serious, wouldn't you say, Em?"

I spun around. "I don't like the way that sounds."

The dimple in Lenny's cheek was showing. He looked handsome in a dark jacket and jeans, his blond hair a striking contrast to his outfit. I skipped down the steps.

"You're so quarrelsome, Emmeline," said Mrs. Gunderson. "Just agree with the man."

He linked his arm in mine. "Yeah, just agree with the man."

I gave him a glare, whispering, "*Dead* is what you'll be if you keep this up."

"Just a minute," called Mrs. Gunderson. "I want to get a picture of you two. You look so nice." She stepped inside her house and popped back out with a little black camera. "Come over here by my tree."

We walked over to her maple, and she snapped the picture.

"Thanks, Mrs. G," said Lenny as we walked to his car. He opened my door, and I ducked inside.

Mrs. Gunderson held up the camera. "You never know when you'll need a picture for the paper."

Lenny shut the door before I could respond. She was still standing on her front stoop as we drove away.

"She drives me crazy," I said, smiling and waving.

"You love her," said Lenny.

"She's nosy."

"*You're* nosy," he said.

I couldn't deny it, though I preferred the word *curious*. Anyway, we had much more important topics to discuss than my neighbor. I told him about my conversation with Officer Beamer. I also told him Tanner's body had been moved.

"Whoever did this was strong enough to carry Tanner, or drag him, to the garden," said Lenny, driving toward the theater. It was only two blocks from campus. Several spots in the parking lot were already taken. Other department chairs must have encouraged their faculty members to attend the exhibit before the production.

"And Tanner wasn't a small guy," I said. "The question is why. We're assuming the killer wanted to replicate the murder in Hamlet, but there might be a second reason."

"Moving the body to a central location makes it harder to figure out where or how he was murdered."

"The campus is one of the only places in town that doesn't have surveillance," I added.

"Right," said Lenny, pulling into an open parking space.

"Keep an eye out for Tanner's understudy," I said. "I want to meet him. To size him up, as it were."

He shut off the ignition. "If we find him, can we go?"

"It'd look bad to leave early," I said.

A smile touched his lips. " 'There is nothing either good or bad, but thinking makes it so.' "

Lenny quoting Shakespeare? I had a feeling this was going to be a long night.

Chapter Eleven

———

A S WE WALKED into the theater, Lenny grumbled about the purchase price. We'd missed the opportunity for rush tickets. I reminded him the faculty discount still applied. Reluctantly, he turned toward the box office, and I continued to the gallery, where I was greeted by a man in a ruffled green shirt, knee breeches, stockings, and a feathered hat.

"Welcome, my lady," he said.

The actors must have been instructed to remain in character. "Hello, kind sir."

"And how does this evening find you?"

"Very well," I said, guessing he was a graduate student. Now I just had to guess what part he was playing. He wasn't a peasant; you could tell that much from his elaborate costume. But he wasn't royalty either. "And who are you to Hamlet?"

He gave a dramatic bow. "I am his dear friend, Horatio, scholar and confidant."

I glanced around the room and saw no one in black. "Where is your good friend?"

"Detained by a last-minute alteration, I'm afraid," he said. "But the Queen of Denmark is standing over there. You might ask her about her son's wardrobe woes." He motioned toward a woman with a red gown and a blue robe that draped over her headpiece. She was talking to a small group of people, and I took a few steps in her direction so that Horatio could greet other visitors. Claudius was at her side, and the ghost of King Hamlet, dressed in armor, looked on vengefully. The ghost of King Hamlet would know the story of his own murder; he was the one to recount it on stage. I moved to his side.

"Hello," I said. "Am I speaking to the king of Denmark?"

"I once was that."

The actor, a young student, was not a very convincing ghost. The makeup and wig didn't do much to transform him from gangly schoolboy to hoary old man. He couldn't have dragged Tanner into the garden any more than I could have.

"But my brother poured the cursed hebenon into my ear as I slept," he continued, "and now owns that coveted title."

Lenny entered the room, and I gave him a wave. He joined me and Hamlet's father.

"You must be the ghost," said Lenny. "I like your armor, though I don't get why you wear it. Don't ghosts usually wear white?"

"My mission is a patriotic one," said the ghost, gripping the hilt of his sword as if ready to unsheathe it. "All of Denmark is in danger."

"And what about *our* Hamlet?" I asked. "Was he in danger from anyone?"

The ghost looked from me to Lenny. Either he didn't understand, or he didn't want to break character.

"She means Tanner Sparks," said Lenny. "Is there anyone here he didn't get along with?"

"How to answer, I do not know," said the ghost.

"Yes or no would be a good start," said Lenny.

"I must bid you good evening," said the ghost. "The safety of Denmark depends on my message, and time is short."

The ghost stalked Claudius and the queen, coming up

behind them unannounced. They turned their heads from side to side, pretending to sense a presence without actually seeing him. The onlookers enjoyed the performance.

"What does that mean?" asked Lenny. "They can't respond as real people?"

I shook my head. "I think they have to stay in character."

I noticed Martha Church, a costume designer from the Art Department, trailing a sulky man in black. She carried a needle and thread. "That must be Hamlet," I said. "Horatio said he had a wardrobe malfunction."

"Mystery solved," said Lenny. "He's big enough to haul two Tanners. Can we go now?"

I ignored Lenny. The new Hamlet was tall and fit, a runner perhaps. Lenny was right: he looked strong enough to carry Tanner to the garden or anywhere else on campus. His dark hair was partially covered by a cap, and he wore a sweeping black robe, scarf, and stockings. Claudius beckoned to him, and he joined the group, to the delight of the onlookers. I hoped the play would be as entertaining as their interactions.

"I want to talk to Martha," I told Lenny. "I met her when Austin died, and as the dresser, she's obviously spent some time with the cast and the new Hamlet."

I crossed the room, and Lenny followed. Martha, a flamboyant woman with a pillow of frizzy blonde hair, wore a seamstress's bracelet with a pin cushion and was sticking a needle into it as we approached. The long sleeve of her purple dress kept getting in the way.

"Hello, Martha," I said. "I hope you remember me. It's been a while."

She looked up from her bracelet and smiled. "Of course. How are you?"

"Good," I said. "This is Lenny Jenkins. He teaches American lit."

They shook hands.

"The costumes look great," I said, taking in the room with

a sweeping motion. "Horatio said Hamlet needed some last-minute alterations."

"He's six feet four," whispered Martha. "It wasn't an alteration. It was a miracle."

"Tanner Sparks was much shorter," I said.

She nodded.

"Well, you did a very nice job." I gave Hamlet a glance. "He looks like most of the other Hamlets I've seen."

"It's not historically accurate, you know," she said, rearranging a pin on the cushion. "Hamlet is the last person who should be in black, as the Danes never mourned anyone—not even their closest relations. He should be in scarlet. But as you just confirmed, it's what audiences expect." She pulled her wide sleeve over the bracelet.

"How does he feel about taking over Tanner's part?" Lenny asked. "That must be difficult so soon after his death."

"It must be," she said, "but you wouldn't know it. It's what understudies prepare for. The worst. They must be ready to go on at a moment's notice. I think that'd be hard, the not knowing."

"Did he say anything … about Tanner?" I asked.

"He has nerves of steel. He was stoic, determined that the play continue." She shrugged her shoulders. "It could be an act. We'll see in an hour."

I hung on to the comment as she walked away. The room was buzzing with activity. The audience members, who appeared to be mostly students and faculty, were interacting with the characters or absorbed in reading about the costumes or scenes from placards on the wall. Two Elizabethan costumes, a man's and a woman's, were adorning department-store mannequins and housed in tall display cases. Another display case was devoted to Shakespeare himself—a poster of the iconic drawing of the bard surrounded by several photos and drawings from historic productions and scenes from Stratford-upon-Avon. Reed stood before that case, hands in pockets, peering in. The man always looked a little sad, but tonight he looked crestfallen. Our loss was minimal compared to his. I felt bad for him.

"Let's go say hi," Lenny said. He must have been thinking the same thing I was.

Reed hardly noticed us approach. He was staring at a picture of Shakespeare's house in Stratford-upon-Avon, according to the caption.

"Hey, Reed," said Lenny. "How's it going?"

He acknowledged us with a nod. "Do you know this isn't even Shakespeare's house?"

"What do you mean?" I asked. It looked like the same white-and-brown, thatched-roof house I'd seen in books. Very English and iconic.

"The gables, the roof, the windows—all constructed between 1858-1864. The nineteenth century! The only thing original are the cellars. This little piece here, this was what was originally dubbed Shakespeare's house. When more tourists and money needed to be accommodated, the pub to the right was bought along with the house to the left. Thus, the monstrosity we have today."

Lenny and I exchanged glances. Reed seemed to be talking nonsense.

"Have you, uh, been there?" Lenny asked.

Reed shook his head. "I learned about it from Tanner. I've studied Shakespeare all my life and had no idea."

"Tanner had a theory," I said. "An unproven theory."

He sighed. "A darn convincing theory, Emmeline. I can't shake it."

I didn't know what hurt him more: the loss of his student or the loss of his Shakespeare. To dedicate a life to the study of someone who might not be the person you thought he was? Devastating. There was no other word for it.

"The important thing is the plays," said Lenny. "They're perfect. Does it really matter who wrote them?"

I admired Lenny's restraint. He wasn't a Shakespeare fan, far from it. He could have said anything but chose to say the right thing.

"Don't you see?" said Reed. "It would change everything. Who we thought he was, who we thought we were. The Shakespeare I know is the quintessential underdog. A man I could root for. A man I could understand. A man I recognized in myself." Reed threw up his hands at the display. "This here, I don't know."

"No one can change who you are," I said. "You're a distinguished scholar I'm proud to know. I mean that," I added, when he returned the compliment with a sad smile.

Hamlet and Claudius started arguing, and our attention turned to them. They were arguing over Claudius's marriage to Hamlet's mother, Gertrude, as the ghost looked on encouragingly. Hamlet unsheathed his sword, a metaphorical flex of his muscles, and when he did, something fell from his pocket. Laughter trickled through the crowd.

I craned my neck to see what it was.

Claudius, a large ruddy student, laughed. "Does Hamlet purpose to kill me with kindness, for it is a beautiful flower he wields instead of a sword."

I took a step closer. A small bunch of yellow flowers lay on the floor.

Hamlet, however, was not laughing. He kneeled down to pick up the bouquet, tied with a string. A note seemed to indicate they were meant for him. Pointing the flowers at Claudius, he said, "Who did this? You?"

"Surely I do not come bearing flowers," said Claudius. The smile on his face diminished as Hamlet glared at him.

"I mean it!" said Hamlet. "Who did this?"

The room grew silent. Though I wanted a better look at the flowers, I dared not move, lest I call attention to myself in the stillness of the room. They were yellow; that was all I could see.

Hamlet picked up the flowers and threw them at Claudius. "I'll get you for this!"

He stormed out of the room, and a ruckus followed. The audience wasn't sure if the scene was part of the performance. Claudius himself looked uncertain, especially when Horatio followed Hamlet.

"What's the deal with flowers?" Lenny asked Reed. "Why's he so upset?"

"It's bad luck to give an actor flowers before a performance," said Reed. "I wouldn't be surprised if that little prank throws off Hamlet's entire night." He wiped his nose with a handkerchief. "Students. They can be ruthless when they want to be."

I took a step in the direction of the flowers on the floor. Everyone's attention was now elsewhere. Just then Claudius picked up the flowers and walked over to the trash can.

"Wait!" I said. Several heads turned, including Claudius's. My mind went blank, and I said the first thing that came into my head. "It seems a waste to throw away fresh flowers. Could I have them?"

"Knock yourself out," he said, shoving them in my hand.

I studied the simple bouquet. Marigolds. Their pungent stink gave them away. A long black hair provided a clue as to the sender. Jacob had black hair. So did Andy. I picked up the strand. But neither had hair this long.

"That's one way to get flowers, I suppose," said Jane Lemort, who appeared at my elbow. She wore a navy dress with black lace that disguised its pretty color. Part of me wondered if she bought the relics at an online specialty shop for medieval aficionados. I didn't dare ask. There was an online beret shop I was quite fond of. I could be Jane in a couple of years if I didn't watch out.

"Jane, I'm so glad you're here."

She blinked, perplexed as I was by the words that had flown out of my mouth.

"These are marigolds, right?" I said. "Do you know what they symbolize, if anything?"

She leaned in and sniffed them, then jerked back. "Yes, these are definitely marigolds."

I glanced at the card. It was addressed to Jacob Heraldson, the student playing Hamlet, but no giver was named. Turning it over, I noticed a Day of the Dead skull insignia. "Are marigolds associated with the Day of the Dead?" The Day of the Dead was November 2 or All Souls' Day in my church. Nowhere near April.

Her pointed chin tipped upward. "Yes, they are. It's said their bright colors lead the dead back to the living."

That was interesting. Was someone trying to lead Tanner's ghost to Jacob?

"But they can also symbolize jealousy, cruelty, and grief in general."

Another interesting connotation. Could Jacob, driven by jealousy of Tanner, have gone after his part in the cruelest way possible? "How do you know so much about flowers?" I doubted that Jane could lift a man Tanner's size—she was way too skinny—but if her muscles were as strong as her zeal for committee work, I couldn't rule it out.

"You must encounter flowers in your classes," she said with a tinny laugh. "I'm not the only literature teacher here."

"A rose, a chrysanthemum, myrtle—nothing like your knowledge. Where does it come from?"

"You got me," she said. "My mom's a florist. I've known the meanings of flowers since I was ten years old and have kept up with the language."

The information moved me, though I couldn't say why. Maybe it was the knowledge that Jane liked flowers. It made her seem more human.

"It *is* a language, you know," she continued. "Just like French or any other. I've talked to the dean about a certificate. There's no reason we can't offer one here."

Now I felt moved—toward the door. I glanced briefly at Lenny. It was all the hint he needed to follow me.

Chapter Twelve

—

I TOLD LENNY about my conversation with Jane as we walked toward the auditorium. Though he thought we had collected enough information on Jacob, I insisted we attend at least part of the play to see if he was shaken by receiving the flowers. This killer was smart: Jacob could have sent them to himself to throw suspicion elsewhere. The only way to know for certain was to see the play. Reluctantly, Lenny agreed. At least Giles could duly note our appearance.

The flowers were in Jacob's pocket. But if he didn't put them there, it meant somebody suspected him of killing Tanner. Unless it was a prank, like Reed said. Either way, one of the actors or someone close to the theater had to have been involved. I'd need to talk to the actors when they weren't in character. Perhaps after the play? I sneaked a glance at Lenny as we scooted into our seats. He caught my look, and I gave him a sweet smile.

"I know that smile." He helped me with the sleeve of my jacket before he sat down.

"What smile?" I said, getting comfortable in my seat.

"The one you give me right before you ask me to do something," he said.

I grabbed his hand as the lights begin to dim. We could talk about that later. The red velvet curtain was lifting and the set coming into view. The most striking feature was the platform of Elsinore Castle, where a guard stood. It towered above the interior of the castle, which had arched windows and a checkered floor. Though dark, the space felt real, authentic. Alexander Schwartz and his set designer, Dan Fox, were pros, and while we lived in a small college town in the Midwest, I defied anyone—namely Felix or Andy—to find a better theater program. I surveyed the audience to see if they were in attendance but couldn't distinguish faces in the dim light.

Hamlet wouldn't appear until scene two, so I relaxed, enjoying the entrance of the ghost. I couldn't think of a more intriguing way for a writer to draw in an audience. Ghosts were mysterious, especially this one, because he wouldn't talk to the guards, yet carried a message. Horatio was skeptical, despite seeing the specter with his own eyes. Watching the interaction, I decided I liked Shakespeare more than I remembered. It'd been a while since I'd seen one of his plays.

"Isn't this good?" I whispered to Lenny.

He leaned in closer. "If you believe in ghosts."

I was puzzled. "Of course I believe in ghosts. Don't you?"

"No."

"What do you think all those souls do while they're stuck in purgatory? Sit still?" I shook my head. "I don't think so."

"I don't have to worry about that scenario," said Lenny. "I'm Jewish."

Hamlet arrived in his "suits of solemn black," and I stopped talking. I analyzed his response to his mother, Queen Gertrude, and the new King Claudius. Jacob knew his lines and recited them well. He was a good actor, charismatic and talented. He made me forget I was watching a play—whose star was possibly a murderer. It wasn't until he was midway through his conversation with Horatio that I remembered the unwelcome gift of flowers. Stumbling on a word, he physically stumbled on the stage, catching himself before falling outright. Horatio, like any good friend would, came to his rescue, improvising a few lines about not meaning to startle him with the news of seeing his father's ghost. But the damage was done. Jacob was still off balance when intermission came.

The lights grew brighter, and I stood to stretch. "I need to use the restroom."

"I see Giles," said Lenny, pointing several rows ahead of us. Giles was sitting with his wife, Katherine, as well as Felix and Andy. "I'm going to say hello."

We parted in different directions, and I made a beeline for the bathroom, but it was too late. The line reached into the hallway. After waiting a few minutes, I decided to take a detour through the gallery. There was a restroom downstairs I could use, and I wanted to check out the gallery again anyway.

The displays were still lighted, and a few people stood around reading placards or peering at costumes. I walked through the gallery, glancing into corners and looking for evidence of who might have placed the flowers in Jacob's pocket. Finding nothing, I scolded myself for thinking there would be clues just waiting for me to find them. My Crimes and Passions course hadn't enhanced my investigative skills; it had only increased my enthusiasm for my hobby.

As I was about to leave, I noticed movement outside the gallery door. Someone darted past, and I exited the gallery in time to see Tanner's girlfriend, Mia, rushing out the front door. Her roommate Mackenzie followed after her. They must've come to watch the play, but why? They'd seen it on opening night. Wouldn't it be difficult seeing Jacob playing Tanner's role? And why leave now? Unless they were the ones who'd planted the flowers to punish Jacob for taking Tanner's part. Then they'd enjoy sticking around long enough to see if their "gift" had done its job of making him flub his lines.

I had to hurry if I was going to make it back before the show began. I walked down the side stairs that led to the downstairs restroom, my footsteps echoing in the empty stairwell. One of the newer buildings on campus, the theater had maze-like turns, twists, and passages that could leave anyone unfamiliar with them disoriented. Fortunately, I'd been in the bowels of the theater a couple times, or I might have hesitated to make the detour. The lower level had no windows, only artificial lighting. The lavatory was close, but if I kept walking, I would find the prop rooms, the dressing rooms, the green room, and the rest of the backstage area out of view of the audience.

Hustling into the bathroom, I was still thinking about Mia and Mackenzie. They were both majors in the Fine Arts Department. It made sense that they were here. They might have been completing a project or … something more sinister. Flowers, flubbed lines? I couldn't help where my mind was going. But neither had black hair. Where had that strand come from?

The theater music started, and the bathroom lights shut off. Still in the stall, I froze. Did the lights shut off automatically when the play resumed? No. Someone was in the bathroom with me. I heard a footstep, then a noise at my door. An object rolled into the stall from underneath. I caught it with my foot. For a moment, I thought it was a bomb because it was round. But it didn't explode.

"What is this? Who are you?"

No reply but the thumping of my heart. Motionless, I listened for a full minute before I dared touch the door. I slid open the latch. The concrete room was engulfed in darkness. I reached for the object by my foot. It was round and hard, plastic. I turned it over in my hands, straining to identify it, but it was pitch black, and I could make out nothing. Plus, I was afraid it was dangerous. I found the entrance of the bathroom and slid my hand up and down the wall, feeling for the light switch. After a futile ten-second search, I pulled open the door. I wanted to get out of there. The dark didn't scare me, but whatever was in my hands did.

Engulfed in darkness, I ran my hand along the cool cement-block wall until I reached the stairwell, which was also pitch black. I grabbed the railing, keeping the object gripped in my free hand. The sound of my heels made an eerie echo as I climbed the metal stairs one at a time.

At the top of the steps, I flung open the door to the main floor, happy to be in the light again. I stood blinking for a second, allowing my eyes to adjust. Then I looked down at the object in my hand and screamed. A skull rolled onto the floor.

"Em! What happened?" Lenny was racing down the hallway.

"It's okay," I reassured him, even though I wasn't sure that was true. "I was in the bathroom downstairs. There was a line up here. When I was in there, someone shut off the lights and rolled *that* under my stall door."

He jabbed at the skull with his foot, as if it might bite. Then he bent down to examine it. Picking it up, he said, "It's not real. It's fake."

I studied the skull. The realization hit me. "Of course it's fake. It's a prop from the play. This is the skull Hamlet talks to."

"Maybe there are such things as ghosts ..." Lenny muttered.

"We need to put it back."

"*We* don't need to do anything," he said, putting his arm around me. "You're shaking."

"But the actors must have it," I said. "And soon."

He led me to the gallery, where he grabbed one of the volunteers and told them to return the skull to the prop table, *now*. When the volunteer asked how he got it, he restated *now* in a very deep voice. That got the student moving.

He turned to me. "Who do you think did it?"

"I don't know," I said. "But I know it was intended for me. Whoever did this saw me go into the bathroom. They took the opportunity to scare me."

"Scare you away from solving the case?"

"Maybe. It could be a warning, like the begonias."

"And the sonnet," he added.

"I can't help but feel guilty." I let out a breath. "The sonnet was the first warning. I should have done more."

"You told Giles," he said. "What more could you do?"

"I don't know," I said. "I could have called Sophie or even Officer Beamer. Maybe they could have identified the killer before they got to Tanner."

"Whoever killed Tanner is playing a game. The sonnet was just the first move."

Lenny was right. I had a feeling the killer was enjoying himself or herself immensely. The sonnet, the flowers, the skull—all embellishments in a real-life game of cat and mouse. I was the mouse.

"So who's good at playing pretend?" he said. "One of the actors?"

"It could be," I said. "They could've seen me go downstairs. I also saw Mia and her friend Mackenzie leave the building. Maybe they came back."

He snapped his fingers. "Andy and Felix are with Giles."

"I know. I saw them, too."

"Anybody else?" he asked, taking my hand.

"Practically the entire English Department, Theater Department, and student body are here."

He pulled me toward the entrance.

"Where are we going?" I said.

"I'm getting our coats," he said. "I think I've had enough drama for one night."

Chapter Thirteen

———

OVER A LATE-NIGHT dinner at Vinny's, Lenny and I had agreed the skull prank had been pulled last minute, which meant the prankster could have made a mistake. I hadn't figured out what that mistake was yet, but I would. After stashing the flowers in Jacob's pocket, he might've seized the chance to frighten me by placing the skull in the bathroom. Unless he wanted the skull to disappear in the first place, throwing Jacob and the entire cast into confusion when they discovered it missing. In that case, rolling it into my stall had been an afterthought, albeit a bonus.

Sitting cross-legged on my couch Saturday morning, I paused mid-sip of my coffee. I had been in the women's bathroom. Could the prankster be a woman? It was possible. The strand of hair in the bouquet was long and black, and I was convinced the person who left the flowers and took the skull were one in the same. Still, it would be easy enough for a man to slip into the downstairs women's bathroom undetected, and Andy's hair was black. Nobody was around, and the lighting was minimal.

Setting down my cup, I grabbed my laptop. I couldn't let

the mystery overshadow my work responsibilities, and Owen Parrish had said he'd email me with the manuscript changes. Sure enough, a file attachment waited in my inbox. I double-clicked on it, eager to see his notes. His comments appeared in red, dozens of them. Starting with the Table of Contents. I hovered over the lengthy note, which said he'd like me to rewrite the concluding chapters; he wanted a happy ending. The resolution wasn't as satisfying as it could be.

I scrolled furiously to the final chapters. Owen was treating the book like a work of fiction. That was why he wanted the final chapters reworked. He liked ending on a progressive note. I would have liked that too, but history wasn't linear; it didn't start at point A and end at point B. Women writers had made progress; that was true. Anyone reading the book would understand that women writers had advanced by leaps and bounds. However, we couldn't take those advances for granted. More progress was needed, especially when it came to promoting diverse voices.

The more I read, the angrier I got, at Owen and myself. He'd found several cringe-worthy errors. As I told my students, everyone needs a fresh set of eyes to look over their work, including me. I was glad for his careful reading. But research, sources, and footnotes had been disregarded—or worse, deleted. Dewberry was a small press that published mostly fiction. They didn't publish academic work, so why did I send them my manuscript in the first place? I wracked my brain for the reason. I couldn't remember. They were on a list somewhere. I was a numbskull who trusted lists. I liked lists. But this one had let me down.

If I approved Owen's edits—did I have a choice?—the book would end with examples of men using initials, instead of names, to disguise their gender, a practice used historically by women. This ending made it appear as if women had overcome their creative barriers. Men imitating them became proof of that. It was a simplistic way to finish the book, and if it wasn't late Saturday morning, I'd tell Owen just that. I closed the file and returned to my email. That was the wonder of technology. I *could* tell him. He might not be in the office, but he was certainly checking messages.

I liked the sound of my fingers on the keys, punching out each word hard and fast. I couldn't compromise my scholarship. I needed to make that understood. I could change words, sentences, or even paragraphs, but disregard the challenges women writers faced today? I didn't think so.

After I hit the send button, I felt much better. I could focus on the rest of my day, which included a trip to campus for an Elizabethan music concert. It was part of the Shakespeare Festival, the part Jane Lemort was in charge of. Despite Jane's involvement, I was looking forward to the event, which would provide another opportunity to investigate Tanner's death. Whoever killed him not only knew Shakespeare's work but used a scene from *Hamlet* to stage his death. An Elizabethan concert seemed like an event the killer would attend.

My cellphone buzzed from the kitchen counter, and I hurried to answer it, thinking it could be Owen Parrish. Had he received my email? I wasn't sure I wanted to find out. I peeked at the screen: Sophie Barnes. "Thank goodness it's you."

"Hi, Professor Prather," said Sophie. "Is something wrong?"

"No, nothing. Actually, one thing, but it has nothing to do with you. I'm publishing a book, and I thought you were the editor. I just sent him a seething email."

"In Business Writing, you said never to do that," said Sophie. "You said give yourself twenty-four hours to cool down before responding to bad news."

"I know," I said. "I wish I'd follow my own advice once in a while. Anyway, it's good to hear from you. I've been wondering about the investigation."

"Officer Beamer told me you were my official contact at the university—for any questions about Shakespeare."

"Of course," I said. "I'm glad to help."

"I knew you would be," said Sophie, conspiratorially. "And I do have a question. It's about the poison used in *Hamlet*. Does it have a name?"

"Hebenon," I said. "The problem is hebenon doesn't exist. *Henbane*—a plant—is the closest scholars have come to naming the poison. They think it's what Shakespeare meant when he wrote hebenon."

Sophie sighed. "This case just gets weirder and weirder."

"Did the coroner test the liquid in Tanner's ear?"

"That's the problem," said Sophie. "It came back plain $H2O$. There are no wounds or evidence of foul play."

"Except the dead body," I said.

"A dead body itself doesn't determine foul play," said Sophie. "We need evidence, and right now, the strongest evidence is the allusion to *Hamlet*. Beamer thinks Tanner might have staged it himself. He played the role of Hamlet. He, better than anyone, would have known that scene."

"Impossible," I said. "Tanner was about to reveal an important breakthrough in his research on Shakespeare. Why would he kill himself?"

"Why does anyone kill themselves?" said Sophie. "His girlfriend said he was upset opening night. Maybe he was unhappy with his performance and recreated the scene in the garden to ensure his death wouldn't quickly be forgotten."

"But his body was moved," I said. "Beamer told me about the blanching."

Sophie muttered something under her breath then said, "Maybe he had help."

"That's still murder, isn't it? Assisted suicide?"

"Why can't we find something then?" She sounded frustrated. She'd been working this case for over twenty-four hours and couldn't call it murder yet. I'd be frustrated too.

"You will," I assured her. "The coroner will get back to you soon with the blood and urine analysis. And I'm sure the toxicology results will yield some information."

"But those tests take forever," said Sophie. "I need something now. His parents want answers, and I don't blame them."

I didn't envy Sophie. I couldn't imagine dealing with grieving loved ones. It was hard enough facing Reed and Giles, knowing how badly they were hurting. "Look, think of it this way. The H2O *does* tell you something. It tells you that the liquid in his ear was a prop, like any other in theater. It wasn't real. It wasn't henbane. You've eliminated one possibility."

The line was quiet for a moment. "Thanks, Professor. You still know how to make me feel better."

"You're welcome," I said. "And I have more news for you. I don't know if it will help or hurt, though."

"Lay it on me."

I told her about the flowers in Jacob's pocket and the skull in the bathroom.

"Whoever we're dealing with is an expert in theatrics," said Sophie when I'd finished.

"Or has gone to a lot of trouble making us believe he or she is an expert."

"True," said Sophie. "Either way, take extra precautions until we figure it out."

I promised I would before I hung up. Then I texted Claudia, asking if we were still meeting at the concert. Though I'd pressed Lenny to attend, he'd refused, saying he'd promised to fix his elderly neighbor's gutters. I peeked out my kitchen window. There wasn't a cloud in the sky. It sounded like a repair that could wait, but he disagreed. He said you never knew when the next deluge would come. He didn't want to see Jane. I knew that was the real reason. As a musician himself, he should put aside their petty squabbles for the greater good of music, and I told him so. But he said he was staying away for the greater good of his sanity. With all the crazy things happening on campus, I could understand.

Claudia said she would meet me there, so I hurried to finish dressing. I slipped into a purple top, jeans, and flats.

With a quick swipe of lip gloss, I was out the door, walking down Oxford Street, the sweet scents of spring pushing away thoughts of death and murder.

The fragrance of apple and cherry blossoms, heady and rich, reminded me how much I loved this time of year. Flowers seemed like a luxury in the heartland. Crops for food, grass for animals, rain for both—those were necessities—but flowers reminded one of the beauty in life, the color and diversity. The variety was appreciated, and townspeople tended to their gardens as if they were pets or children. They referred to their perennials as people. I once heard Mrs. Gunderson call her snapdragons *tired* after a thunderstorm. They required rest from the relentless winds.

My thoughts changed when I came upon Mia and her roommates' house. Since Tanner's death, flowers evoked a new emotion, the opposite of delight: fear. Someone had used them to scare me and Jacob. I might never look at flowers the same way.

Alice walked out the door, and my mood lifted. I was thankful she lived there. It was nice to see a familiar face, even if I didn't know her from my classes. She was smart and approachable. If I asked her for help, she would give it. It felt as if I had an *in* with her roommates. "Hey, Alice. Heading to campus?"

She stopped mid-step. Even though it was Saturday, she was toting a backpack. She smiled, her brown eyes tawny in the sunlight. "No way," she laughed. "I'm on my way to work out."

"I'm going to the Elizabethan music concert." I motioned toward campus. "How's Mia doing?"

Alice joined me on the sidewalk. "She's okay. It will take some time."

"And how about you and the others?"

"Good," Alice said. "Well, not good, but better than Mia."

I nodded in understanding. "You and Tanner were both in the English Department. I imagine you had some classes together."

"Not even one," she said. "He was a PhD student. I'm getting my master's in TESOL. But like you said, we were in the same department, and his girlfriend is my roommate. I feel terrible about what happened."

"How long had Mia and Tanner been dating?"

She wrinkled her nose. "A year? No, wait … Mackenzie dated him first. That's how they met. So I guess Tanner and Mia dated maybe six months."

"That had to be a little awkward," I said.

"You said it, not me." Her eyes were small but full of intelligence. I liked her sharpness.

"Did Tanner and Mackenzie still—"

"I hope not," Alice was quick to answer. "You could ask Mackenzie. She'll be at the concert. Just don't tell her I told you. I don't want her to think I'm gossiping behind her back. That would make life miserable for me."

"I won't mention your name."

Alice started toward her car and stopped. "It's just not right, what happened to him. You know what I mean? He should still be alive."

The depth of her disillusion was reflected in her clear brown eyes. It wasn't fair. Tanner was a young student, like her. If he could die young, maybe she could too. The look made me even more determined to find Tanner's murderer.

"I know." I couldn't think of anything else to say.

"Anyway, I'd better get going. I'm late for my barre class." Alice unlocked her car doors.

"Have a good workout."

She got into her car and drove away, and I continued toward campus. I wished I'd been able to soothe her concerns. But I had no answers—yet. She'd given me a direction to pursue, however. She said Mackenzie and Tanner used to date, which meant Mia wasn't the only one close to Tanner. The waitress at the pub said he was flirting the night before his death. Could Mackenzie have been one of his pursuits? A love triangle might explain his jealousy. If he was cheating on Mia, he might think Mia was repaying him in kind. I could ask Mackenzie about it at the concert.

Cars were already lined up on the street parallel to the museum. Soon others would crowd Oxford Street for a parking spot, extending the line all the way to my house. Scholars had flown in for the conference, and attendees had paid for tickets. The festival attendees who knew about Tanner's death believed it was a tragic accident—an isolated incident. After all, the word "murder" had not yet been spoken.

A bustle of people congregated under the huge ash tree that spread its branches over the fountain outside Harmony Music Museum. It was the perfect day for a spring concert, warm with little wind, and concertgoers talked and laughed as they greeted one another. Claudia waved from one of the chairs that'd been placed in rows near the fountain, and I hurried to join her. The musicians had almost finished setting up, and the chairs would fill quickly.

"Thanks for saving me a seat," I said, tucking my backpack under the chair.

"I knew you'd be running late."

"I'm not late," I said. "I'm right on time." I motioned to her outfit. "Love the dress, by the way." Claudia wore a maxi dress that brushed the ground with its colorful, floral-patterned fabric. In her hair was an elaborate rose-blossom barrette. I had the feeling that getting dressed was an event at her house, not last-minute or rushed, as it always ended up being for me.

"Thank you. I adore purple on you," she said, returning the compliment.

I adored purple, too, and all the other bright, bold colors. "I ran into Mia's roommate, which held me up a little." Seeing Claudia's puzzlement, I added, "Tanner's girlfriend, Mia. She lives right down the street from me. That's another roommate." I pointed to the girl setting up with her viol, a precursor of the violin. "Mackenzie. She used to date Tanner. It seems like he got around. A real *player*, if you know what I mean."

She adjusted her flower barrette. "Do me a favor. Strike that word from your vocabulary."

"Why? I used it correctly."

She gave me a look. "Correct—but still awkward."

Jane, her dress black with a high neck, approached the microphone, and the crowd quieted. After thanking us for coming, she began her lecture. "Music was very important in Shakespeare's time," she said. "Shakespeare made over five hundred references to music in his plays and poems. *As You Like It* and *Twelfth Night* had six songs each, and many of his sonnets were put to music." It was a fascinating lecture. I couldn't help but think of the Beat poets and how music, too, accompanied their poems, though in a different century. Of course it would be difficult to find two more different styles.

Jane finished her lecture by introducing the musicians and their instruments. Mackenzie played the viol, one musician played a fife, another a cornet, and—could it be?—Jane Lemort played a lute. I hadn't dreamt it after all. She must have mentioned it during one of our conversations. She was fond of listing her accomplishments. I leaned back in my chair, arms crossed, bracing myself to witness yet another of her achievements. I couldn't wait to tell Lenny.

Chapter Fourteen

—

CLASSICAL MUSIC ISN'T my favorite, but the concert was excellent, lute and all. I had to give Jane her due for putting on a solid performance, and the other musicians as well. On top of being a popular softball player, Mackenzie was outstanding on the viol and I supposed the violin as well. During introductions, Jane mentioned that Mackenzie had been invited to play with the symphony, and considering today's performance, no wonder. She must have spent hours practicing. That might explain her and Mia's presence last night in the theater building, which housed the Music Department as well. It also made her a suspect in the bouquet and skull pranks. She could've given Jacob the flowers and placed the skull in the bathroom. But to what avail? I could understand seeking revenge on Jacob as motivation for the flowers, but why target me? I'd done nothing wrong. If anything, I was on her side, trying to solve Tanner's murder. Unless she was the murderer. In that case, we were definitely on different sides.

The performance over, I clapped loudly, partly to blow off a little steam. I was starting to understand Sophie's frustration. Each step forward in the case meant another one back.

Hopefully talking to Mackenzie would constitute a giant leap forward.

"Lenny should have been here," said Claudia. "Where is he?"

"Cleaning his neighbor's gutters," I said. "Don't worry. I'm sure he'll get a full recap on Monday." I nodded toward the stage, where Jane was accepting praise on behalf of the group. "Let's go add our congratulations."

"First applause, now kudos for Jane?" She shook her head. "Did something happen to you today?"

"As a matter of fact, it did," I said, scooting out of the row. I explained about the email from Owen Parrish and my quick response.

"Go back a sec," said Claudia. "You signed the contract with Dewberry without telling me?"

I couldn't deny it.

"I thought we agreed I was the published author here. You were going to talk to me and Gene before signing the contract."

"I know," I said with an irritated wave of my hand. "But I was going to sign it anyway. Why waste time? You know me. I like getting things done."

"You and the rest of the Midwest," she muttered.

"The point is, I don't like his revisions," I said. "His comments lead me to believe he didn't read the entire book, or if he did, he skimmed it."

"You said yourself they don't publish nonfiction," said Claudia. "That should have been a red flag."

"Regardless, we're past red flags. I'm on fire here."

She smoothed a flyaway strand of hair. "You'll have to make the changes. You signed the contract."

"And if I don't?" I asked.

"They don't have to publish your work. Period."

I didn't like that answer. I couldn't handle the thought of the work remaining unpublished now that the call had come and the contract had been signed.

"Promise you'll talk to me before responding again," said Claudia.

I couldn't promise anything. It was our turn to bestow congratulations on Jane Lemort.

"That was a wonderful performance, Jane," I said. "I really enjoyed myself."

"Me, too," said Claudia. "I wish I would have brought my kids."

"Thank you." She glanced over my shoulder. "Where is Lenny? I hardly see you apart these days."

Jane liked bringing up the topic of our relationship whenever she could, especially in front of other faculty members. She knew I'd been cautious about dating Lenny—a colleague and my best friend—in the beginning, but that was months ago. I could talk about it in front of anyone now.

"He couldn't make it," I said. "He sends his regrets." I noticed Mackenzie putting her viol in the case. "Excuse me. I want to congratulate Mackenzie before she leaves."

Claudia gave me an enigmatic look. If she'd dared show me how she really felt, she'd have outright glared. Now she would have to wrap up the congratulations with her least-favorite colleague on her own.

I hurried over to Mackenzie, who was snapping shut her instrument case. Her wheat-colored ponytail dipped over her shoulder. "That was a fantastic performance. I just wanted to tell you."

She glanced up and smiled. "Thank you."

"I didn't realize you'd be at the concert," I said.

"Really?" She stood. "It was on the poster."

"I must have missed it."

"Most people think of me as a softball player." She hoisted her instrument case onto her back. It had two straps that allowed it to be carried like a backpack. "More people attend games than performances, I guess."

"That's the truth," I said. "Games get better advertising too."

She nodded in a distracted fashion. I'm sure she wondered how long I was going to keep her and to what purpose. I kept my tone casual as I continued, "And how are you doing with Tanner's death? I heard you used to date him, so it must have hit you hard."

She glanced over my shoulder before answering. The crowd was beginning to dissipate, and we were nearly alone. "That was a year ago. We were still friends, though, so it's hard."

"Did you break up because of his attraction to Mia?"

She smiled, showing two small dimples. Like her hair, her fresh complexion was natural. She wore very little makeup. "We broke up because of his attraction to everyone."

Her statement confirmed what others had implied about Tanner. While he enjoyed flirting, he didn't want his girlfriend flirting. Such behavior seemed controlling and manipulative. "His wandering eye didn't bother Mia?"

"I'm sure it did, but she loved him. She put up with a lot."

"Maybe she was fed up," I said.

She understood the implication. "Not Mia. She defended him no matter what. It was pathetic, honestly. His moods were getting worse, but she blamed it on the play. After it was over, she insisted he'd be better."

Her description reminded me of the argument the night before his death. "Someone at the bar saw Tanner arguing with a man in glasses. Was it over Mia?"

She snorted. "You mean Denton Smart. It was sad how Tanner turned on his friend. I don't think Denton even knows how to flirt, but Tanner was jealous of him. Denton's really intelligent. He knows a lot."

I agreed. On our panel, he'd radiated intelligence. He'd said he could prove de Vere lived much longer than the historical record said, which meant de Vere could have written the later Shakespeare plays. If true, he had the evidence Tanner needed to make his case against Shakespeare. Why would Tanner chance an argument with him? I needed to find out more about Tanner's work. I could accomplish that with a trip to the library. "Are you sure they were arguing about Mia?"

"Positive." Mackenzie's plain face was open and honest. "That night, Tanner told Denton to stay away from Mia. Denton left. Tanner tried to get him to come back, but he wouldn't. He was really upset."

Just how upset was he? I needed to find out. "I have to get to the library, but it was a really great performance, Mackenzie. I hope to hear you play again sometime."

"Thanks," she said. It was all the permission she needed to join a friend.

I returned to Claudia, who was now talking to Giles. Jane had disappeared and so had the sour look on Claudia's face. She and Giles were discussing Felix's keynote address, taking place this evening in the small, but regal, lecture hall in Stanton. The English Banquet would follow at Bluff View Restaurant. Giles wanted to make sure all faculty members would be in attendance, since he would be bestowing next year's scholarships and awards.

"We'll be there, won't we, Em?" said Claudia.

"I'm looking forward to it," I said.

Giles acknowledged our responses with a murmur of appreciation.

"I'm headed to the library," I continued. "Anybody going in that direction?"

Claudia shook her head. "I need to get back to the kids. They have science projects due on Monday, and we haven't even started them."

"I'm meeting Felix inside." Giles pointed toward Harmony. "There's an afternoon panel on Elizabethan art, if you'd like to join us."

I'd had my fill of Elizabethan culture for one afternoon. "Sounds interesting, but I really do need to take care of a few things before this evening. I'll see you at the lecture?"

They both nodded, and I started toward the library. The blue of the sky was intense, like cornflowers, providing a stunning canvas for the white peaks of Stanton Hall on this beautiful spring day. Had it not been for the garish crime scene tape surrounding Shakespeare's Garden, it would have been the perfect backdrop for a small Midwestern college.

I paused for a moment at the gate. Pink flowers lined the path to a reader's paradise. Complete with benches for sitting and blossoms for smelling, the garden invited passersby to put away their busyness and open up a book. The refurbished bust of Shakespeare would watch over them in silent approval.

If only the bust could speak—he would tell me who killed Tanner. I still pictured the young actor posed on the bench, a ghastly reenactment of a scene from *Hamlet*. Could I ever sit on that bench, could anyone, without thinking of Tanner? I doubted it.

Students had piled flowers, cards, and candles at the entrance, a shrine to a life ended too soon. My eyes focused on a single red rose. It was next to a bouquet of wildflowers wrapped in clear cellophane, the kind purchased at the local grocery store. Beside it was a yellowing piece of paper, dull in contrast to the flowers. I picked it up. It was a page ripped from *Hamlet*, the famous "To be, or not to be" soliloquy. In the speech, Hamlet contemplates suicide. Did its placement here suggest Tanner killed himself? Or was it chosen as a memento from the play because the lines were the most recognizable?

A breeze swept through campus, lifting the page from my hands. I grabbed it and returned it to the pile, unable to shake the feeling that someone was watching me replace it. It was a prickle that began at the base of my spine and traveled all the way to my neck. I glanced around. No one was there. Still, the eerie feeling persisted all the way to the library. It was instinctual, irrational fear. Even in my previous encounters with murder, I'd never experienced anything like it. My body was warning me of danger. What that danger was, though, I couldn't say.

I fought the temptation to run. Reason told me the day was

warm, the campus was picturesque, and I was wearing my good heels. It could see no hazard at all. And yet, there was the warning, like a hand on my back, pushing me forward.

Chapter Fifteen

—

I CHECKED MY fear and pulled open the library door. Maybe I was losing my nerve. Or maybe I was losing my touch. I had several clues to the killer's identity—the sonnet, the flowers, the skull—yet I couldn't work it out. It was like putting together a five-thousand-piece puzzle without the corner pieces. I needed to build the framework first. When I did, I was certain the rest of the pieces would fall into place.

Since it was Saturday, the library was sparsely occupied but not deserted. A few students worked at tables while librarians shelved books or answered questions. I logged on to a computer near the copy machines and pulled up the library catalog. Tanner's PhD dissertation was incomplete; it wouldn't be printed because he wasn't alive to defend it to his dissertation committee. The killer had effectively killed his work. But I did find his master's thesis, because he'd done his coursework at Copper Bluff. Unfortunately, a thesis couldn't be checked out, but I could read it in the library. I hoped it might give me clues to Tanner's later research.

After finding the call number, I climbed the stairs to the third floor, where the books were dusty from disuse. I released a breath I didn't know I'd been holding. Surrounded by towering bookshelves, I felt safely ensconced in a place where no one could touch me. Now that I was feeling more like myself, it didn't take me long to find the red leather book with Tanner's name on it.

I skimmed through the first few pages as I took it to a study alcove. As the title suggested, it was about Shakespeare, but the table of contents suggested the work analyzed Shakespeare's plays rather than discussing the author himself. I slouched into a chair, skimming pages for information. Histories, comedies, tragedies. They were here, but where was Tanner's allegation that Shakespeare wasn't Shakespeare? Maybe that idea hadn't come until he began work on his PhD. I turned to the last chapter, coincidentally on *Hamlet*.

Many scholars purport that *Hamlet* is autobiographical, that the author inserts himself into this play more than any other. Tanner asserted the same, but with an acknowledgment of a contradiction. How could William Shakespeare, a man of lowly origins, write about the struggle between social obligations and personal desires with such depth and understanding? It was here I found the first mention of de Vere, a man who led a double life, according to Tanner. De Vere was a court favorite and a minor poet, a husband and a philanderer, a father and a murderer. Wait. Had I read that right? Yes, according to Tanner's thesis. At eighteen, de Vere killed Thomas Brincknell. Hamlet, too, commits murder. He's responsible for five deaths in the play.

I leaned back in my chair. De Vere *did* resemble Hamlet. He was polished, as Ophelia claims, but also full of offences, as Hamlet himself admits. In fact, the description sounded a lot like Tanner. On the outside, he was an accomplished actor and scholar. But he, like de Vere, was also known to treat people cruelly.

The chapter ended on a melancholy note, with Tanner questioning whether Shakespeare really wrote the plays. It was not the assertion presented so confidently at the conference; the tone was that of a fledgling scholar, deflated and disenchanted. Coming to the end of the thesis and finding the contradiction, Tanner could no longer summon the enthusiasm so prevalent in the acknowledgments and first chapters. No wonder he'd hoped to exact revenge on Shakespeare scholars, who he now believed knowingly propagated a myth. But what of his proof? Had he really found evidence that proved de Vere faked his own death? I shut the book. I'd have to ask Denton that question, and fortunately, I knew just where to find him.

Denton worked at the medical library, a fact I'd noted in his bio when I was preparing for our panel. Today was Saturday, and I guessed he put in most of his hours on weekends. Returning Tanner's thesis to the shelf where it belonged, I started for the M.M. Scott Medical Building. It was newly refurbished, thanks to the gift of a young doctor who'd had a noteworthy breakthrough. She'd created a drug that reduced transplant rejections significantly and credited Copper Bluff for her outstanding education. I enjoyed seeing her picture whenever I visited the building, which wasn't often. It had a large auditorium for lectures and an impressive library with serious-looking gray texts.

As I surmised, Denton was working today. He was seated at the front desk, staring at a computer screen. A book lay open at his side. I greeted him with a cheery hello.

He looked up from the screen, his glasses hanging off his nose. "Professor Prather, right?"

"Good memory," I said. "This is a nice library. I don't know if I've been in here before."

He took off his glasses, rubbing the bridge of his nose. He looked less scholarly with them off. "It's a good job. It's quiet here, and I get a lot of studying done. What brings you in?"

"Actually, you do," I said. "I wanted to ask you a couple of questions about your research on Shakespeare."

"My research is in molecular biology, actually," he answered.

"My presentation on Shakespeare was recreational. I like his work, and I'm interested in genetics, as a hobby."

Brightness radiated off him like sun off a mirror, and I had no trouble believing he researched genetics in his spare time. He probably also crunched algebraic equations. Suddenly my reading hobby seemed a bit frivolous. "But you've put some time into researching Shakespeare's true identity. During our panel, you mentioned having evidence to support Tanner's theory."

"I did, but I wish I hadn't." He cleaned closer to the ledge that separated us. I could smell his aftershave or cologne, something nautical. "After our presentation, Felix Lewis cornered me in the lobby. He told me not to associate with Tanner. He said doing so would put a red X on my back. I wasn't sure what that meant, but now my enrollment in the summer research program has been put on hold."

"Do you think there's a connection?"

"What do you think?" Denton said. "There has to be."

Felix didn't know anyone on campus except Reed, and Reed had nothing to do with the medical school. I couldn't see how Felix could have him booted out of a summer research program. "Did you tell Tanner?" I asked.

"Of course," said Denton, "He was ecstatic. He said to have a Shakespeare authority like Felix Lewis threaten me proved how close we were to solving the authorship mystery."

"And were you?" I asked.

He glanced at a professor passing by. After the teacher was gone, he continued, "If the test results match, then the answer is yes."

"What exactly are you testing?" I asked. "You never said in the panel."

"No, I didn't, and I don't know if I should say anything now." He returned his glasses to his nose. A sheen of perspiration glinted off his forehead. "Tanner is dead."

"And you think you might be next," I said.

His eyes widened behind his spectacles. "I didn't say that."

"You didn't have to," I said. "I can see you're afraid."

"Not just about that … everything. My education, my career, my future. I've spent years in med school. I can't risk throwing all that away."

I stepped as close to the counter as possible and leaned in. "Look, Denton, you may be smart, and your last name might be Smart, but you're missing the obvious point here. You won't have a future if you're dead. Tell me what you and Tanner were into. Maybe I can help."

He tilted his head, as if deciding how to proceed.

"You can trust me," I said.

He started talking, but in a whisper. "A few years ago, a letter with Edward de Vere's signature was auctioned at Bonhams—that's an auction house in London. The document itself was worthless, just a record of an annuity left to a servant. What was interesting was the person who bought it: one of de Vere's ancestors. The ancestor wished to see if the signature matched the handwriting in a letter he had in his possession, dated 1610."

"Wait," I said. "De Vere died in 1604." The only reason I remembered the year was because it was the crux of the entire controversy. One of Shakespeare's plays referred to an event that took place after 1604, so Shakespeare scholars claimed that proved de Vere couldn't be Shakespeare.

"That's the official date of death, but there's always been a question surrounding de Vere's final resting place." Denton took off his glasses and wiped them with a handkerchief; meanwhile, he nonchalantly scanned the area to make sure no one was listening. "One of de Vere's cousins said de Vere was exhumed and reburied at Westminster at a later date. Some say that's the real date he died."

I thought it made sense. Why would de Vere's body be moved to Westminster years after his death? I could think of no reason. "So, did the signatures match?"

"One hundred percent," said Denton, pronouncing each word distinctly. He leaned back in his chair, satisfied with impact of his revelation.

It was a heck of a nugget, the golden wrapper in *Charlie and the Chocolate Factory*. No wonder Tanner and Denton had been so excited during the Shakespeare symposium. I would've had a hard time keeping the news to myself. They had to be waiting on something else. "The signatures match, but is that conclusive? There's no way to *prove* de Vere was alive in 1610, is there?"

A smile touched his lips, his bright eyes sharper than ever. The look gave me pause. "There is now."

Chapter Sixteen

———

Denton explained that when de Vere's long-lost relative took the letters to a handwriting expert, the expert noted a dark spot on the parchment and theorized it was blood. Elizabethans used quills, quills that required sharpening before use. Penknives were invented for this very reason. The expert speculated that de Vere might have nicked himself while sharpening the quill. The difference in ink weight supported the theory of a newly sharpened instrument.

Tanner Sparks's timing was impeccable. According to Denton, he and Tanner traveled to England last summer. Tanner was reading de Vere's letters at the National Archives when he met de Vere's relative. They were the perfect partners, both dedicated to debunking the Shakespeare authorship myth and giving de Vere his rightful place in history. When Denton returned from a backpacking excursion in Edinburgh, Tanner introduced them, and a plan was hatched.

"When we met, I told de Vere's relation I could test the blood on the parchment against his own DNA. If the DNA shared the right markers, it would prove de Vere was alive in 1610 to write the late plays."

I waited for the conclusion. The story was better than the mystery novel on my nightstand. "So? Did the DNA indicate they were related?"

He frowned. "It isn't that easy. The relative didn't want the letter compromised, so I had to use extraordinary caution. I had one chance to get it right. The nice thing was the letter had been impeccably preserved. But it took time to isolate the DNA. Because of the implications of the research, however, I'm in the process of testing multiple genetic markers, STRs, and SNPs."

"What are those?"

"Sorry," he said. "Short tandem repeat and single nucleotide polymorphisms."

That cleared it up. "Have any markers matched?"

He remained silent, but there was that smile again.

"So they have," I said, a statement rather than a question.

"It would be rash of me, as a scientist, to leap to conclusions before all the evidence is in."

But I wasn't a scientist. I was leaping like a gazelle, making connections between de Vere and the letter and Tanner and the murderer. De Vere had been alive in 1610, which meant he could have written the later Shakespeare plays. Tanner was killed because he knew it and would reveal all as soon as the tests were complete. But wait …. Wouldn't Denton have been the more obvious victim, the one with the ability to prove Tanner's theory? The one who could *still* prove it? Even so, Denton wasn't a writer. He was a medical student. I didn't think his plans included publishing a book on Shakespeare.

Denton was watching me. The corners of his not-quite-so-bright eyes were etched with worry. "I see you understand why I haven't told anyone."

I nodded slowly. "Have you told the police? Maybe they could protect you."

"I tried to explain the project, but the officer was more concerned with my whereabouts the night before Tanner's death. I went to the bar with Tanner opening night. That was a mistake."

If Denton explained his research to Officer Beamer, Beamer might not have understood the implications, especially before talking to me. I would need to make him aware of the seriousness of the claim. "Mackenzie said you and Tanner got into an argument that night. What happened?"

A student approached the desk to ask Denton a question. I took a step to the side, waiting for them to finish.

After the student was gone, Denton continued, "It wasn't even an argument. I didn't argue. Tanner yelled at me, and I listened. He thought I was flirting with Mia." He gestured to himself. "Do I look like the kind of guy who would flirt with Mia?"

He was fit, young, and good looking. I didn't see why not.

He took off his glasses and waved them at me. "I don't expect you to see it, but I'm a nerd. If I'm not in class, I'm here. Mia wouldn't be into a guy like me. She's incredibly popular, and she's in love with Tanner—or was. His jealousy got the best of him that night."

"You don't think there was something else making him act that way?" I asked. "Alcohol or drugs?"

"I've never known him to drink …." His words trailed off as he appeared to think back to Thursday night. His eyes snapped back to mine. "He *was* sick to his stomach that night. Or at least I thought he was. He spent a lot of time in the bathroom."

Was it an excess of alcohol or another poison making him ill? Sophie would soon have the results from the blood taken postmortem. They would tell us for certain. Until then, I was adding nausea to slurred speech and clumsiness. "Did you see him again after you left the bar?"

He shook his head. "No, that was the last time."

"Are you going to continue with the DNA tests?"

He put his finger to his lips, again scanning the room for listeners. "De Vere's relative is paying me for the work. I have to finish it. I don't have a choice."

I fastened the buttons on my coat. "I didn't realize. Can I ask how much?"

"Fifty thousand dollars."

I stopped buttoning my jacket.

"It sounds like a lot, but research costs money," said Denton. "Tanner and I were splitting the payment."

"And now?" I asked.

"I'll be the sole recipient of the funds."

After a brisk walk home, I grabbed a bite to eat before getting into my car. Fifty thousand dollars was a lot of money. It would cover several years of tuition at our small campus. I wanted to get Lenny's opinion on Denton's approaching payday. I also wanted to see if Lenny was really cleaning Mrs. Baker's gutters. A turn down Park Street told me he was. I could see his blond head a block away. Standing on the roof with a hose, he gave me a wave as I drove up. I didn't wave back; I didn't want to encourage any dangerous moves on his part. Thankfully the house was a small ranch, like his, and if he fell, he probably wouldn't break his neck.

"I knew it," he hollered. "Checking up on me again." He walked to the ladder, propped near the side of the house, and climbed down.

"I don't think it's safe up there," I said. "The roof looks old."

"That means it's well constructed." He wiped his hands and neck with a towel. "I'm done anyway. Come in while I shower."

I wanted coffee at Café Joe. I told him so.

"It'll take five minutes."

I followed him into his house, an olive-green ranch with comfortable furniture. I noticed sheet music, half-filled with musical notes, propped up on his keyboard. Lenny played the piano and guitar and also wrote music, though he could be shy about sharing his compositions. I pointed to the music. "You working on something?"

"Yes." He threw the towel he was carrying over a chair.

"Can I hear it?" I asked.

"It's not ready."

"You always say that," I complained.

"Because it's always true. But this one's close."

I didn't press him. I knew that would be futile. Plus, I wanted him to get through with his shower so we could go to Café Joe. I shooed him toward the bathroom. Taking my point, he started in that direction. I camped out in his recliner in the living room, picking up a half-finished mystery novel lying on the end table next to the chair. Ten minutes later, he returned, fully dressed with wet hair.

I held up the book. "I'm rubbing off on you, aren't I?"

He sat down on the couch, pulling on his socks. "More than I would like to admit."

I put down the novel. "I have lots to tell you. I'll fill you in on the way."

In the car, I told him about my conversations with Mackenzie and Denton. I also told him about the page from *Hamlet* I found in the garden. I was right in the middle of explaining the eerie feeling that followed when he interrupted.

"—But was she good?"

"Was who good?" I asked.

"Jane," he said.

I turned onto Main Street. "Quite good. The lute is kind of like a tinny guitar. I liked it. It was soothing." I gave him an impatient glance. "Can I continue with the eerie feeling now?"

He rolled down his window. "Sure."

"I can only describe it as wanting to run."

"That *is* eerie," he said. "You hate exercise."

I pulled into a parking spot in front of Café Joe. "I'm serious. I think someone was watching me."

"I don't like it, Em. These last few days have been weird, even for you. The sonnet, the skull, now this. It's too much of a coincidence."

"Someone is playing a very dangerous game, and they consider me their opponent."

"Why?" he asked.

I reached for the door handle. "That's what we need to figure out."

Inside Café Joe we ordered two coffees and two fudge brownies. Penelope Dobbs, a pastry chef I'd met over Christmas, had just opened Pen's Patisserie a block over, and the coffee shop offered some of her desserts. The dark brownies, stuffed with chocolate chips, looked ooey-gooey delicious. I grabbed extra napkins on the way to a table.

We selected seats in the sun by the window so we could enjoy both the indoor and outdoor views. Café Joe hosted poetry readings, language clubs, and art exhibits. Colorful prints painted by local artists dotted the walls. Always changing, the paintings could be plucked down and purchased, as could the homemade greeting cards and pottery near the register. Taking my first sip of coffee, I realized why I liked the café so much. It was a reflection of Copper Bluff—small, eclectic, and diverse.

"Try it," said Lenny, holding up his brownie. "It's delicious."

Famous for my sweet tooth, I didn't need persuading. I took a bite of the brownie, and a chocolate dream came true in my mouth. Unable to speak, I moaned in agreement.

"Pen can really bake." He washed down his brownie with a sip of coffee.

I dabbed my lips with a napkin. "I'm glad her dad decided to give her the loan for the store. With confections like these, she's going to make a fortune."

Out of the corner of my eye, I noticed Sophie Barnes approaching the café. All business, she was dressed in slacks and a jacket, her brown hair tied in a knot at the nape of her neck. I guessed she didn't have to wear a police uniform now that she was a detective, but she still looked like a cop. I tapped on the window and waved, but she didn't notice me. She was too focused on getting coffee—probably to-go.

"Sophie!" I said as she rushed through the door.

She stopped and turned toward our table. "How are you guys?"

"Good," I said. "How are you?"

"Em thinks someone's stalking her," Lenny said.

I gave him a look. Why was he sharing my concerns with Sophie?

"I thought you should know," he said.

Sophie's brow furrowed. "Is that true? Do you think someone's stalking you?"

I rushed to assure her *stalking* was too strong of a word. "A few times, I've felt a presence. That's all."

"Dead or alive?" asked Sophie.

It was a fair question. "Alive. It's as if someone is toying with me." I shook my head. That wasn't exactly it either. "Forget it. It's nothing. I want to know if you have Tanner's initial blood results back."

"Just now," she said. "I'm on my way to the station."

"And?" I pressed. "Were they helpful?"

"Not as helpful as I'd hoped," she said. "His pH levels were elevated, which could be for any number of reasons."

"What about alcohol? Did he have any in his system?"

She hesitated to answer.

"Remember, Beamer said you could consult me on this case."

"He said I could consult you about *Shakespeare*," she corrected. "But no, Tanner didn't have any alcohol in his system, which confirms what we were told. He didn't drink."

"The waitress at the bar said he was slurring his words," said Lenny. "He stumbled on his way out the door."

"And," I was quick to add, "Denton said Tanner spent a lot of time in the bathroom that night."

Sophie shrugged. "It wasn't because of alcohol."

"What about marijuana?" Lenny asked. "Is that a possibility?"

"Cannabinoids aren't included in routine blood draws," said Sophie. "It's on my list of things to ask for on Monday. Beamer had to pressure them to get this information to me quickly."

That made sense. Reed found Tanner Friday morning, giving the lab one working day to run initial tests. Specimens were usually collected within twenty-four hours. The nice thing about living in a small town was that Beamer could communicate with the coroner and staff directly. Maybe not so nice for the coroner's office.

Sophie glanced toward the register. "I'd better order my coffee. I'm meeting Beamer at the station in fifteen minutes."

"Of course," I said. "Thanks for filling us in."

"Be careful, okay?" Sophie said. "Until we figure this out, you can't be too cautious. Don't go out alone." She nodded toward Lenny. "Use the buddy system."

After she left, Lenny gave me a smile. "Where do you want to go next … buddy?"

Chapter Seventeen

—

The only place I wanted to go was home. The coffee and brownie had revived me enough to grade papers—or at least quizzes. Felix's keynote speech was at seven o'clock and dinner at eight. That left me a good chunk of time for grading. On my dining room table, I arranged two stacks: essays and quizzes. Then I set out my highlighters, pencils, and handbook. I felt very organized. As I took a seat, Dickinson decided to join me. Her plans didn't include organization. She batted down one marker after the other—yellow, pink, blue—with her orange paw, then the rubber bands. I was gathering them off the floor when my cellphone rang.

It was Dewberry Press. My earlier email came back to me in a wave of nausea. What had I said and how strongly? I was too panicked to remember. "Hello?"

"Emmeline, this is Owen." His voice was full of exasperation.

"I know. Hi." Dickinson gave me a look that relayed how stupid she thought I sounded. I pulled her off the table and onto my lap. I didn't know why I couldn't speak coherently to him. Every time a Los Angeles area code popped up, I became tongue-tied.

"I received your email," Owen continued. "I didn't think the call could wait until Monday."

Good. I was glad he could sense the urgency of it.

"I'm only going to say this once. The book is too long. The final chapters need to be revised. It's not a question of *if* but *how*."

"Too long?" This was new criticism.

"Too long, too wordy, too much," said Owen.

Sensing my irritation, Dickinson jumped off my lap and onto the dining table. She started working on the rubber bands again. "I hardly think three hundred and fifty pages can be considered too long. I have appliance manuals longer than that."

"It is," he said. "Long books don't sell. You want the book to sell, don't you?"

Of course I wanted the book to sell. But this wasn't a large press. You didn't see many of their titles on the shelves of bookstores. Were sales really driving his decision? Or was it his experience with fictional titles? "Yes, I do, but—"

"You read, don't you?" he asked.

What kind of question was that? I was an English teacher. "Every day."

"You want to feel satisfied when you finish a novel, right?"

"Yes, but this isn't a novel," I said. "And some novels are quite disturbing."

"The ones you read in college, maybe," said Owen. "Not in real life. Readers want a happy ending. Your ending isn't happy."

"That's because there's still work to be done in the field!"

He let out a sigh. "Save it for another book, okay? Make the changes this week. Our graphic design department is working on a mock-up cover. They'll take into consideration your requests from the questionnaire we sent. Look for it soon."

This week? If I wasn't in the middle of a murder investigation, it might have been plausible, but there was no way I could rewrite the ending this week. But what other option did I have? Like Claudia said, I'd sealed my fate when I signed the contract. I had to make the changes or not publish the book. "I don't feel good about these changes."

"Leave the feelings to me," said Owen. "Stick to words. I'll be in touch."

He clicked off the phone, leaving me staring at the screen. "Did you hear that animal? He said I should stick to words. Then he hung up on me."

Dickinson looked up from the rubber band.

"I'm sorry," I said as I lifted her off the table. "That was offensive to animals."

Grading made the time drag, and I was glad to get up from my chair two hours later. When the papers tested my patience, I switched to the quizzes. When the quizzes irked me, I had no choice but to bemoan my students' reading habits, or in this case, lack thereof. Dickinson listened to me recount stories from my own studious college days for about thirty seconds before she fled to the bedroom, leaving me with no one to talk to. That's when I decided to tuck the papers away and get ready for Felix's keynote speech.

I was looking forward to it. A month ago, I'd started revisiting Shakespeare's plays in preparation for my panel. Before that, I'd have been humdrum about the lecture. Now, as I put on my long pink dress and gray-and-pink-flowered scarf, I was excited for the event. Whoever killed Tanner knew a lot about Shakespeare. It made sense that the killer would attend tonight's lecture. Felix was a noteworthy scholar in the field. If the murderer was a Shakespeare aficionado, he or she wouldn't pass up this opportunity.

I swiped my lips with Petal Pink lip gloss and stashed it in my purse. I tied my trench coat as I walked down the steps of my bungalow. The clear, warm day had turned cloudy and cool, but the event was only two blocks away. Lenny would drive us, and perhaps other faculty members, to the banquet afterwards.

Crossing the quad, I noted the dim light from the old-fashioned lampposts. Just waking up, they would watch over the campus like sleepy parents. With their warm light, they made the campus feel safer, friendlier. I glanced about. This was the place I knew and loved. The bench where the begonias had sat was empty. The paths were filled with smiling people. Two stories of Stanton Hall were shining with yellow light; the prettiest building on campus was now the busiest. The university was its pleasant self.

I scooted through the doors on my way to the formal lecture hall, where André Duman, a French professor and old friend, was handing out programs. Dressed in a fitted jacket and black beret, he was handsome, his cheeks flushed. When wasn't he handsome and flushed? He was passionate—though Lenny hated it when I used that word to describe him. Lenny preferred *excitable*. Either way, I was surprised to see him handing out programs. Though his office was in the building, he had no other connection to the event I was aware of.

"Hello, André," I said. "It's good to see you."

He took my hand and kissed it dramatically. "It is always good to see you, *mon amie*." He lowered his voice. "Even if the circumstances are highly irregular."

"What's the matter? Has something happened?"

"Something has happened all right," he said. "They have me working like a student tonight." He gestured to the student handing out programs at the other door. "Like the undergraduate!"

"Why?" I asked.

"Because I don't have a department, they treat me like an errand boy. Go here, go there, André." He threw his hands in the air. "*Mon Dieu!*"

André had been petitioning for a French department since I first met him. At one time, I was sure he would succeed and I would teach French literature courses. But the department hadn't happened, and judging by the look on André's face, it wasn't a possibility in the near future. "They undervalue you, André. I'm sorry. Come sit with me and Lenny when you're finished. We will save you a seat."

"I will be the last one in the auditorium. That is for certain."

I gave him an encouraging smile.

"By the way, you are a vision in pink," said André. "Lenny is the lucky man."

I thanked him, taking a program and entering the hall. It was as intimate as an auditorium could be. Its cream-colored walls, burgundy seats, and warm wood invited scholars to listen to anyone fortunate enough to stand at the podium. It was reserved for special events, events such as Felix's keynote address.

Felix was seated on the stage with Giles, who would probably introduce him. Reed Williams was also on the stage and perhaps would say a few words. President Conner was seated next to Reed. Was he there to lend support, or was he a Shakespeare fan himself? We would soon find out.

A quick glance down the aisle told me the English Department was well represented. Faculty members and many of our students were in attendance. Lenny was in the middle of the auditorium. Andy was seated on his left, but several spots to his right remained open. I hurried in to join them, saying hello to the other faculty members. I sat next to Lenny, placing my purse on a chair for André.

"Nice dress," said Lenny. "Pink is your color."

"Thank you," I said. "Hi, Andy."

"Hello." Andy wore a black shirt and suit jacket and an oversized gold watch.

I motioned to the stage. "No speech tonight?"

Andy shook his head. "Felix said I could say a few words about my book, but I wanted tonight to be about him."

How kind of you, I thought. "Your book has gotten enough buzz anyway, right?"

Andy feigned indifference, but his blue eyes lit up. "I can't complain. *Publishers Weekly* gave it a starred review. How about you? Do you have a publication date?"

Lenny and I shared a secret smile. Andy had dropped the *PW* review into the conversation like a five-carat diamond, a sizeable nugget to appreciate.

"Not yet," I said. "As you know, the publishing process takes time." I had a feeling, however, that our experiences were vastly different. "Did you know Tanner had plans to publish his work? Reed told me. He was in his final stages of research."

"I never saw his manuscript, but I have to admit, he did his homework." Andy crossed his legs. "He told me he'd gone to England and met one of de Vere's descendants. I didn't realize."

"You think his theory had merit?" asked Lenny.

"I think he went to a lot of trouble," said Andy. "I don't think the work was viable. You know it could never be accepted as serious scholarship."

I gritted my teeth, and from the look of his jaw, Lenny did too. It angered me that even with Tanner dead, Andy wouldn't acknowledge the value of Tanner's research.

"Come on," said Andy with a chuckle. "You don't take it seriously, do you? I know you want to be supportive of your students, but even they knew Tanner was wasting his time. Remember that undergrad at the symposium? She called him a hack."

I thought back to the panel. "I don't recall that."

"The one with the long black hair?" He leaned in. "Anyway, if students recognized its pointlessness, shouldn't we, as professors?"

"I don't think one has to do with the other," I said. "Having a degree doesn't automatically make me right."

"But it gives you more expertise," said Andy.

I couldn't argue with that, and neither could Lenny, although he wanted to. Giles was approaching the podium, and André had entered the hall at last. I gave him a wave. He joined us, whispering apologies as he scooted through the row.

The lecture was an intriguing mix of Felix's personal story and Shakespeare's work. I enjoyed it when scholars revealed personal connections to their research, and Felix did. He had first come to Shakespeare as a child, hanging around the theater in his small English village. His parents were impatient with their imaginative young boy, and he found himself thinking of the actors and stagehands as playmates. They never shooed him away or discouraged his fun. They became his family and the theater his home.

No wonder Tanner's claim irked him. The longer Felix talked, the more Shakespeare sounded like a substitute for loving parents. Felix was older, of course, and his generation had different challenges than mine growing up. Still, I couldn't shake the feeling that he'd had it rougher than most. Hearing Shakespeare declared a fake would be a personal blow. Like being told he was adopted.

After Felix finished, we gave him a hearty round of applause. Andy stood and clapped, and many of us joined him. I noted the pride in Andy's eyes. Usually he reserved that look for his own work, but he revered his mentor. He would protect Felix's feelings at any cost. I was glad to see he admired someone other than himself.

"Would you like to join us at the English banquet, André?" I asked, putting on my coat. "It's at Bluff View Restaurant, and no one will notice an extra guest. We have a private room and a nice buffet lined up."

André gave me a little bow. "Thank you. I am like the boat without the anchor, floating and drifting."

"Don't be so dramatic," said Lenny. "Join us for a beer—or a glass of wine. They have the local stuff. They make it right here in South Dakota."

André made a face. "I have tasted the wine you speak of, and it does not excite the palette. I think, *mon ami*, South Dakota should stick to the corn and soybeans."

I chuckled. Many states tried their hand at growing grapes,

but very few did it well. André would probably say France does it best. His family owned a winery in Bordeaux. "Come for the conversation, then," I said. "We need to catch up, and Giles mentioned wanting to talk to you the other day."

"I always enjoy talking to Giles," said André. "And you and Lenny, of course. Okay, I will meet you there."

André left, a tiny smile on his face. I was glad to see him feeling better. A dinner with friends was just what he needed.

"Do you need a ride, Andy?" Lenny asked. "I'm taking Em and anybody else who needs a lift."

"Thanks," said Andy. "That'd be great."

As we gathered our things, I noticed Mia and her roommates leaving. Denton and Mia were walking together, apart from the rest of the group. They were deep in conversation, and I wondered about what. Had Tanner been right to be suspicious? Were Denton and Mia more than friends? Denton assured me they weren't, but he could have lied to protect himself. Cheating with Mia would give him another motive for murder. But Mackenzie had corroborated his account at the bar. She said Denton and Mia were just friends. Still, at this point I didn't trust anyone to give me the full story. She herself might have remained on friendly terms with Tanner.

We stopped near the stage to discuss driving arrangements with Giles. He said he and Katherine would take Felix and Reed. Claudia and Gene were taking Thomas and his wife, Lydia. My ears perked up at the mention of Lydia's name, for I'd only met her once. I relished the chance to talk to the woman who'd made herself scarce the moment she moved to Copper Bluff. Thomas said she worked out of their home, but one had to eat and shop. Yet I'd never seen her in the grocery store or café, the book or coffee shops, or the regular places townspeople bumped into one another. Lydia was another mystery to me, one I wanted to solve.

Chapter Eighteen

—

Lenny and Andy talked about Tanner as we drove to the restaurant a few miles outside of town. I listened, trying to learn as much as I could about Andy from his comments. I gleaned that he and Tanner had been better friends as undergraduates in Iowa than I first realized. Their friendship cooled when they applied to graduate school, each moving in different directions. Tanner wanted to attend school in Denver, Andy said, but was rejected. Andy was accepted, creating the first ripple in their relationship. Although Tanner wouldn't admit it, he was jealous, at least according to Andy. I believed Andy. It would be hard seeing your friend attend a school that gave you a pass.

"You didn't keep in touch with Tanner after you moved?" I turned to Andy, who was in the backseat, staring out the window. Perhaps he was thinking of Iowa. A lot of the farmland in the Midwest looked alike.

"Maybe for the first month or so," said Andy. "He moved to Copper Bluff, and then we both got busy with our graduate work. Felix took me under his wing right away. He had plans for me the moment I started the program. I owe everything to him."

"Did he give you the idea for the Shakespeare book?" asked Lenny, navigating a turn.

"The idea was mine," Andy replied, sounding offended. "It's why I was admitted into the program in the first place."

That made sense. Felix would be thrilled to have a student writing a book about the relevancy of Shakespeare in the twenty-first century. From what'd I'd seen at our campus, graduate students were gravitating toward less traditional topics. They were interested in under-represented authors and under-studied subjects. Andy was an old-school scholar who thought like Felix. They could collaborate on the Shakespeare book for the five years it would take Andy to finish his PhD. With the book coming out in the fall, they wouldn't want to chance competing with or being contradicted by a new discovery in the field. But would they go so far as to kill Tanner so that he couldn't publish his work? That's what I needed to determine.

Lenny pulled into Bluff View Restaurant, a white building that hugged the edge of the bluff. The sun had almost disappeared behind it. Only faint streaks of pink remained in the sky, giving the horizon a rosy glow. *This is what people mean when they say spring is in the air*, I thought as I got out of the car. For me, the color of spring was pink. Pink like the cherry blossoms. Pink like the color of my cheeks when Lenny took my hand as we walked up the stairs.

The hostess pointed us to the room reserved for the English Department. The dinner was a nice way not only to end the Shakespeare conference but also to celebrate our students' accomplishments. Many students would be receiving awards and scholarships after dinner. The buffet at Bluff View was one not to miss; the restaurant was considered the best in town and for good reason. Besides serving great food, the establishment was elegantly furnished and had the best views in our area.

Tonight, white lights outlined the oversized deck, a sure sign that summer was on the way. Lunches were already being served outside. Soon, dinners would be too. But for now, guests would have to be content with taking a drink on the deck to soak up the last rays of daylight before the sun set.

"This is nice," said Andy, glancing around the room.

The surprise in his voice irritated me. Copper Bluff might not be as large as Denver or Detroit, but it had fine dining, too. "They have great food."

"There's André," said Lenny. "It looks like he found a wine he could drink."

Swirling a glass of red wine, André was standing next to a table where many faculty members were already seated.

"Good idea," said Andy. "Where's the bar?"

I pointed out the door we'd just entered.

After he left, Lenny said, "That was nice of him to ask us if we'd like a drink."

"He only thinks of himself," I said. "It drives me crazy."

"I hear you," said Lenny. "If he name-dropped one more book reviewer in the car, I was going to smack him. You want a glass of red?"

"Let's set our coats down first. Seats are filling up quickly."

We joined the English faculty, choosing chairs near the end of the table. Giles, Felix, and Reed hadn't arrived yet, but the rest of the faculty was there, including Thomas Cook and his wife, Lydia. I glanced over the people seated between us. Maybe I'd have a chance to talk to her when we went through the buffet line. I was brainstorming conversation starters when Lenny interrupted my thoughts.

"Are you thinking about switching seats?" Lenny's blue eyes twinkled. He knew exactly what I was thinking.

"Have you ever talked to Lydia?" I whispered. "I've only seen her once."

"Never," said Lenny. "They say she's a hermit."

"Who says that?"

"Thomas's students," said Lenny. "They say he talks about her in class sometimes."

I nudged Claudia, who was seated on my other side. "Have you ever talked to Lydia?"

"Occasionally," said Claudia. "Why?"

"What does she do, for a job, I mean?"

"She works from home." Claudia took a sip of her white wine. "A lovely person."

"Students say she's a hermit," I said.

Claudia gave me a sidelong glance. "And we can vouch for how much *they* know."

"But what does she work on, from home?" I pressed.

"I don't know, Em," said Claudia, setting down her glass with a plunk. "Maybe you'd like to interrogate her before dinner."

"She'll wait until dessert," answered Lenny. "It'd be bad manners not to let the woman eat first."

They shared a chuckle at my expense.

"I'm just curious, that's all," I said. "I'd like a chance to get to know her."

"Sure," said Lenny.

"How about that wine now?" I said. Andy had returned with a cocktail, but much to my amusement, all the seats at our table were filled. He'd have to sit with the other grad students.

Lenny stood. "I'll be right back."

In the meantime, the guest of honor arrived and was welcomed with a nice round of applause. He, Giles, Katherine, and Reed took their reserved seats at the head of our table, officially beginning the night. Standing to join them, I congratulated Felix on his lecture. "I loved hearing about your childhood and the theater. I dream of seeing an English village like yours someday."

"Thank you," Felix said. "Those were formative years, if somewhat painful at times. But we English are known for keeping a stiff upper lip, right? My childhood served me well when facing adversity. Have you ever been abroad?"

"Almost." I glanced at André, a few seats away. Last spring, we were scheduled to take a group of faculty members and students to France, but a professor died in-flight—murder, it later turned out—grounding the plane. I hoped one day for a chance to see France and the town of St. Émilion, where my great-great grandmother (and namesake) had lived. With the cost of airfare and hotel, it wouldn't be any time soon.

Giles provided Felix with an explanation. He nodded toward André. "André is from France. He organized the trip."

"That reminds me," I said to Giles. "I asked him to come tonight. I know you tried to reach him last week and failed. I hope you don't mind."

"Not at all," said Giles. "I need to talk to him about the English as a Second Language Program. With Professor Davis leaving us unexpectedly, I'm looking for a replacement for next year."

"André would be perfect for the job," I said, getting excited. It was too late in the year for Giles to conduct a proper search for the position, and André needed a department. It was a win-win for both of them.

"I'm glad you agree," said Giles. "Let's just hope André does."

The buffet opened, and I quickly said my goodbyes and took my seat. Lenny had returned with my wine, and I told him the news while we waited in line for food.

"I suppose that means I'll learn more French curse words," said Lenny. "I have to admit I'm kind of excited."

I chuckled. André tended to curse in French when he was frustrated. "Giles is going to talk to André tonight. I don't think André knows. I'm so excited for him."

"He's worked hard," said Lenny, taking a plate. "He deserves it."

"No chicken parmigiana?" I said, checking out the entrées. "Dang." Bluff View was known for its excellent chicken parmigiana.

"Don't look so glum," said Lenny. "There's cheesecake."

I glanced down the buffet. Lenny was right. The end of the line was a dessert lover's mecca. I gathered my meal and sped toward the desserts, reaching for the chocolate mousse and cheesecake.

"You can't possibly eat both," said Claudia.

We started for our table. "It's chocolate and it's cheesecake. One dessert."

"You're worse than my kids."

I believed it. Her kids were like miniature adults, well-mannered and disciplined.

After dinner, Giles made a short speech, then gave Felix a token of our appreciation—a painting of Copper Bluff, signed by the artist. Felix shook his hand, thanking Giles for the gift. He also thanked Reed for inviting him and Andy to campus as special guests.

Andy stood and raised his cocktail high in the air. "To the good people of Copper Bluff!"

As we raised our glasses, Lenny whispered, "I think he's drunk."

I agreed. If he wasn't drunk, he was headed in that direction. I should have warned him about the well drinks. When grad students bartended on the weekends, the drinks were strong, especially when their friends were present.

I noticed Lydia walk to the deck after her dish was cleared. Now was my chance to get to know her better.

"I could use some fresh air," I said to Lenny. "How about you?"

Lenny stood. "If by getting fresh air you mean cornering Lydia on the deck, I'm game. I'd like to know who taught her to slip in and out of places like a ghost."

Lenny helped me with my coat, and Claudia reprimanded us with a look. "You know you're getting as bad as Em, right?"

"I'm supporting her interests," said Lenny. "It's what any good boyfriend would do."

I beamed at him.

Claudia shook her head as we walked past her.

The evening was clear, and the stars sparkled like silver confetti in the night sky. The land was as flat as the horizon, the two melting together into a vastness that made me feel small. This close to the bluff, I could hear the river flowing down below, the burble of water over the rocks. The murmur of people on the deck couldn't quell the distinctive sound, so rare on the Great Plains.

Near the edge of the deck, Lydia stood with her back to us, her narrow shoulders covered in a thin sweater. While others formed small groups, Lydia was alone and appeared comfortable in her aloneness. With the crush of people inside, maybe she needed to get away. For a moment, I reconsidered approaching her, and in that moment, Thomas Cook joined us on the deck. He greeted us with a hearty hello.

I returned his greeting. In the few years Thomas had been on campus, he'd changed. *We'd* changed. The first time I met him, he came off as East Coast intelligentsia, bragging about his hip dissertation. He was friendlier now—though still very au courant. One glance at his slim-fit jacket and perfect highlights told you that.

"Not a bad way to end the conference," said Thomas. "I enjoyed dinner thoroughly."

"The night isn't half-bad either," said Lenny. "I can't believe how warm this spring has been."

"I'm sure we'll pay for it sometime or another," said Thomas.

We were talking about the weather like real South Dakotans.

Thomas glanced at Lydia. "I'd better see how Lydia is faring. She was worried the gluten-free option wasn't really gluten-free."

"We'll join you," I said.

We started in the direction of Lydia, who jumped when Thomas touched her arm.

"Sorry," she said to Thomas. "You startled me."

Lydia was thin and tall. Maybe that's why she seemed frail.

Or maybe it was her eyes. Studying her, I wondered if that's where Lenny got the idea of a ghost. There was something behind her melancholy expression, a painful memory that time couldn't heal, perhaps.

"We're having a great time," said Lenny. "Right, Em?"

Whatever Lydia had said, I'd missed it. Lenny was prompting me to answer. "Wonderful," I said. "How about you? Thomas said your gluten-free meal might have been misrepresented."

"I think so," said Lydia. "When you're gluten intolerant, it's impossible to get a decent meal out."

No wonder I didn't see her around town. "I suppose you eat in most nights?"

She nodded. "It's the only way to know if the meal's been prepared correctly."

"Thomas says you work from home, too," I said.

She and Thomas shared a smile. "You're right, Thomas. She *is* inquisitive."

"I'm sorry," I said with a chuckle. "I don't mean to pry into your business."

"Not at all," said Lydia. "I'm teach online history courses for a college in Rhode Island."

"I didn't realize," I said. "I love history."

"You'll have to enroll in one of her classes," said Thomas, putting his arm around her. "In Massachusetts, she received the Teacher of the Year Award."

She brushed aside the accolade. "That was a long time ago."

"That's cool," said Lenny. "You should teach something on our campus."

"I know the history chair," I added. "I'd be happy to talk to her."

Lydia shook her head. She looked genuinely worried. "No, please don't. I mean, I'm happy where I am."

Thomas must have seen the question on my face. "Thank you, Emmeline. It's a kind offer, but like Lydia said, she's perfectly happy teaching from home."

The deck door burst open, and I turned to see what was

causing the commotion. It was Andy, and it looked as if he had refilled his glass more than once. He might be a burgeoning author, but he was still a graduate student. He didn't know when to curtail his drinking. We'd all been there. I wasn't going to judge.

"I think I like Andy when he's drinking," said Lenny. The group followed Lenny's eyes, which were on Andy. "He's much happier like this."

Maybe a little too happy. He was swerving around clumps of people like an indie race car driver. It might be time to get him home. I didn't want him to embarrass himself.

"We're his ride," I explained to Thomas and Lydia. "We'd better get him back. I don't want him getting in trouble with Felix. It was really nice talking to you, Lydia. I hope to catch up with you again sometime."

"Yes, I'd like that," said Lydia.

Lenny was saying his goodbyes when I heard the crash. It appeared we hadn't intervened in time after all. Andy had run into a table and fallen flat on his face, spilling his drink.

Chapter Nineteen

———

ANDY COMPLAINED ALL the way back to Copper Bluff. His head, his stomach—everything hurt. He was certain he'd contracted food poisoning. I assumed the complaints were excuses for falling at Bluff View Restaurant. He was embarrassed, and why wouldn't he be? His reputation as an upright young scholar disappeared as quickly as his drinks. Nothing was wrong with the food. If there were, we'd all be sick, I told him.

Andy let out a loud moan from the backseat, and Lenny rolled his eyes. He was losing patience, and so was I. The quicker we got him back to the hotel, the better. Lenny stepped on the gas, and soon we were at the edge of Copper Bluff, stopping at the first light into town.

"Where are you staying?" Lenny asked.

"The Happy Rest Motel," said Andy. "But take it from me, it's anything but happy and restful."

"It's only for one more night, right?" I said. "You leave tomorrow."

"Thank god," said Andy. "This trip has been a good reminder of why I left this area in the first place."

"Will you be back for Tanner's funeral?" I asked.

"We weren't close anymore," said Andy. "Why would I go to the funeral?"

To see your victim one last time?

Lenny turned into the motel parking lot. "He was your friend."

"I don't have friends," said Andy with a laugh. "My success has made me an outcast."

Thank goodness we were about to be rid of him. I couldn't tolerate one more minute. He was more exasperating drunk than sober. "Is Giles taking you to the airport?" I asked.

He didn't answer, and I wondered if he'd passed out. I looked in the backseat. His eyes were closed but fluttered open.

"Hmm?" said Andy. "Oh yes. Our plane leaves at three."

"Safe travels to you both," I said as Lenny pulled into a parking spot. "I look forward to reading your new book."

"Get some sleep," said Lenny. "You'll feel better in the morning."

Andy sat up and looked out the window. He mumbled his thanks as he stumbled out of the car. He held his stomach all the way to the door.

I gestured to Andy. "You don't think it's food poisoning, right?"

"Not unless you get food poisoning by drinking Captain Morgan."

"Right," I said. "And we feel fine."

"Better than fine," said Lenny.

I smiled. "I talked to Owen Parrish again. He insisted I rewrite the ending."

"Are you going to?"

"What choice do I have?" My block was quiet except for a boom, boom, boom coming from down the street. Somewhere students were celebrating to a strong bass beat. I just hoped they didn't celebrate all night. I had grading to finish tomorrow.

"What did you think of Lydia?" Lenny asked.

"I don't know," I said. "I have a feeling Thomas is protecting her from something, but I don't know what."

"Us?" said Lenny with a laugh.

I gave him a shove.

"Something in her past?" Lenny said.

I nodded. "She was petrified when I said I could get her in touch with the history chair. Did you notice that? I wonder what happened."

Lenny stopped in front of my house. "If I know you, you'll find out sooner or later. Let's just make it later, okay? I hear a bottle of vino calling our names."

After Lenny left, I had a hard time falling asleep. Actually, I didn't even try. Wearing sweatpants and a t-shirt, I lay reading in bed, shoving various pillows behind my head to get comfortable enough for sleep. It was impossible to relax. First, the bass beat still thudded somewhere in the vicinity. Second, I had too much on my mind, mainly Tanner's death. He'd been murdered for knowledge, love, or money, which didn't narrow down the motives or the suspects. Andy was leaving tomorrow, and so was Felix. If they had anything to do with Tanner's death, how would the police catch up with them? I wished I'd had more time to talk to Andy—and that he'd been capable of coherent conversation when we dropped him off.

My friendship with Giles also weighed heavily on my mind. Giles had given me the green light to investigate, and I had nothing to show for my efforts. Then there was the little matter of truncating my book to end on a more positive note and reduce the word count. The thought of deleting all those hours of work made me want to punch Owen Parrish in the face, but I settled for fluffing a pillow. Eventually, after I flung it to the floor, I decided to take a walk to ease my mind—and tell the music lovers down the street to call it a night.

The air was still, and as I descended my stairs, I waited for a breeze to surprise me, bursting between a house or building like a thief absconding with his ill-gotten gains. But the wind was silent. The only sound was the thumping of the stereo in the distance. It wasn't an angry sound; it was like the beating of a heart, pumping constantly whether we were asleep or awake. It was the pulse of a college town, refusing to conform to schedules or nightly rituals.

Soon I realized the party was a block over. If it hadn't quieted by the time I was finished with my walk, I would take a detour and ask them to shut off their music. Right now I was enjoying the spring night and the promise of summer. Everywhere I looked, the campus landscape was returning to life. Vibrant colors scrubbed away the brown and gray, with newly planted flowers along the pathways and budding bushes ready to bloom. Cherry trees scented the air, and the maple tree on the corner, the one I thought of as a friend, had returned to its former leafy glory like the note of a robin, strong and certain.

As I walked to Harriman Hall, I felt part of the change, as if I, myself, was coming back to life. I'd made it; we all had. We'd endured heavy snowfalls, icy roads, and subzero temperatures. Spring, this beauty around me, was our reward.

Since buildings were locked at ten, I took out my keys as I opened the heavy outer door with a shove. I liked the peacefulness of my office, my home away from home. Sometimes I would grade papers, read, or simply enjoy the scent of honeysuckle wafting into my window. Tonight I had a book in mind I wanted to consult, one about Shakespeare. It was a slim volume my mother had given me in college, and I liked its conciseness.

Despite the cool night, my office was stuffy, insulated by all the books. Leaving my keys in the doorknob, I flicked on my two lamps, one on the desk and one standing. Then I began searching my shelves for the Shakespeare book. Originally, my books had been organized by literary periods. During my three years on campus, however, they'd rearranged themselves according to use. I rarely referenced my Shakespeare collection, so finding the one I wanted was easy.

Holding the book, I flopped into my floral-patterned chair in the corner alcove. A cricket chirped in the distance, keeping me company. I flipped to the chapter on *Hamlet*, which contained summary and analysis. I couldn't say what I was looking for. I only had a dim recollection of something I'd once read to guide me. A lot of my academic searches started this way. I'd read something in a book and now wanted to reread it. It was the reason I never threw anything out, no matter how obscure or unrelated to my field.

Halfway through the chapter, I began to wonder if I had the wrong book. Then I found it, a line in Hamlet highlighted with yellow marker: "That one may smile, and smile, and be a villain!" The line is aimed at Claudius, King Hamlet's brother and murderer. But I found myself thinking of Tanner, who was also a great performer. What I knew about him had to do with performing—the actor, the scholar, the victim—but who was he, really? The analysis pointed out that performance and authenticity are important themes in the play. I decided they were important in my investigation as well.

How long I read I couldn't say. Shakespeare had never captured my heart as completely as a romance novel, so it probably wasn't very long. I woke up feeling refreshed and very, very warm. A couple of sticky blinks told me the sun was out and that I'd spent the night in my office. In my jogging pants. Terror-struck at the thought of my colleagues seeing me this way, I sat up, and the Shakespeare book fell to the floor. The clock on the wall read ten. I remembered it was Sunday; thankfully, no one would see me creep out the door in my joggers. If Barb caught me like this, I'd never hear the end of it.

I hurried down the stairs. The door to Harriman Hall was still ajar. I chided myself for my irresponsibility. I'd worked there three years. I knew the door stuck. I should have pulled it shut when I came in. Oh well. No harm done. I shut it now.

My cellphone buzzed as I walked toward Oxford Street. It was Lenny.

"So this is weird," he said.

"What?" I glanced around. Could he see me leaving the campus?

"Andy *did* have food poisoning," said Lenny. "I just left the hospital."

"What the heck? Why didn't you call me?"

"I didn't want to wake you," he said. "Andy called me at four this morning. His stomach was killing him, and he needed a ride to the hospital. He's really sick."

I hurried across the crosswalk. "Is he going to be okay?"

"I'm sure he will be," said Lenny. "He was back to his old self-righteous ways. He said he knew he'd eaten something rotten. He was completely vindicated. What's that noise? Are you outside?"

"I fell asleep in my office," I said. "I'm just walking home."

The line was silent for a moment. "I don't like you going to the campus in the middle of the night, alone. It's dangerous."

"I'm sorry you feel that way," I said.

"I'm serious, Em. I worry about you." I'd never heard Lenny sound this angry.

"I know you are," I said, approaching my cheery yellow bungalow. "But you also know I have insomnia. I need outlets." I waved at Mrs. Gunderson, who was sweeping her front steps.

Lenny let out a breath. "Find other ones—at least until Tanner's murder is solved."

I spotted something purple on my porch. "What's this? Did you leave me something?" I bent down to inspect the flower.

"Leave you what?" asked Lenny. "What are you talking about?"

"A pansy ..." I said in a voice barely above a whisper. I didn't need Jane to tell me what it meant or the connection to Shakespeare. A pansy was for thoughts.

Chapter Twenty

—

I SPUN AROUND, the miniature flowerpot in hand. "Who did this?" I yelled at the neighborhood. There was no answer from the psychologists next door, nor the family across the street. Lenny, still on the line, told me to calm down. I tossed the flower over the front railing of my stoop. Now it was in my yard, the petals still picture-perfect. I stomped down the steps, walked into my yard, and crushed them with my tennis shoe. It was then I noticed Mrs. Gunderson staring at me. Mrs. Gunderson, the eyes and ears of our block—who was I kidding?—the entire town. I'd have to explain.

"I gotta go, Lenny. I'll call you back after I shower." I clicked off the phone and turned to Mrs. Gunderson.

"I know you have a hard time growing plants, Emmeline, but really, that was uncalled for." Mrs. Gunderson, wearing navy-blue pants and a flowered top, held a plastic watering can in her hand. Her dog, Darling, lay near her Hostas, and I read judgment on his spoilt mug.

"It's not that," I said. "Someone is messing with me. They keep leaving me flowers, notes, clues that I can't piece together. Have you seen anyone around my house this morning?"

"I went to church at eight thirty," said Mrs. Gunderson. "So I haven't been home the entire time, but I haven't seen anyone near your house. Rest assured, if I did, I would ask them what they were doing. I'm not afraid to call out hooligans when I see them acting up."

I knew she meant what she said. I'd seen her approach students, neighbors, and police officers with the same idea: it was her neighborhood and she would decide what did and did not happen on her block. "Just be careful," I said. "Something very strange is going on, and I don't want you involved."

She set down the watering can with a plunk. "I most certainly *will* get involved. I'm not as old and frail as I look."

She looked anything but old and frail. With pink lips, curled hair, and church clothes, she was more put-together than I was most days. She had a strong will that went along with her sturdy polyester pants. "I'm just saying, if you see something, call the police. I don't know what kind of creep I'm dealing with. I have no idea where these came from."

"Why don't you check the price tag?" Mrs. Gunderson said, approaching my yard. Darling followed.

"That's a really good idea." I bent down and turned over the plastic pot. The price tag had been removed. "Nothing."

Mrs. Gunderson leaned over my shoulder. "Those are pansies."

I nodded. "I know."

"There's only one place in town that would have them out so early," said Mrs. Gunderson. "Petal's Place."

"Petal's Place," I repeated. Of course. It was too early for pansies and many other flowers. Lots of Midwesterners didn't put out flowers until Mother's Day, the gold standard for planting season. But Petal's was the flower shop downtown and the only place that offered blooms year-round. I could easily check there. Someone might remember who bought the pansies. "Thank you, Mrs. Gunderson. You've been a great help."

"You're welcome," she said. Darling showed his gratitude by peeing on my tree.

After a quick breakfast and shower, I called Lenny back. Since our earlier call, he'd driven Felix to the hospital to see Andy, and he was on his way to my house. Maybe it was fate. Andy and Felix wouldn't be able to leave town after all. If they were connected to Tanner's murder, I had more time to find out. One thing was certain: Andy had nothing to do with the pansies. He had an airtight alibi.

Dickinson made a good show of running up to Lenny when I opened the door, as if she had been the one to suffer insult and injury. Meowing, she told her story of her night all alone in the house. *If only she could tell me who'd left the pansies at my door*. But this wasn't Agatha Christie's *Dumb Witness*. My pet would be the last animal in the world to help me out.

"So, while you were away, your stalker came to play," said Lenny, scratching Dickinson's ears.

"It's probably a good thing I wasn't here." I seized the opportunity to bolster my position in our earlier disagreement. "Who knows what would have happened if I hadn't taken that walk."

Lenny stopped petting Dickinson and stood. He took a step closer. All six feet of him was in my space when he touched my chin. "I don't want to fight."

I didn't want to fight either, not with him sending shivers down my spine.

He brushed my lips with his. "Okay?"

I nodded.

"Good."

I wondered what I had just agreed to. Taking a step back, I refocused on my afternoon plans. "I'd like to go to the hospital to see Andy. I can't believe he really had food poisoning. But first, I want to stop by Petal's Place downtown. Mrs. Gunderson says it's the only store in town with pansies."

"It's a small store," he said. "The cashier might remember who bought them."

"Exactly," I said, slipping on my tennis shoes. "Let's go."

Lenny's old Ford Taurus sputtered to a start, and soon we were driving toward Main Street. I saw the problem with my plan the minute we approached the stoplight. Like most stores, Petal's Place wasn't open on Sundays. My questions would have to wait until tomorrow.

"Shoot," I said. "It's not open."

"So, where to now?" said Lenny.

"The hospital," I said.

Lenny grumbled. "I just came from there. It's going to look really weird when I show up again."

"I'll say I wanted to see Andy."

He looked skeptical. "Because you guys are such good friends."

"We drove him home—and he called you for a ride." I shrugged. "I think that constitutes friendship."

"I don't understand why you want to go," said Lenny. "He's just going to rub our faces in our poor judgment. He told us he was sick last night. We should have believed him."

"I *still* don't know if I believe him," I said. "Nobody else got sick, and it was a buffet."

Lenny turned toward the hospital. "So … what are you saying?"

"I'm saying it might not be food poisoning."

"Why don't we let the doctors be the judge of that." Lenny put the car in park.

"That's what I'm doing," I said.

"Helping the doctors judge if Andy has food poisoning?" said Lenny. "I'm sure they'll appreciate your input."

I opened my car door. "I want to make sure they don't jump to a conclusion, that's all. I need to make them aware of the connection between Tanner and Andy."

"We're not sure a connection exists."

"We're not sure a connection *doesn't* exist, either," I said, arranging my scarf. "Andy's illness could be attempted murder."

Lenny raised one dark eyebrow, a skill I coveted. "I don't know, Em. Think about all the trouble Tanner's murderer went to. The garden, the scene, the liquid in the ear. How could he botch this murder so badly?"

"I don't have all the answers," I whispered as we entered the hospital. "That's why I'm here." The facility was cold, quiet, and sterile. It smelled like latex and disinfectant. It made me sick with its pungency.

After learning Andy's room number from a volunteer, we took the elevator to the second floor. I hoped he felt better. The last thing I wanted was to walk in on him while he was throwing up. Felix being there was a good sign, though. He would have called Lenny for a ride if Andy was too ill for visitors.

Andy's door was half closed, and Lenny knocked on it softly. "It's Lenny and Em. Can we come in?"

"Sure." The voice was Felix's.

As we entered the dimly lit space, I was surprised by the gravity of the situation. Andy was hooked up to an IV as well as a machine that monitored his vitals. His cheeks were pale, and the skin around his eyes ashen. Had someone told me he was the same scholar from the Shakespeare conference, I wouldn't have believed them. He didn't respond when we said hello. His lips turned up as if he were attempting a smile, but then he reached for his stomach. The action seemed to physically hurt.

"It looks like he's taken a turn for the worse," Lenny whispered in my ear.

"How's he doing?" I said to Felix.

"Not as well as we'd hoped," said Felix. "I thought we might be able to make our flight today, but it will need to be rescheduled. Which isn't a problem," Felix added when Andy's eyebrows lifted.

"Did the doctor say how long it'd be?" asked Lenny.

"She's not sure," said Felix. "If he doesn't show signs of improvement soon, they're going to test for bacteria. If it's positive, the health department will need to be notified of a possible outbreak."

"I'm so sorry, Andy," I said. "Is there anything I can do?"

"Call the authorities," said Andy between gasps. "Tell them to shut down that cesspool of a restaurant."

I didn't enjoy hearing him call one of the nicest restaurants in town a cesspool, but I bit my tongue. The guy was in pain. He was allowed a few choice words about Bluff View. "Do you have any idea what food caused it? Did you start getting ill right away?"

"Not right away." He closed his eyes. "Not until after dinner. It could have been anything. Maybe the salad."

Several cases of contaminated Romaine lettuce had been reported in the last year, but I'd had the salad, too, and I felt fine. We hadn't been seated at the same table. Perhaps different batches of lettuce had been served.

His eyes flew open, and he grabbed for his emesis bag. That was our cue to leave. We all rushed out of the room, almost colliding with the nurse outside Andy's door. He was a brick wall, and just as sturdy as one. My bumping into him didn't faze him.

"Stomach again?" The nurse wore green scrubs, a badge, and carried a small phone.

I nodded.

"Hey, Zeb," said Lenny. "How are you?"

"Professor Jenkins," said Zeb, holding out his hand. "Good to see you. I didn't realize Andy was an English professor."

"Not yet," said Lenny. "He'll graduate in May from Denver, though. Felix, here, is his advisor." Felix nodded in acknowledgment before scooting off to get a drink from the water fountain.

"No wonder those guys weren't familiar," said Zeb, after Felix left. "I didn't recognize them."

"How is Andy?" I asked. "He seems really sick."

"Food poisoning can be pretty dangerous," said Zeb. "Most

people don't realize, but symptoms can persist for several days. The Zofran should have helped with the nausea. We might need to increase his dosage."

"We all ate the same buffet last night," I said. "Does that mean we can all expect to get sick?"

"Not necessarily," said Zeb. "It might have been something he ate earlier in the day. Many times it takes hours for food poisoning to catch up with you, though certain strains, like staphylococcus aureus, can wreak havoc in as little as thirty minutes."

He made a good point. Andy could have eaten something for lunch that affected him at dinner.

"But you think it *is* food poisoning?" asked Lenny.

"For now," said Zeb. "If he doesn't get better, the doctor might need to look into other possibilities, including an antibiotic for a bacterial infection." Zeb's phone began to ring.

"Is it okay if we check back later?" Lenny asked.

Zeb nodded. "Sure thing. I gotta take this."

Felix returned from the water fountain, and we updated him with the information Zeb had given us.

"Am I correct in assuming it might be several days before we can leave?" Felix asked, looking toward Andy's room. His gray hair was parted perfectly to one side.

"It's possible," I said. "If I were you, I'd wait to rebook my flight. I'm sure he'll improve by tomorrow."

Felix scratched his neck. "This trip has been one bloody disaster after another. First, the young actor, now Andy. They say big cities aren't safe, but I wonder."

"Your lecture was fantastic, if that makes you feel any better about the trip," I said.

"And Giles said your book is selling really well in the bookstore," added Lenny.

I wasn't the only one doing damage control. Lenny didn't want our big-name scholar leaving Copper Bluff disgruntled either.

"Thank you," said Felix. "I'm glad to hear it. Now, if you don't mind, I'm going to sit with Andy. He's been like a son to me these past few years. I don't want him going through this ordeal alone."

"Please let us know if we can help," I said. "We can be here night or day."

"Night or day?" Lenny said after Felix left. "Isn't that a bit drastic?"

"You know what they say: drastic times, drastic measures."

Lenny took out his keys. "I should have known that was coming."

Chapter Twenty-One

MONDAY ARRIVED LIKE a bouquet of flowers—a gaudy one splashed over my mock-up book cover. When I received the email from Owen Parrish at my office, I thought maybe he'd reconsidered his harsh words about my final chapters. From the looks of the cover, though, he was punishing me for my resistance. It looked like an outdated romance, cluttered with pink and purple flowers. The font was ornate. Whoever had created the cover obviously hadn't read the book or taken my suggestions into consideration. The subject was women's writing, but that didn't mean the scheme needed to include pink and purple tones or a cutesy font. I hated it when women's scholarship wasn't taken seriously.

I shut my laptop and pushed back my office chair. "Ridiculous!"

"Everything all right over there, Emmeline?" said Giles from beyond our adjoining door.

"No, it's not," I said, gathering my books. I had to teach class in fifteen minutes. Closing the door behind me, I marched into his office. "My editor just sent me a mock-up of my new book cover, and it's hideous."

Giles crossed a foot over one knee. "It can't be that bad."

"It has flowers all over it."

"You like flowers," said Giles.

"Yeah, in my yard—not on the cover of a scholarly book!" I readjusted my backpack.

"You'll just have to tell him it's unsatisfactory," said Giles. "They'll need to come up with something else."

"He doesn't listen to me." I tried not to let my exasperation show, but I could feel beads of sweat forming on my forehead. "He wants me to delete a bunch of stuff and revise the ending. He's like a hundred years old."

"That seems old to still be working." A smile curved Giles's lips.

I chuckled at his dry sense of humor. "You know what I mean. He's been working there forever, but this is a different kind of book from what they normally publish, which is fiction. I don't know if he's even read it."

"Just be patient," said Giles. "Contact him after you've had a chance to cool down."

"I'm on my way to my 101 class right now," I said. "I'm sure it will be downright icy in there when I hand back papers."

"Oh, and Emmeline?" said Giles as I turned to leave. "I'll be out this afternoon if anyone asks. I promised Felix I would take him to the hospital to see Andy."

"Andy's still sick?" I couldn't believe he was so bad he needed visitors. He'd been in the hospital since early Sunday morning. Why wasn't he recovering?

Giles let out a sigh. "I'm afraid so. Felix says he's worse than yesterday."

"That's not right," I said. "If it's food poisoning, he should be feeling better."

"Tell me about it," muttered Giles, sounding very unlike himself. "I have a feeling this will be their last trip to Copper Bluff."

I wasn't heartbroken over the pair not coming back. I was

worried about Andy's illness, though. It would be bad news for Bluff View Restaurant and even the university if Andy didn't get better soon. His nurse, Zeb, said they might test his blood for bacteria. Maybe they'd start an antibiotic today if he didn't improve.

With class on the third floor of Stanton Hall, I had to get going. I told Giles to keep me posted and hurried across the quad. As I walked up the stairs of Stanton, my steps became stomps. Owen Parrish and his book cover were heavy on my mind. I could think of a hundred things to say to him in the moment, but chances were, when I talked to him, my words would dissolve into a series of angry headshakes. Despite its scholarly tone, the book had a lot of my heart in it. That's what stung. It was like I was defending a family member, since the idea was one I had grown up with in my college years. I would fight for it as fiercely as I would a close relation.

I paused on the landing of the stairwell, smiling. It was funny how often Lenny's words came to mind, how often they cheered me up. Frequently, he teased me about being an only child, replacing siblings with books. Maybe I had done just that with my scholarly work.

I kept walking, reminding myself of our upcoming trip to Petal's Place. Every day I looked forward to seeing Lenny, to talking and planning and dreaming. We'd been dating only four months, but it was hard to imagine life without him. It was as if he'd always been a part of my life. I wondered if he felt the same way.

I shook off the possibility. Lenny went through girlfriends like I went through coffee filters, and for me, dating included a revolving door. But these last three years had built a foundation, a friendship that was unbreakable. I hoped our bond was too.

My students were waiting for me when I stepped into the classroom. I heaved my backpack onto the table as a few stragglers found their desks. Returning papers, I heard some groans. Many professors waited to give back papers until the end of the class to avoid the grumbling. For the next fifty minutes, I would face an uphill battle taking their minds off their grades and getting them to focus on their final papers. But I managed it with the help of a few controversial topic ideas. In groups, they debated those instead of my grading scale, and as I walked to my next class across the hall, my backpack was lighter and so was my mood.

Until I overheard a discussion near the stairwell. Mia and her roommate Hailey were talking to a male student. The volume was increasing, and I moved toward the group to make sure nothing was amiss. That's when I realized the man was Jacob, the student playing Hamlet now. Jacob saw me and fled down the stairs. Hailey crossed her muscular arms, which were emphasized by a team volleyball tank top. Mia, dressed in a long vest and leggings, shouted after him, "Goodbye!"

"You've been through one heartache," said Hailey. "Why make it two?"

Mia turned her attention to Hailey. "How can you say that? Tanner's not even buried yet. I have no plans to date anyone."

"It doesn't make it less true," said Hailey. "If you still can't see how they're alike, maybe you need counseling."

Mia chided her, "With a school counselor? I saw the brochure you left for me on the table. I'm not an idiot."

"I don't know what you're talking about. I didn't leave you anything." Hailey shifted her weight awkwardly from one foot to the other.

I decided to step in. I didn't have much time before my next class. "Is everything okay? Was that student bothering you?"

Mia brushed back the tendrils of blonde hair that had come undone from her high bun. "It's fine. He's from the theater."

"Are you sure?" I asked.

Mia smiled. "I'm sure."

I wasn't as sure, so I tried to keep the conversation going. "I thought I recognized him from the play. Jacob, right? Did you guys enjoy Dr. Lewis's speech?"

"I did," said Mia. "He kind of reminded me why I got into art in the first place. Theater was his refuge. Art is mine."

"I thought the talk was too long," said Hailey. She was the most pragmatic of the group, interested more in backstage workings than what was said on stage. "At least he had a cool accent, I guess."

"Right?" said Mia. "I love the way he talks."

A student came up on my left. He was in my next class and seemed to need to talk to me. "I have to get to class, but let me know if I can help in any way at all. Asking for help is a sign of strength, not weakness. Losing a friend or loved one is hard. Remember that."

"Thank you, Professor Prather," said Hailey. "We appreciate it."

AFTER CLASS, I went back to the English Department. I had an office hour, which meant, as long as students didn't stop by, I could contact Owen Parrish. I had cooled down enough to make an outgoing call. At least until I pulled up the picture of my book cover again. Staring at the pink and purple eyesore, I could feel the angry feelings well up again. Just because this was a book about women didn't mean it needed flowers, pastels, or animals on its cover. I huffed a breath. It didn't reflect the work of these women—or mine, for that matter. And Owen Parrish was going to hear about it.

"What the hell is that?" said Lenny. He was standing at my side with a bag of food from Roca de Taco.

"It's a collage of every stereotype women have fought against for the last hundred years," I said, pivoting my chair in his direction.

"That's putting it kindly." Lenny took the corner alcove chair. "It looks like the Disney princesses threw up on your screen."

"Thanks for your opinion," I muttered.

"Sorry, I just got off the phone from my sister," said Lenny. Lenny's sister had two little girls who recently graduated from Nickelodeon to Disney. He knew more about tiaras and wands than I did.

"I brought lunch," he added. "Everything is better with salsa—even ugly book covers."

I thanked him as he handed me a grilled burrito. "Did you remember to add—"

"Jalapeños?" he said, handing me a container of salsa. "Of course. I think I know what you like by now."

Yes, he did. But did he know how much I liked his company and how often I found myself wondering about what he was doing? I pondered those questions for the next several bites.

"I assume you're going to talk to Owen about the cover," said Lenny. "It looked like you were formulating a sinister plan when I walked in."

"Plot is more like it," I said. "I'm struck dumb by his nasal voice. Last time we talked, I could hear my earring clattering against the phone."

"That's not like you," said Lenny. "Why does this guy have you spooked?"

I shook my head. "That's the million-dollar question." I added salsa to my burrito. "I suppose I don't like disappointing people."

"Like who?"

"My parents, for starters," I said. "They've told the entire neighborhood. They act like my book is going to be a *New York Times* bestseller."

"Don't worry about them," said Lenny. "They'll love you no matter what. So will—"

A knock on Giles's door interrupted our conversation. "Professor Giles is gone for the afternoon," I hollered from my desk.

Alice, Mia's roommate, poked her head into my office.

"Oh hi, Alice," I said. "Can I help you with something?"

"I didn't mean to interrupt," she said. "I just needed to talk to

Professor Giles about my schedule next year. I want to switch up some classes."

"Sorry," I said. "He won't be back this afternoon. You should be able to catch him tomorrow, though."

"I'll stop by in the morning," said Alice. "Will you let him know?"

"Sure," I said. "Before you go, can I ask you something? It's about Mia."

She took a step into my office. The sun caught the highlights of her lovely cranberry hair.

"I overheard a conversation she had with Hailey," I said. "Something about counseling. I wondered if Mia might need help from a school grief therapist. I could put her in touch with someone."

Alice thought for a moment. "That's funny. I saw the Health Services brochure on our table. That must have been what it was about."

"So, Mia knows where to get help if she needs it?"

Alice nodded. "The university sent out emails, too. I can mention it, though, if you think it will help."

"Thank you," I said. "It might be better coming from a friend."

She gave me a little salute. "I'm on the case, Professor Prather."

After she left, I turned to Lenny. "I like her, you know that?"

The dimple in Lenny's cheek showed. "You like anyone you can wrangle into your world of detection and mystery."

Now it was my turn to smile. "That must be why I like you so much."

Chapter Twenty-Two

BEFORE WE WENT to Petal's Place, I needed to call Owen Parrish. I couldn't focus on anything, even Lenny's cute dimple, with the cover art on my mind and computer screen. I told Lenny to shut the door on his way out so I wouldn't be disturbed. Then I took a deep breath and dialed Owen's number. He sounded more annoyed than ever. I wanted to hang up the instant he picked up. But I'd completed more difficult tasks than making a phone call. I'd brought three killers to justice. Surely I could tackle one unfriendly editor.

"Hello, Owen. This is Emmeline Prather, and I'm calling about the mock-up cover I received this morning." So far so good. My voice was strong and clear, and my hoop earrings were silent.

"If you have concerns, you need to schedule a call," said Owen. "I'm very busy."

"I'll remember that for next time," I said. "Since we're on the phone now, can we talk?"

"What is it?"

"The cover is a little … flowery." I stared at the tangle of blossoms on my screen, trying to describe the problem. "I don't think it relays the message we want to convey."

"What message?"

"The early ways women found to express their creativity," I said. "This book is about voice."

"Gardening is a form of creativity," said Owen.

My earring jangled, and I switched my black office phone to the other ear, determined not to let his unexpected responses distract me. "True, it is, but it's not one of the forms I discuss in the book."

He sniffed. "Maybe it should be."

Was he kidding? The book was about writing, women's writing. I was starting to believe he really hadn't read it. Or he was joking. I attempted a chuckle. "It would hardly fit with the theme. Anyway, if we could try another cover, one with fewer flowers, that would be great."

"Everyone likes flowers," he said.

"Purple and pink flowers? I don't think so."

"The cover will appeal to women."

"It doesn't appeal to me, and I'm a woman." The statement hung in the air like smoke from a gun. I was glad I'd said it because it was true. It was my book, after all. I'd written it. I'd spent hours with it. He acted as if it had materialized out of thin air, as if my opinion didn't matter at all. Well, it should.

"What *would* appeal to you, Emmeline?"

I'd never detested the sound of my name so much. I might have been a two-year-old. I refused to be talked to like a toddler. "I'm glad you asked. I would like to see some form of writing, perhaps letters and a fountain pen or a typewriter. Something that conveys the art of writing."

He puffed out a breath. "I'll talk to our designer and get back to you."

"Thank you," I said. "I appreciate it."

"Please don't call again without an appointment."

The line went silent, and I was glad I didn't have to respond. I'd won a small battle. I wanted to end on that happy note.

Lenny opened the door. "You were great."

"Were you listening outside the door?" I asked.

"Yep, and you held your own against that jerk."

I pushed back my chair. "I did, didn't I? He's going to talk to their designer and get back to me."

"Good." He reached for the gray knit sweater on the back of my chair, holding it out for me. "We can go to Petal's Place now. It's too nice to be inside."

Locking up, I noticed the hall was quiet for a Monday. No one was coming in or going out, and a familiar mustiness hung in the air. It was the disuse of summer, already settling into the cracks in the walls, the crevices of floorboards. When the warm air arrived, it would slowly fill the void left by students, leaving scholars to peruse their favorite tomes in peace for two blissful months. Then the cold fall air would snap their attention back to teaching, and the blithe summer days would go much more quickly than they'd come.

Thomas Cook stood in the hallway outside Barb's office, and seeing him reminded me to ask him about the sonnet submitted for the contest. He was our resident expert on rhetoric and studied violent language on campuses. He and I had collaborated on a paper last semester that had recently been accepted by a prestigious scholarly journal. He might have some insights into the poem that I hadn't considered.

Lenny and I greeted him with hellos. He explained that he was waiting for Barb to finish her phone call. Most likely she was talking to her niece. She spent most afternoons gabbing with her about her kids.

"It might be a while," said Lenny.

"Tell me about it," said Thomas.

"I didn't get a chance to ask you something the other night," I said. "Mind if I ask you now?"

"I'm in no rush," said Thomas, putting his hands in the pockets of his sleek jacket. "Obviously."

"Great," I said. "A submission came into the sonnet-writing contest that warned of trouble. At the time, Claudia wasn't concerned, but with Tanner's death happening shortly thereafter, I wondered if you might look at it. I gave the original to Giles. I have a copy in my office."

"Sure, I'd be happy to. When?" asked Thomas.

I appreciated his willingness to give it a look. "We're on our way out, but are you in tomorrow?"

"I'll be here in the morning, around ten," said Thomas. "I'm meeting with a student."

"I'll stop by your office afterwards." I turned to Lenny. "Do you want to be there?"

He shook his head. "Iambic pentameter is not something I set my alarm for."

Thomas laughed. "I hear you. I'm not a big fan either."

"By the way, I enjoyed visiting with Lydia at Bluff View," I said. "I wish she'd let me talk to the history chair. It'd be nice to have her on campus."

He tilted his head. "She likes working from home."

"She might like it here better," said Lenny. "You never know."

He glanced into Barb's office. "It looks as if she's off the phone. See you tomorrow, Emmeline."

Once we were in the stairwell, Lenny gave me a look. "Did you notice how he brushed off my question? I wonder why he doesn't want her teaching here."

"There's something we don't know," I said. A blast of cold wind hit my face as I opened the back door of Harriman Hall. I quickened my pace to Lenny's car.

Lenny unlocked the doors. "So many mysteries, so little time."

PETAL'S PLACE WAS owned by Petal Petersen, whom I'd met last Christmas while poinsettia shopping. She had the loveliest— and the most expensive—red and white plants in town. They were also the healthiest, for I still had mine in my bay window. A Christmas fanatic, I wasn't about to throw my poinsettia away just because the season had ended. Even Dickinson was resigned to it being there. She hadn't touched it for months.

Petal's Place was packed with colorful blooms, and as we passed under the creaky wooden sign that marked the entrance, it was like entering another world, a world of gardens and high tea and stolen kisses in gazebos. I almost forgot we were here because someone had left me an ill-intentioned pot of pansies. The idea seemed silly in the midst of so much beauty. How could the gesture feel sinister? It occurred to me that maybe it wasn't. Unlike begonias or marigolds, pansies had a pleasant meaning. Was it possible they were a gift, sent by an admirer? Someone who liked me? In the context of other recent events, I doubted it.

"Claudia was right," said Lenny. "Your eyes are violet."

I smiled. Maybe the enchantment of the place was rubbing off on Lenny, too. Or maybe it was the purple hydrangeas I was standing next to. "Do you see any pansies?"

"Not yet," said Lenny. "Let's look around."

The store was small, with several nooks and crannies. Every corner was stuffed with plants, potpourri, or plush animals to send as gifts. The delicious smells changed from one nook to the next—roses, then lilies, then carnations. But no pansies.

"Em, over here," called Lenny. On the other side of the store, he'd found the perennials and annuals. As I approached, he held up a pot of pansies identical to the one I'd found on my porch. "Is this it?"

"It is." I turned the pot around, looking at it from all sides. I was certain of the match.

"Aren't those gorgeous?" said a peppy voice. "I just put them out on Saturday. Sorry, I didn't hear you come in. I was in the backroom."

It was Petal. I remembered her heterochromatic eyes, one blue and one brown. They were distinctive, just like her flower shop. "Yes they are," I said. "I was given one yesterday."

"How nice," said Petal. A heavy canvas apron covered her

top and jeans. She must have been cutting or arranging flowers when she heard us come in.

"Normally, it would be," said Lenny. "But this was different. Someone's been leaving flowers as signs, messages. The pot of pansies was left on Em's doorstep overnight."

"Out in the cold? Terrible." Petal brushed her blonde pixie hair off her forehead. "Who would do such a thing?"

I could tell Petal took the carelessness personally. "We thought you might be able to tell us. If you just put them out Saturday, maybe you remember someone buying one."

She bit her lip while she considered the question. "I was here Saturday morning and then left to do a wedding. I don't remember selling any." She paused. "I don't have a security system, but I could review the receipts for that day. Maybe someone used a credit card. Would that help?"

"That would be great," said Lenny.

We followed her to the cash register then waited while she reviewed her list of sales. The local radio station crackled over the speakers. An announcer reminded listeners of the upcoming party at Harmony Music Museum for Shakespeare's birthday on April 23. Free and open to the public, it was the final event before the folio left campus.

"Let me check one other place," said Petal and disappeared into the backroom. I could see her looking through rolls of receipts near a file cabinet. She returned with a shrug. "Sorry. According to my receipts, I didn't sell any."

"Does any place else in Copper Bluff have pansies?" I asked.

"I don't think so," said Petal. "I'm usually the first because I have space for them indoors."

"Thanks for the help," I said. "We appreciate it."

"I hope you find whoever left them," said Petal. "It's not nice to leave flowers out in the cold."

Lenny and I shared a look. Disregard for flowers might be the least of this person's sins.

Chapter Twenty-Three

—

I DIDN'T TEACH on Tuesdays or Thursdays, but that didn't mean I didn't work. If I wasn't in my office, I was usually grading papers or writing my own essays for eventual publication. This being Tuesday, I was up early, rewriting the last chapters of my book. It was a difficult process, one I couldn't completely reconcile myself to. Dickinson was in my office and heard the grumbling and saw the headshaking. After deleting a few sentences, I would turn to her for comfort. With a squint of her eyes, she would assure me that I was the last person on earth to be right about anything. So I continued deleting and rewriting until I'd cut thirty pages and added seven.

I sent the file to Owen and pushed my office chair away from the desk. Revision was hateful. I was not hearing the happy voice that told me to write all these wonderful pages in the first place. A devil sat on my shoulder. Then he'd jumped into the chair and had his way with my manuscript at last. I hoped he was happy. I certainly was not. But I trusted the writing process enough to know I would be when the project was finished.

My phone was buzzing on the counter when I deposited my coffee cup in the kitchen sink. It was Lenny. Maybe he'd decided to come to Thomas Cook's office with me after all. "Hello?"

"You know I can hear it in your voice when you're smiling?" said Lenny. "That's why I love calling you."

I attempted a straight face and failed. "You got me. I am."

"I called to tell you that Andy is really sick," said Lenny. "I just got off the phone with Felix, and the antibiotic they started isn't helping. Andy's worse than ever. Giles is teaching, so I'm taking Felix to the hospital. I wondered if you wanted to go with me."

"Shoot," I said. "I would, but I promised Thomas I'd meet him at his office. Remember? You go and see what you can find out. Call me when you're done."

"I will," he said. "Be safe."

"You, too." I ended the call, more convinced than ever that Andy's illness wasn't food poisoning. None of the people at the banquet had gotten sick, including faculty members or students. If something was wrong with the food, that would have been discovered. Even if it was food poisoning, Andy should be feeling better by now, not worse. Nothing they did was helping. I'd bet my summer vacation it was because the doctors hadn't found the underlying cause.

As I was tucking my phone into my blazer pocket, it rang again. This time it was Claudia. She was making arrangements for Shakespeare's birthday party and wanted my input on the desserts. My suggestions included chocolate, chocolate, and more chocolate.

"And don't forget coffee," I added. "Get it from Café Joe if you can. The university's coffee is weak."

"Chocolate and coffee," said Claudia. "I got that. But what about finger foods? I need a vegetarian option."

"Cucumber sandwiches are always nice," I said.

"You're right," said Claudia. "Shakespeare's English. We should have tea."

"Who said anything about tea?" I said.

"Plus, Felix is English," said Claudia. She was talking to herself now. I heard her scribble something on a notepad. "Thanks for the ideas, Em. This helps."

"Don't forget: chocolate and coffee. You can't go wrong with that combination."

She promised she wouldn't before she ended the call.

I slipped my purse off the coat hook and started out the door. I needed to meet Thomas at ten, and it was a quarter till the hour. I stopped, went back, and grabbed my keys, noticed the full trash bag, and grabbed that too. Tuesday was garbage day, and the trash needed to be in the alley this morning if I had any hope of it getting picked up. Even though Mrs. Gunderson hated it when I put the garbage out early, I always did. Otherwise, I'd forget it, as I'd almost done today.

The air was chilly, and after I placed the bag in my receptacle, I buttoned my blazer. The air was cold, the kind of cold that brought sleet and sometimes snow. I checked the sky: steel gray. *Oh no.* I didn't want a snowstorm ruining our above-average spring. Ice now would freeze buds and break branches. The thought was inconceivable, and I shook it off and started toward campus. It was too warm for snow. Maybe rain. Possibly sleet, but not snow. I noticed Mrs. Gunderson's garbage receptacle was open. I would shut it—just in case.

As the lid clanked down, I hesitated and turned back. I didn't want to snoop, but something had caught my eye. I reopened the lid. It was just as I thought. Through a clear bag, I could see a container of antifreeze. I looked at Mrs. Gunderson's tidy white house. Was she still driving? I shut the can and kept walking. She had a spiffy black Cadillac tucked away in her garage. I'd seen the car but had never seen her drive it. For all I knew, she took it for a late-night drive every evening. I chuckled aloud. More likely, she kept her car as immaculate as she kept her house. I crossed the street, a smile still on my face. Mrs. Gunderson under the hood would be a sight to behold.

Before going to Thomas's office, I stopped at mine to pick

up the copy of the anonymous sonnet. Giles's door was open, so I grabbed the poem and poked my head in. "Alice Hudson stopped by yesterday to make a schedule change. I told her I'd let you know."

"Thank you," said Giles. "She got ahold of me. Guess whose class she wants to add?"

"Whose?" I said.

"Yours," he said. "It sounds as if you've made an impression on the student. She had good things to say about you. Nice work."

"Thank you." Singing my praises to my boss? I was really starting to like that girl. "Did you hear about Andy?"

"I did," said Giles. "Felix called, but I told him I couldn't miss class this morning. I'm glad Lenny could take him. I wonder why Andy's not getting better. It seems every time Felix checks on him, he gets worse."

A new thought entered my head. I took a step into Giles's office. "Like Munchausen's Syndrome. You've heard of it, I assume."

"Of course." The three grooves in Giles's forehead grew more pronounced. "It's when someone makes another person ill, usually a child, to get attention. That's not what you think Felix is doing, do you?"

"It's possible," I said. "If Andy has food poisoning, he should be better by now, and he's not. The only one who has been with him at the hospital is Felix. If someone's making him worse, it could be him."

"But why would he do that?" asked Giles. "He's his mentor and colleague."

"Andy was friends with Tanner at one time," I said. "He might know something about Tanner's death. If Felix was involved, Felix could be trying to silence him."

"But Felix is his advisor. He thinks of him as his own child."

"That's what I'm saying. He might not be trying to kill Andy, at least intentionally, just keep him quiet. But, as is often the case with Munchausen's, he could be doing irreparable harm."

Giles nodded, and his sweep of brown hair fell over his forehead, covering the wrinkles.

I checked the clock on the wall. It was a few minutes after ten. "I'm late to meet Thomas. I have to go, but Lenny told me he'd call when he was done at the hospital. I'll let you know what I find out."

"Thank you, Emmeline," said Giles. "It's a great relief to know you're asking questions. I'm confident you'll have the answers soon."

I flashed him a smile as I scooted out the door. I wished I were as confident. My mind was spinning with possibilities, yet only one person killed Tanner, a person who reveled in the planning, the details, and the game. The killer was a formidable opponent, but like Giles said, I had justice on my side. Truth was like grass rising from the hard ground in spring, natural and good. Murder would never be natural or good. It took effort to keep evil hidden.

"There you are," said Thomas as I knocked on his door. "I was starting to think you'd forgotten about the sonnet."

I took off my coat. "I wish. It seems I'm in my own personal Shakespearean hell these days. I dreamt I was Hamlet last night."

Thomas put down the paper he was reading, placing it on the tidy stack on his desk. His office was neat, noticeably so, and decorated with modern touches like a steel lamp and framed picture of New York City. The room was just as cool as its occupant. "Hamlet," he repeated. "That makes sense. He's trying to find his father's killer, just as you're trying to find Tanner's killer." He tapped his fingertips together. "Just don't wind up dead."

"Thanks," I muttered, smoothing out the copy of the poem on his desk. "This was turned in to the sonnet-writing contest. The last stanza in particular is troublesome."

I leaned back and let him study the poem. I knew what

it said. I could probably recite it from memory if I had to. Thomas would see it with fresh eyes. I didn't want to taint his impression with mine.

"The person you're looking for has an enormous ego," said Thomas. "He's probably smart but not social. He doesn't play well with others, because he distrusts them, and has high aspirations. He might distrust technology, too. He knows it leaves a trail, which is why he wrote this by hand."

I blinked. "Where are you getting all this?"

"Handwriting analysis," he said, not looking up from the paper. "I wrote a paper on it."

Thomas wrote papers on everything. Maybe if I weren't so busy solving murders, I'd write more papers. "I assumed the all-caps were a way to disguise the writer."

"A valid assumption, except when people disguise their handwriting, the line is smoother because they write more slowly. This shows wide variation in thickness, which means the author might naturally write in all-caps."

I was intrigued. Thomas wasn't analyzing what it said but how it was said. A fresh perspective indeed.

He brought the paper closer to his face. "This is interesting. The slant of the letters varies. The author might have a psychological problem."

"You think?" Obviously the person had a problem if he or she murdered Tanner.

"I'm serious." Thomas put down the paper. "You need to be careful. Whoever you're dealing with might suffer from schizophrenia or another mental condition. You wouldn't realize it until it's too late."

His words sank into my bones, pushing me down into the chair. They confirmed the uneasiness I'd felt since Tanner's death. "Do you think the poem was intended for me?"

"Taking into account everything else you've told me—the flowers, etcetera—yes, I do. The person might admire you, but calls himself a foe." He leaned toward me. "He's issued you a challenge. Don't trust anyone, especially your students."

The look in Thomas's eyes changed, and I had the feeling he was speaking from personal experience. Usually cool and reserved, Thomas revealed emotion that wasn't there before. In a moment I understood it was about Lydia. All of it: why Lydia taught online and not in person, why she rarely left the house, why Thomas studied violent rhetoric. She had been frightened, perhaps was still afraid, and he was looking for answers. "What happened to Lydia?"

A small smile crossed his lips. "I knew you'd find out one day. I just didn't think I'd be the one to tell you."

"You can trust me," I said. "I know what it means to be afraid."

"I know," he said. "But I also know your curiosity is insatiable. If I tell you, I want the story to stop with my explanation. Promise me you won't take it any further."

I promised, and he proceeded to tell me what happened. Lydia wasn't always so shy and retiring. She, like him, had been a young professor on campus, excited to have a job in the big city. Unlike him, she was from a small town in Indiana. He said it singled her out in a way that made her more vulnerable. She wore her sweetness on her sleeve. One night on her way home from class, a man tried to assault her, but she'd had a whistle and blown it. Campus police showed up just as he was dragging her away. The man fled before they could catch him. Police were convinced he was the same man who'd assaulted many young women in the area. This assault had the same MO. After that, she started receiving threatening calls and letters. Police said the perpetrator couldn't deal with the fact that one of his victims escaped. So they moved away, but she still feared for her safety, and so did Thomas.

I let out a breath. It was a terrible situation, one I deeply sympathized with. "Does she still receive letters or calls?"

Thomas shook his head. "No. We picked Copper Bluff

because of its remote location. I've tried to assure her he will never find her here, but it's hard for her to believe it."

"I'm sorry." I knew it was all he wanted me to say, and I wanted him to understand I wouldn't interfere.

"Thank you, Em." He caught himself by surprise. "It's okay if I call you Em?"

I smiled. "Of course. That's what all my friends call me."

Chapter Twenty-Four

—

O N MY WALK home, I realized that Thomas and I shared a new comradery. For some reason, we'd always felt like adversaries, though it wasn't clear what we were on the opposite sides of. I suppose there was some academic jealousy on my part. He was the young professor I'd always thought I'd be, camel-hair coats and all. And I was just me, immersed in a mystery and now a love story that was all-consuming. I realized life was becoming more interesting than my career, and I was fine with that. Although the career part was heating up too, with my book about to be published. Which reminded me, I wanted to check my email before Lenny arrived to take me to the hospital.

I hustled inside and grabbed my laptop from the coffee table. Like a notice of a library fine, a new book cover was waiting for me to open it, to see how much I would pay for my remarks to Owen. A great deal, from the looks of it. A fleshy woman sat on a garden bench with a book in her lap, her eyes half open. Was she waking from a nap? Hung over? It was hard to tell. She certainly wasn't writing.

A honk sounded outside, and I shut my laptop. The cover

would need all my attention … later. Right now, I needed to figure out what was going on with Andy. I grabbed my jacket and hurried out the front door.

"Wait until you see my new cover," I said, buckling my seatbelt. "Owen emailed me another mock-up."

"Better?" said Lenny, pulling away from the curb.

"Worse."

Lenny gave me a look. "You're exaggerating."

"There's cleavage."

"Oh god." He turned onto one of the two main streets in town. "I thought you'd made progress."

"I thought so, too. I did make progress with Thomas, though." I told him about the handwriting analysis and Lydia.

"I always wondered why he came here from the East Coast," said Lenny. "It makes perfect sense."

"I think I can use what he said about the killer's handwriting. If the person habitually writes in all-caps, he or she should be easier to locate. Some evidence must exist on campus."

Lenny shut off the car in the hospital parking lot. "There's something personal about all this that I don't like."

"It's your feelings for me, that's all." Lenny knitted his dark eyebrows in concentration as I tried to explain. "We're dating now. It's normal for you to feel more protective of me and I of you."

"Chasing criminals is not normal," said Lenny. "I'm not dating a cop. I'm dating an English professor."

"One who was asked by her chair to investigate." I squeezed his hand then reached for the door. "I'll be careful. I promise."

We walked into the hospital and up to Andy's room, where Felix waited outside. The nurses were running another test on Andy. I told Felix that Giles would be up after his class, and he thanked me and Lenny for all our help.

"Andy isn't getting better, and I'm starting to wonder if it's on purpose," I said, deciding there was no reason not to tell Felix my theory. If he was the one causing Andy's illness, he would know I was on to him and stop. If he wasn't responsible, he might be able to help me figure out who was.

"What are you saying?" said Felix, his hawk eyes narrowing. "He's making himself sick on purpose?"

"Not at all. I'm saying someone *else* may be making him sick on purpose."

"Rubbish," said Felix. "Why would anyone want to do that? We don't know a person in town."

"Em thinks Andy might know something about Tanner's murder," said Lenny. "That's why we're here. She's hoping to talk to him, to see if we can determine what it is he knows, and whether that it is enough to make the killer strike again."

Felix shook his head. "Impossible. He's much worse than yesterday. He's incoherent." He took a step closer to us. "Personally, I think the doctors are running out of ideas. If they don't figure out what's going on soon, I'm worried Andy will die."

The nurse stepped out of Andy's room. It was Zeb, Lenny's old student.

"Can I go back in now?" asked Felix.

"Sure," said Zeb. "The tech is just finishing up."

After Felix was gone, Lenny asked Zeb how Andy was doing.

"Not good," said Zeb. "His kidneys are failing."

A woman came closer with a food tray. Lenny's eyes were on the tray.

"So, not food poisoning?" asked Lenny.

"Not food poisoning," said Zeb, stopping the food ambassador from making her delivery. He told her Andy wouldn't be eating. "The doctors think it's something else. Do you have any idea what he might have gotten into? Anything at the school ... a pesticide or chemical?"

"Not a clue," said Lenny.

Gotten into. Chemical. An alarm went off in my head. It was the same words the vet had used when Dickinson had become ill three years ago. They asked if she might have wandered into a garage. Antifreeze was poisonous to pets—and people. That's when it clicked. "I do."

They turned to me in surprise.

"I think he was poisoned with antifreeze," I said.

"And you figured this out when?" asked Lenny.

"Just this second," I said. "Listen. Today is garbage day, and I noticed a container of antifreeze in Mrs. Gunderson's garbage. I've thought of it on and off all morning. You know she doesn't drive, so why was it there?" I turned to Zeb. "When you mentioned 'getting into' something, I remembered what the vet said a few years ago. He said my cat might have gotten into antifreeze from an open garage. Alcohol was the antidote, which might explain why Andy isn't dead. He was drinking the night he got sick."

"I always knew alcohol was a good thing," said Lenny.

"It makes sense," said Zeb, turning over the hypothesis.

"You think the person who poisoned Andy dumped the evidence in Mrs. Gunderson's garbage?" said Lenny.

"Think about it," I said. "The person had to do something with the evidence. Why not put it in an old lady's recycling bin?"

"Especially if she lives right down the street," said Lenny.

"Exactly," I said. "Mia lives a block away. Either it's her, or someone who wants me to think it's her."

Zeb grabbed his phone. "Stay here. I'm calling the doctor."

While Zeb made the call, Lenny asked, "Why would someone poison Andy? Like Felix said, they don't know anybody in town."

"It's just like we thought," I said. "He must know something about Tanner's murder, something he doesn't know he knows."

Zeb returned. "We're running a blood test. If it's positive, we'll start Antizol right away."

"You've run a thousand blood tests already," said Lenny. "Why didn't antifreeze show up?"

"Because you have to look for it," said Zeb. "You have to test for it specifically."

"If the test is positive, will Andy be okay?" I asked.

"Probably," said Zeb. "Antizol works within three hours. The worry is he'll sustain permanent organ damage." His phone rang. "I need to take this. I'll let you know what happens."

"I'm going to call Sophie," I said after Zeb left. "She needs to get over to Mrs. Gunderson's house and pick up that container before it's too late."

"Good idea," said Lenny. "I'm going to see if I can snag one of those food trays."

I pulled out my phone. "Really?"

"I didn't eat lunch."

Watching Lenny stalk the food ambassador, I dialed Sophie's direct number, and she answered on the second ring. I told her what I'd found this morning and the connection to Andy's mysterious illness. She agreed to go to Mrs. Gunderson's house.

"When will you know for certain it's antifreeze poisoning?" asked Sophie. She was typing on her keyboard.

"Soon," I said. "They are running the blood test now."

The typing stopped. "Antifreeze poisoning: clumsiness, nausea, vomiting, slurred speech. It sounds like what you're describing."

It also described Tanner the night of his death. The only difference was that Tanner hadn't been drinking; there was no alcohol to hinder the poison's efficacy. The murderer used the same poison with different results. Imagine the killer's surprise to find Andy still alive. "Sophie, you need to contact the medical examiner. I think we've just found what killed Tanner Sparks."

Chapter Twenty-Five

—

ANDY'S TEST CAME back positive for ethylene glycol, the poison in antifreeze, and the doctors started Antizol immediately. I told Sophie as soon as I heard. She was still waiting on Tanner's organ test. The medical examiner was testing his liver because the poison would be most prominent there. In the meantime, Sophie had gone to Mrs. Gunderson's house to confirm the antifreeze wasn't hers. It wasn't, but the garbage had already been collected. I didn't think it really mattered. Whoever deposited it there had been careful; there wouldn't be fingerprints. Had it been Mia or one of her roommates? Or was it someone who wanted me to think it was?

Lenny and I talked over the possibilities while sipping a glass of wine at my house that evening. Giles had shown up at the hospital, and we ended up spending most of the afternoon surrounded by people. We needed time to ourselves to think and talk. If we could figure out when Andy ingested the poison, we could figure out the killer. The problem was, depending on how much he drank, his first symptoms would appear from thirty minutes to twelve hours later, which didn't exactly narrow down the timeframe. I thought he'd consumed it at the banquet because that's when his behavior changed. Lenny insisted we couldn't be certain.

"It's a nice night for a walk, and Mia lives right down the street. Let's pay her a visit."

I started to object, and Lenny put down his glass of Cabernet. "She dated, fought with, and probably killed Tanner. Plus, she lives close to Mrs. Gunderson's house." He shrugged. "Occam's razor: the simplest solution is usually the right one."

I put on the flip side of the record we'd purchased secondhand from This and That. "But nothing about this murder has been simple. The sonnet, the staging, the flowers—somebody spent a lot of time orchestrating Tanner's murder."

"But not Andy's," said Lenny. "Andy's was spur of the moment. Otherwise he'd be dead."

"You're right." I snuggled close to him on the couch. "Something must have panicked the killer into taking action. But what? What does Andy know that we don't?"

Lenny put his arm around me. "A lot, I'm sure."

I chuckled. "You make everything better, do you know that? Even murder."

"Same." We were quiet for a few minutes, enjoying our wine and Cole Porter. Then I heard scratching. Dickinson had decided "Anything Goes" did not go with her current mood.

"That's our cue," said Lenny. "Let's take that walk."

"I'll get my purse."

"You haul that thing wherever you go," said Lenny. "Why? What could you possibly need while walking around the block?"

I couldn't think of a thing, but I was good at making stuff up. "If, for instance, I fell and needed an antiseptic for my wound, I would have one on hand."

"You *have* been drinking," said Lenny. "I guess a fall is possible."

I punched his arm as we walked out the door. We didn't get

very far before Mrs. Gunderson stopped us. Dressed in a pink-and-white housecoat and wearing a crown of pink curlers, she stood on her front stoop like a queen looking down on her kingdom.

"Emmeline, I didn't see you come home." She motioned for us to draw nearer, and we obeyed. "There was a cop at my house today—a lady cop."

"Sophie Barnes, I know. I sent her."

"She said someone used my trash receptacle." She crossed her arms. "That's not the proper way to dispose of chemicals."

"We have bigger problems than recycling violations, Mrs. G," said Lenny. "Whoever threw it away might be a murderer. You need to be extra cautious until they are caught."

"Humph!" said Mrs. Gunderson. "If I catch them fooling around with my garbage can, *they'd* better be cautious. My husband left me a gun, and I know how to use it."

The thought of Mrs. Gunderson wielding a pistol was downright scary. I worried for her garbage collector. "Seriously, please be careful. The police are close to catching the person. Just be vigilant."

"You can count on it," she said, letting the door close.

"I imagine the lights will be on full blast tonight," said Lenny as we continued down the block.

"I have no doubts." Mrs. Gunderson was a huge fan of lights. She said they deterred criminals, but not this one. Someone had sneaked antifreeze into her garbage undetected. Was it Mia or one of her friends? We were about to find out.

Mia's house was mostly dark, but a light shone from one of the front rooms, maybe the parlor. I could see the outline of a large, leafy plant. Since it was a nice night, I'd hoped Mia and her friends would be out in the yard, like lots of other college students. But they didn't appear to be home.

"Let's knock," said Lenny.

"And say what?"

"That you're just checking in," said Lenny. "You're her

neighbor—and a professor. Plus, you said someone mentioned counseling."

That was true. It wouldn't seem that unusual for me to follow up.

We walked up the crooked front steps, the slant of the porch noticeable as I rang the doorbell. I turned to Lenny and shrugged. Maybe no one was home. We had started to leave when I heard the first steps. Mia opened the door.

"Hi, Mia," I said. "I was taking a walk and wanted to check in to see how you're doing."

"Ah ... thanks," said Mia. "I'm good."

"Your friends have been supportive," I said.

She nodded.

"That's good." I struggled for a transition.

Lenny jumped in. "Hey, do you have a car?"

And he thought *I* was indiscreet.

"Yeah, why?" she said.

"My low coolant light is on, and my car won't start. I thought maybe you had some antifreeze."

She pulled her rope of blonde hair over her shoulder. "No. My dad does all that stuff in the summer."

From behind her, Jacob stepped forward. Mia moved over to make room for him, allowing us a peek inside. I'd had no idea he was there with her. He must have been listening from the hallway or living room.

"I can take a look at it if you want," said Jacob. "I'm pretty good with cars."

"Thanks, man, but I think I'll ask around." Lenny smiled. "I don't want to intrude on your night."

Lenny could play the cool professor whenever he wanted. I was completely jealous. I sort of wondered if Jacob was too. His eyes were narrowed on Lenny. Maybe he knew something about the antifreeze. Or maybe he didn't like seeing his new girlfriend talking to a cute professor. Hailey had warned Mia she was stepping into the same situation. If Jacob was spending time at the house, though, he could have easily deposited the antifreeze in Mrs. Gunderson's garbage can. Plus, he might not know I lived next door.

If only Lenny's car were really low on coolant, I would have an excuse to ask more questions. Tomorrow I would need to get back to the theater. *Hamlet* was no longer playing, but I would find another reason. The graduate exhibition spotlighting student artwork opened tomorrow. I wondered if Mia and Jacob would be there.

"Will your art be on display at the graduate exhibition tomorrow?" I asked. "I'm eager to see it."

Mia smiled. "Yes, one of my costume designs is going to be used in *Twelfth Night* at the Hayes Theater in New York. They're announcing it tomorrow."

"Congratulations," said Lenny. "That's good news."

"Yes, congratulations," I said. "I'll try to stop by."

"Thanks, and thanks for checking in," said Mia. "It's kind of nice having a professor right down the street."

"Unless you're in her class," said Lenny. "Then it's not so nice. She'd be stopping by with her red pen."

Mia laughed. Jacob crossed his arms.

"Not true," I said. "Have a good night."

She shut the door, and we returned to the sidewalk to finish our walk. Something was bothering me, but I couldn't put my finger on it. I looked back at the house. Maybe that was it, the creepy old two-story. A day didn't pass that I didn't look at the windows and think of them as eyes staring back at me. The weathered paint, the sinking porch, the flapping shades. It didn't take much for me to imagine a ghost living there. But a murderer? I was starting to wonder.

Chapter Twenty-Six

—

IT TURNED OUT I didn't need to set my alarm. I woke up early Wednesday morning in a cold sweat. I'd dreamed I was on a garden bench, much like the one on my mock-up book cover, and a vine had twisted up the bench and around my ankles. It had reached my shoulders by the time I awoke, struggling to free myself from my bedcovers. I sat up and switched on the lamp on my nightstand. Dickinson squinted in my direction. Then she returned to looking out the window, where I could hear the swish of Mrs. Gunderson's broom as she brushed it over our shared pathway. The woman was like the town itself: indestructible. Wind, weather, flood, or murder couldn't keep her from her morning chores.

Nothing could keep me from calling Owen Parrish either—except the time zone. It was two hours earlier on the West Coast, but that didn't prevent me from sending an email. After drinking an extra-large cup of coffee, I sat down with my laptop and wrote a polite but firm email requesting the cover be changed. My dream was literally turning into a nightmare. I'd gone from elated to deflated in exactly one week. I'd changed the ending, but no way was I going to change my mind on this mock-up.

When the hour reached a respectable eight a.m., I prepared for the rest of the day. The art reception was over lunch, which meant I would go to the theater following classes. The morning was cool, so I wore a navy and white sweater with my trouser slacks and a pair of open-toed shoes. For months, my clothes hadn't mattered. Shapeless, dull, and warm, they were functional but nothing more. Picking out a pair of shoes that weren't boots was a treat, and although I was no fashionista, I admired my ensemble in the mirror, liking the way my red toenails looked against the navy shoe. A great pair of shoes made anything seem possible, even solving a murder.

After shrugging on my camel-colored trench coat, I was out the door, bracing myself against the cold spring morning. The sun was bright but the wind fierce, and tears stung my eyes as I walked briskly down the street. Mia's house was quiet, but someone was up. They had lifted the shades. I pulled my coat tighter. Even in the yellow sunlight, the house was dreary and battered. As I crossed the street to campus, I dismissed an ominous feeling. I had lots to do today. The last thing on my mind should be the rental on the corner.

As I entered Stanton Hall, the warmth rushing to my fingers, I saw André emerge from the crowd. He looked dapper as always in his dark shirt and gray beret. Though about to enter the door to the Foreign Languages Department, he stopped when he saw me. He reached for my elbow and led me to an empty alcove by the water fountain. "I have news."

"Okay, but I have class," I said as we walked.

"This will only take a minute." He stopped and faced me. "You know Giles and I spoke at the banquet. You recommended the meeting."

"Of course, I remember." I guessed at what the news was, but I let him tell me.

"He is a most pleasant man, as you know," he said. "He's

been very kind to me over the years, and he's paid me another kindness." A smile reached across his face.

"What is it?" I asked, hoping the news was what I thought it was.

"He's asked me to direct the Teaching English as a Second Language program next fall. Beginning in September, I will be a member of the English faculty."

"That's wonderful, André!" I said. "I'm so excited for you."

"I'm excited, too," he said. "Finally, I will have a place of my own—right next to you and Lenny!"

"I know Lenny will be thrilled." *Thrilled* might have been an overstatement, since Lenny wasn't as charmed by André's French heritage as I was. There had been a time when André might have even been a rival. But Lenny would be excited that, after years of trying to create a French department, André would finally have a home. It wasn't the home he'd dreamed about, but it was a home all the same.

"We will talk more later?"

"You can count on it." I started toward the towering stairwell then turned back. "And congratulations, André. You deserve this."

He smiled. "Thank you, Emmeline."

The next fifty minutes dragged by. I was counting the seconds until I could leave for the theater. I wasn't the only one. A third of the class was staring out the long, sun-filled windows. It was getting to be that time, the time when sitting in a classroom seemed like sacrilege. The days would only get warmer and the homework more hurriedly done. I needed to keep them focused as long as I could. Once May hit, the gates of pandemonium would officially open. I reminded them of the test on Friday, and they snapped back to attention.

My next class was better, probably because their grades were worse. The end of the semester had thrown them into a panic. Like some classes were, this one had been notoriously truant. Sports, parties, and other important matters had kept them away, and the upcoming test was their Hail Mary. I appreciated their improved behavior. Their studious note-taking and intelligent questions made me forget, momentarily, about the graduate reception. It wasn't until the first backpacks were unzipped that I remembered I had somewhere else to be.

I, too, packed up my supplies—my textbook, my grade book, my personal box of chalk. You never knew when a rogue scholar would steal all the chalk in the building to get out of notetaking. My backpack pocket buzzed, and I checked the number. It was Sophie Barnes! I answered right away.

"Your hunch was right," she said. "Tanner died of ethylene glycol poisoning."

I leaned against the podium. "I knew it."

"That's why the pH levels were high," said Sophie. "I should have known it, too."

"Don't beat yourself up," I said. "There's no way you could have known what to test for. The nurse told me yesterday it doesn't show up on a routine blood test. If I hadn't found the antifreeze container in the trash, we still wouldn't know."

"Thanks." She exhaled a breath. "Beamer says we can't assume the antifreeze found in Mrs. Gunderson's trash was the murder weapon, but I can't help it. Why else would it be in her receptacle when she doesn't drive?"

"Why else, indeed," I said. "What I don't understand is why Mrs. Gunderson's house and not someone else's?"

"I think I can answer that," said Sophie. "From what I can tell, Mrs. Gunderson is a very organized person with a set schedule. Once her trash was out, there would be no reason for her to go near the garage. She'd have no idea it was there."

"True," I said. The next class was starting to file in. I threw my backpack over my shoulder and started toward the door. "But I live right next to her. Didn't the killer think it was risky leaving it within arm's reach of a known sleuth?"

Sophie chuckled. "Maybe you're not as well-known as you think."

* * *

DESPITE THE COLD day, the art gallery was stuffy. It was as if all the artwork on the walls were taking up not only space but air. Besides pictures, there were sculptures, statues, and costumes. I saw Mia's costume right away. It was a lovely black, white, and gold gown, and as I drew closer, I noted it was designed for Olivia in *Twelfth Night*. It had to be the one she mentioned last night.

Though the room was filling quickly, I caught sight of Mia, dressed in a peasant top and wide-legged jeans. She was admiring a statue as she talked to Denton Smart. Next to her, he didn't look like the reserved scholar from the law library. Basking in Mia's attention, he exuded a new confidence. His serious brow was relaxed, and he looked almost happy. He might not be so happy if he knew Mia was my primary suspect in Tanner's death. She fit into every scenario I'd recreated.

It would have been easy for Mia to slip the flowers into Jacob's pocket. She was a costume designer and had access to the actors' wardrobes. She could also have been the one to place the skull in the bathroom. I had seen her and Mackenzie leave the theater, but maybe that had been a ruse, and she had returned soon after. Plus, Mia could have easily placed the antifreeze in Mrs. Gunderson's garage. Maybe Lenny was right; maybe it was Occam's razor. If only I could explain the strand of black hair, the puzzle would be complete.

The dean of the School of Fine Arts approached the podium, and attendees began taking their seats. Three modest rows of folding chairs had been arranged, and as I took a chair, Lenny breezed in, smelling like the wind. He dumped his messenger bag in the chair next to him.

"You're such a nerd," he whispered. "What are you doing in the front row?"

I gave him a look. "I want to hear what's being said. It may be important."

He mouthed the word *whatever*.

As it turned out, it wasn't as important as I thought. The

dean spoke for two minutes before handing the microphone over to the chair of the Art Department. Near the end of her speech, which outlined many of the graduate students' accomplishments, the chair announced Mia's good news. Hoots and hollers accompanied the clapping, and I turned to see Mia's roommates standing in the audience. Denton was there, too, and Jacob. I listened to the dean's closing remarks, but my mind was on the group. They were bright students and artistic, too. I'd go so far as to say they stood out in that regard. How could it be that one of them was a murderer? Experience told me it was possible, even probable, but I didn't want to believe it. Jacob was the lead in *Hamlet*, Mia had sold a design in New York, Denton was in med school. Then I realized it was those very qualifications that made them good suspects. Whoever had killed Tanner was not only smart but sneaky. He or she was playing a game of matching wits. My only hope was that I played the game better.

When the dean had finished, Lenny and I made our way to the refreshment table. We were both disappointed to see only coffee and cookies.

"Oatmeal raisin?" said Lenny, pointing to my cookies. "This is a change."

"I didn't get lunch," I said. "I need something nutritious."

Lenny stacked four chocolate chip cookies on his tiny plate. "I guess budget cuts are affecting everyone."

I nodded. In our department, Barb had become a dictator over the copy machine. We had a budget for paper, and we had to stick to it. When our copies ran out, our cards were suspended, and we had to give specific reasons for why additional paper was necessary. Giles advocated for PowerPoints and class webpages to disseminate information, and I did a good deal of uploading. Still, I copied many stories that weren't in our textbook and had done battle twice this semester to get my account reinstated.

Denton was pouring a glass of lemonade from the dispenser,

and I took the opportunity to ask him about his Shakespeare research. Last time we talked, he was close to confirming Edward de Vere's DNA. I asked him now how the project was progressing.

He took a sip of his lemonade before answering. "I'm finished."

"And?" I prompted. "Was it de Vere's letter?"

"Yes." His voice was no louder than a whisper.

If he was excited about the information, it didn't show. The eyes behind the glasses conveyed the same cool intelligence they had the first time I met him.

"So, that means de Vere was alive at the time the late Shakespeare plays were written," said Lenny, exhibiting far more excitement.

"You told him?" asked Denton.

"Don't worry," I said. "He won't say anything. He's my boyfriend."

"Hey, that's the first time I've heard you call me your boyfriend," said Lenny.

I smiled.

"It sounds nice," he added.

"Anyway," I said to Denton, who was waiting on our side conversation, "what will you do now?"

Denton shrugged. "Finish med school. I have the money now."

"You're not going to continue the research?" I asked.

"What research? Tanner was the Shakespeare expert. I'm just a lab rat." Denton threw his Styrofoam cup in the trash can. "Besides, I've come to the conclusion that it's best to leave well enough alone. Some mysteries are better left unsolved."

I wholeheartedly disagreed.

Chapter Twenty-Seven

—

As Denton walked away, I thought maybe someone had gotten to him, someone like Felix or Andy, and convinced him to stop his research. Tanner's death alone was enough of a deterrent. If pressured or threatened, he might have been persuaded to withdraw from the controversy. He had a lot at stake, including a medical degree, and as he said, he was a scientist, not a literary scholar. I couldn't blame him for not continuing. Still, I was disappointed. The sleuth in me wanted to know if Shakespeare was really Shakespeare. His results might not have answered the question definitively, but they would have brought the world closer to knowing the truth.

Jacob was standing next to Mia and her friends, and Lenny and I took a step in that direction. Dressed in black and wearing a dour expression, Jacob reminded me of a storm cloud. Actually, he reminded me of Tanner. He had the same brooding personality. He was less able to keep a lid on his emotions, though. Tanner was a natural. Jacob had to work at it. Judging by the way he clenched his fists at his sides, whatever Alice was saying irritated him.

"Congratulations, Mia," I said as Lenny and I approached the group. "It's a lovely gown. I'm so glad we got an opportunity to see it."

"It's cool," said Lenny. "Good job."

"Thank you," said Mia. "And thanks for coming."

"No problem," I said. "I promised another student I'd drop by."

"You get your car working?" Jacob asked Lenny.

"I did," said Lenny. "Thanks."

The question threw me. Luckily, it hadn't thrown Lenny.

"Was it antifreeze?" said Jacob.

The word entered the conversation like a dart. I flinched.

"I added a little water to the radiator," Lenny said. "It's fine—for now, anyway. I need to get it into the shop."

My phone buzzed in my pocket, and I was relieved for the break in the conversation. I checked the caller ID. It was Owen Parrish. I excused myself from the group before answering.

"You didn't like *this* cover either."

These were the first words out of Owen's mouth. Not hi, hello, or how are you. I wasn't sure how to answer. "Hi, Owen. The cover is concerning, yes."

"There are fewer flowers," said Owen.

"That's true, but there is also a Victorian lady sprawled out on a bench. I don't see how she relates."

"She's reading," he said. "We want people to read your book."

"People looking for a historical romance?" I shook my head. "I don't think so. They would surely be disappointed. I know. I read a lot of historical romances."

"I'm not sure what you want from me," said Owen.

How about a normal conversation, for starters. "I would like to see a nonfiction book cover that matches the theme of the book."

"I will see what else we can come up with that would satisfy you."

Owen released a stream of air right into the mouthpiece. I held the phone back from my ear. "That would be nice, thank you."

Owen didn't respond.

I looked at my phone screen. The jerk had hung up.

Mia and her friends had dispersed, but Lenny was waiting for me, chewing the last of his cookies. His face was a combination of a smirk and a smile. I swear I could put him in the middle of a maelstrom, and he'd find a way to paddle happily ashore. I'd probably drown looking for a compass.

"Owen hung up on me," I said.

"I figured," he said. "I saw you glaring at your phone."

"What am I going to do?" I said.

He dusted off his hands. "Exactly what you're doing. He'll change it. Just be patient."

"That's easy for you to say. Your name isn't on a book with cleavage."

"Actually, I don't think I'd mind that so much."

"Ha ha," I said. "Very funny."

He put his arm around me. "I couldn't resist. I love it when your lips do that little thing they're doing. Do you know it was one of the first things I loved about you?"

There was that word again. Love. Every time he dropped it, I felt like I might swoon. It was ridiculous. "No … I … uh, didn't know that."

"The second was the way the curls at your temples escape no matter what contraption you tie them into." He touched a curl behind my ear. "These."

I swallowed. "I see."

"And the third was the way you eat candy with wild abandonment. The moment I saw you tear into a king-sized Snickers at a faculty meeting, I said, here's a girl after my own heart."

Now I laughed. "They're very satisfying."

"It's been a wonderful ride, hasn't it Em?"

"It has," I said. "I'm glad it's led us here."

"Who knows where else it will lead?" His navy eyes searched mine. "Some journeys take a lifetime."

"Or longer."

He smiled. "Or longer."

My response had answered a question in his mind. What the question was, I wasn't sure. We'd both played the field and lost when it came to love. Relationships had been disappointing at best, soul-killing at worst. Maybe he was asking if I still believed in the journey, in finding the one person who completed me. I did, and though maybe it was my vast experience with romance novels talking, I believed he did, too.

The theater director breezed through the door, and I refocused on Tanner and his unsolved murder. I wanted to ask Alexander about the skull in *Hamlet* and who would have had access to it. I called his name, and he turned and strode in our direction, his barrel of a belly leading the way.

"You spend a lot of time in the theater," said Alexander. "I'm starting to think you might need a job."

"Heck, no," I said. "You will never get me up on that stage."

"There are other things you can do," he said.

"That's what I want to ask you about," I said. "Well, not *that* exactly but something related. I have a question about the prop department."

"If this is an excuse to try on the Marie Antoinette wig—" began Alexander.

"It's not." I cut him off before he could tell Lenny about catching me in the wig before one of our meetings. I had a bigger head than I thought, and it didn't come off easily.

"Someone put the skull from *Hamlet* in the downstairs women's bathroom, under Em's stall," said Lenny. "She was the only one in there. We're still wondering who did it."

"Friday night," said Alexander. "I remember. Someone ran it down to the theater. A volunteer. I was livid to see it gone."

"That's right," I said. "Lenny had a volunteer return it."

"Who had access to the props that night?" asked Lenny.

"Anyone in the play, of course, and anyone backstage. We have tables near the tabs, where props are easily accessible.

Nobody else is allowed back there during a performance."

"Tabs?" said Lenny.

"The side curtains," Alexander clarified. "In *Hamlet*, the skull comes in during Act V."

"This happened during intermission, before Act V," I said.

"That's brazen," said Alexander. "The skull was on the opposite side of the theater from the restroom. Whoever took it would have to be familiar with the tunnel that runs under the stage. We use it to cross without being seen."

"So it's someone who *knows* the theater, not just enjoys it," I said.

"Precisely." Alexander waved at a colleague who called out to him. "Let me know if you catch the punk. I'd like to have a word with him. He might have ruined my entire performance. Excuse me."

I was glad to hear my safety was his chief concern.

"Well, that narrows it down," said Lenny after Alexander was gone.

I grabbed Lenny's arm. "*It does*. Think about it. Felix or Andy don't know our theater. They've never been here. If Alexander is correct, it means they couldn't have murdered Tanner."

"You're right. It has to be someone else." Lenny gazed around the room. My eyes followed his from one clump of people to the next. Nibbling cookies, drinking lemonade, exchanging back-pats—they all appeared harmless. His eyes stopped on Mia, who was smugly admiring her creation for *Twelfth Night*. Alice was admiring it, too. Mackenzie and Hailey were engaged in a side conversation. Jacob looked bored, and Denton watched from the sidelines. Dressed in a plaid button-down and jeans, he was as distinct in his plainness as they were in their flamboyancy. He wasn't directly involved with the theater, nor was Alice. But any of them was familiar enough with the campus to pull off the trick.

Chapter Twenty-Eight

LATER THAT AFTERNOON, I received an unexpected email from Owen Parrish. I was grading online discussion posts when a beep notified me of the arrival. I switched over to my inbox and was pleasantly surprised to find a new book cover waiting for me. The font was the same, but the sleepy woman was gone. A bouquet of old-fashioned roses was placed over a typewriter. Still, I liked the typewriter. The bouquet wasn't bad either. I'd have preferred it smaller, but if the last week had taught me anything, it was compromise. The book was no longer mine alone. Publishing meant getting used to people's input.

I sent off a quick reply, thanking him for the change. He responded with a release date, and I was thrilled. The book would be published next year.

After the news, it was hard to go back to my online discussion, but I had forty student responses to read, and their quality and length varied. Some students wrote impassioned posts filled with adjectives and metaphors. Others left one or two plain lines to gnaw on.

It was late by the time I finished. The dinner hour long past and my brain blurry, I ordered Chinese food from Dynasty and turned on the classic movie channel. When my cashew chicken arrived, I was thirty minutes into *Lawrence of Arabia*. I grabbed a fork (I could never get the hang of chopsticks) and, putting my feet up on the coffee table, dove into the containers of food.

Though I liked sand as much as the next person, my eyes were tired from reading online, and I must have dozed off near the end of the movie. It shouldn't have come as a surprise that my dream involved the good-looking Peter O'Toole and a tent. I woke with a start. The house was dark and the TV blank. Dickinson lay at my feet, not budging. She hadn't made the sound. I rubbed my eyes and sat up. A noise came from the alley.

I grabbed my empty containers of chicken and rice and walked to the kitchen. Tossing them in the trash, I squinted out the back-porch window. I could have sworn my car was running. A stream of smoke was coming from the garage. How could that be? I took my keys down from the hook near the door. That's when I noticed my car key was missing. Because I rarely drove, I had no idea when the key had been stolen. The other keys were all accounted for.

Stopping only to slip on my sandals, I raced out to the garage. If someone thought they were going to steal my car, they were sadly mistaken. It was a '69 Mustang, a classic my uncle had sold me. There was no way I could show my face in Detroit again if the car was taken.

"Stop!" I yelled as I rushed out of my house. "Right now, stop!" I ran to the single-stall garage. I looked inside, but nobody was there. The car was running. I came closer. It was empty. Maybe I'd scared off whoever it was. *And Lenny said I wasn't athletic.*

I pulled on the handle of the driver's door. It didn't budge. I peered inside. No one was in there, but the door was locked. I walked over to the passenger door. It was locked also. *Great.* I didn't have another set of keys. I went back to the driver's door and tried again. Nothing.

I had a small toolbox, which I bent down and opened. The nice thing about owning a classic car is that security isn't the best. I was certain I could get inside with a tool. But which tool? I fumbled through the box, unsure of what to try.

Suddenly, the garage door shook, and I turned around to see it slam to the ground. I sat on my haunches, frozen with fear. After a second, I rushed to the door and pulled. Like the car doors, it was locked. But the long metal bar that looped through the locks was on the outside of the door. I pulled harder, chiding myself for not updating the old carriage house into a proper garage. It still had the shake & shingle siding and was as solid as a brick. With no windows, it felt like a wooden tomb.

I tried not to panic. I'd seen enough movies to know panic ended in tripping, falling, and general disaster. I ran back to the toolbox and grabbed the hammer. Although it pained me to do it, I struck at the driver's side window of my Mustang. To my surprise, nothing happened. Not even a crack. I struck harder, over and over. A few dings appeared in the glass, giving me hope. But the action left me dizzy, breathless. I told myself I had time. I wouldn't die instantly from carbon monoxide poisoning. I smacked it again, choking on the fumes.

Images of my parents, Christmas, and Lenny swam in my brain. I willed them away. The glass cracked further, but I felt tired, unenthused about my progress. I forced myself to hit it again. It was as if I was watching the action from outside my body, floating somewhere above myself. It was a pinprick against the window, and I begged myself to hit harder. The hammer slipped out of my hand, and I watched it fall to the ground. I tumbled too, grabbing for anything, the side of the car, watching my hand slide against the red paint.

A shot rang out, and I wondered if this was death, the last moment of consciousness not a light but an alarm signaling the end of life on earth. Then a light did start, low to the ground, rising up, up, up. I blinked lazily, wondering who from the other side was there to greet me. It was a woman in curlers. My grandma? This woman had a gun. Why would anyone need a gun in heaven?

"Emmeline! Get out of there right now!"

It wasn't grandma. It was Mrs. Gunderson. Did she rule heaven and earth? No, I was still alive. I stumbled toward the door, and when I got closer, she grabbed my hand, and I skipped along the hard gravel ground. She was surprisingly strong. Her thin arm was like a life preserver jerking me to the safety of my lawn. The last thing I remembered was the feel of her hand in mine and her words in my ear: "Hang in there, dear. You don't want to die a spinster."

I awoke with an oxygen mask over my face. Officer Beamer was there, and Lenny, too. They were talking. I was in the hospital, the emergency room. A blood pressure cuff was squeezing my arm.

I lifted my mask. "Thank god you're here. Someone tried to kill me."

"Put that back on," said Lenny, rushing to my side. "She's awake," he said to the nurse.

"Leave that on, Ms. Prather," said Beamer. "We're aware of the situation."

A woman in scrubs asked me how I was feeling, assuring me I could talk with the mask on when I tried to lift it again.

"I have a splitting headache. Otherwise, I feel okay. Where's Mrs. Gunderson?"

Lenny clasped my hand. "She's in the waiting room. We couldn't get her to leave."

I blinked back tears. "She saved my life."

"We know," said Mr. Beamer. "What happened?"

I relayed the story, leaving out the dream of Peter O'Toole and the tent. "I must have awoken when I heard the car start, or maybe it had been running for a while. Either way, I ran out to the garage to find it idling. Someone stole my key."

"We noticed that when we shut it off," said Beamer.

I groaned. "Did you break the window?"

"Yes, but it was broken already," said Beamer.

"My uncle is going to kill me."

"Cars can be fixed, people can't," said Beamer. "We're just glad you're safe. Did you lend your car to anyone lately?"

I shook my head.

"Leave your keys anywhere?"

I considered the question. I didn't use my car much, and I took my keys two places: home and the college. I hadn't left them at either place. I shook my head again.

"No wait, you did," said Lenny. "That night you walked to your office and fell asleep. Remember? I bet you left them hanging in your lock."

Lenny couldn't let that night go, could he? I retraced my steps from that evening: walk, campus, office, sleep. I *had* left them in the lock. Plus, I arrived home to a pot of pansies on my doorstep. It was the closest my stalker had come. The person must have followed me. "You're right. The keys were in my door all night. I haven't used my car since then."

"You're in grave danger, Ms. Prather," said Beamer. "Until this killer is caught, I don't want you going anywhere without someone else." He glanced at Lenny. "Maybe him."

"You got it," said Lenny. "I won't let her out of my sight."

His words never sounded so sweet.

Chapter Twenty-Nine

—

I WAS RELEASED from the hospital the next morning. Thankfully I didn't have to teach on Thursdays because I had a thousand forms to fill out before I could leave. When Lenny drove up to my house, Mrs. Gunderson met us with an enormous pot of chicken noodle soup. Lenny took the slow cooker inside while I hugged her for the second time. Her body was as stiff and unyielding as it had been in the hospital, but I didn't care. This wiry, strong, nosy woman had saved my life. I still couldn't think of it without tears filling my eyes.

Inside, Lenny was making himself at home. Without saying a word, he was keeping his promise to stay by my side until the killer was found. Seeing him feed Dickinson and make coffee was oddly gratifying. Maybe it was the carbon monoxide hangover, but I felt as if I could watch him forever. It was comforting knowing he was there for more than the day.

"So, one thing," said Lenny as he brought us our coffee. "I have a student conference at eleven. I want you to come with me." He glanced at me over his cup.

If he thought I was going to argue, he was mistaken. Seeing my life almost fade away in a cloud of smoke made me not want to be alone right now. It also gave me a new appreciation for being alive. I knew what it meant to nearly lose a life—mine—and I was more determined than ever to solve Tanner's murder. Whoever had killed him had also attempted to kill Andy and me. I was putting together the events the way I put together puzzles, twisting and turning until I found the answer that fit.

"Good idea," I said. "It's a beautiful day, and I'd like some fresh air. I still feel like I'm in a fog."

"The thought of last night." Lenny exhaled a breath. "I can't get it out of my head."

"Every time I think of it, I get angry," I said. "How dare someone taunt me with flowers, follow me to my office, trap me in my own garage. I swear I'm going to find whoever's doing this, and I'm going to find them today." I checked my enthusiasm. "Or tomorrow at the latest."

"We're going to find them *together*. This has to end."

Lenny was right. I needed to end it before someone else was killed. Mrs. Gunderson and her gun couldn't be everywhere. I set down my empty coffee cup. I needed to ready myself to catch a killer. A shower and tennis shoes were most certainly in order.

An hour later, Lenny and I walked out the door, toward campus. The robins had never sounded so lovely. They reminded me it was a privilege to be walking on these legs, seeing with these eyes, smelling with this nose. The apple trees, bursting with white blossoms, perfumed the day with their exuberant scent. Against the blue sky, the blooms were as fresh as the morning. I grasped Lenny's hand, turned to him, and smiled. "Isn't it a gorgeous day?"

"It is," he said, returning my smile.

"I mean, it's chilly, but the cold air is helping." I motioned to my head. "My brain feels so much clearer."

"Thank God you weren't hurt." Lenny was still looking at

me. "I like it when you wear your hair down. You should wear it that way more often."

I threaded my fingers through the curls springing over my head. "I may never wear it up again, you know that? It feels good this way. It feels *real*."

"Next time I see it in a ponytail, I'm going to remind you," said Lenny.

"I'm not kidding," I said. "Something has changed in me. I can feel it. I feel more alert, more alive."

"The world had better watch out."

"You're dang right it better," I said. Even his dimple looked cuter.

As we walked past Mia's house, a dark outline took shape in the window. I stopped and stared. The plant. *That's* what was different. I'd walked by the house for three years. There'd never been a plant in the front window. It had been placed there in the last couple of days. I *was* feeling sharper.

"What are you looking at?" said Lenny.

"That plant," I said. "It's never been there before. It's new."

"So?" said Lenny.

I shook my head. "So I don't know. Why would someone buy a big plant like that just before moving out? The house is for rent."

"It was for sale?"

"I don't know—yet." We started walking again. "But I'm going to find out."

"Take it easy, Em," said Lenny. "You just got out of the hospital. Don't push yourself too hard."

Seeing the worried look on his face, I reassured him as we crossed the street.

The buzz started before we reached campus: the slamming of car doors, the bursting of laughter, the shuffling of feet. Energy begot energy, and I found myself walking faster toward Harriman Hall. I wanted to tell Giles I'd narrowed down my list of suspects. He would be glad Andy and Felix were no longer at the top. Which reminded me to check on Andy's health. He had started the antidote; hopefully he was feeling better and could talk to me about Tanner's death. He knew something that had put him in danger. Would it be safe to come to tomorrow's birthday party? April 23 was the date both Shakespeare's birth and death were celebrated. Though the precise birth date was unknown—he was baptized April 26, 1564, which made April 23 a good guess—scholars knew for certain Shakespeare died on April 23.

The thought brought me to Denton. I couldn't believe he wasn't continuing his Shakespeare research. Well, a piece of me could. It was hard to see one's favorite author discredited— as Tanner himself had found out. Besides, the controversy had cost Denton plenty already. His summer research program had been put on hold, and he was worried about his future. The fifty thousand dollars was the compensation he needed to distance himself from the trouble. Though it was possible, I didn't believe he'd tried to kill Andy or me. He was moving on. Why would he commit murder?

Lenny stopped at the entrance to the English Department. "I'll be right down the hall, meeting with my student. Don't leave without me, okay?"

"I won't," I said. "I'm going to talk to Giles. I'll wait for you in my office."

He gave me a peck on the cheek before turning in the other direction.

"That's the look of a woman in love," said Claudia, who had breezed up behind me. In her fitted pants and a floral shirt, she was dressed in the height of fashion, as always.

"I can't deny it," I said, watching Lenny open his office door.

"What?" said Claudia. "Subterfuge is your middle name."

I laughed. "You know it, I know it, and I'm starting to think Lenny knows it." I lowered my voice. "Do you think he … feels the same way?"

"You're kidding, right?" Claudia adjusted the clip in her hair, rolling her eyes at me. "Incredible. You're not. Walk with me."

"To my office," I said. "I need to talk to Giles, and I don't want Lenny to hear us."

Once we were in the safety of my room, Claudia said, "Lenny loves you. He's loved you for a long time. He's waited for you for a long time, too. It might seem fast, but it's not. If you'd watched it from the sidelines, as I have, you'd agree. It's moved at a snail's pace." She was leaning against the table with her arms crossed. It was the stance she took when she wanted to be taken seriously. Used to talking with her hands, she kept them tucked under her armpits to prove she wasn't being dramatic.

"It doesn't seem fast," I said. "That's the thing. It's as if every moment has led up to this. Like … fate." I thought of the events that had brought me here: my first conference, my first interview, my first murder. If anyone would have told me five years ago that I'd be living in a Copper Bluff, teaching English, I wouldn't have believed them. Yet here I was.

"I've told you never to use the F word," said Claudia. "Relationships are work, and you're in a serious one."

I hung up my coat. "Maybe it's the near-death experience, but I think you're right. I think it's destiny."

"I said it was *work*, not destiny—what? What near-death experience?"

I refocused on our conversation. "It was nothing. I mean, it was something, but I'm fine. I was trapped in my garage with the engine running, but Mrs. Gunderson fired her shotgun to open the door and saved me. I was released from the hospital this morning."

Her shoulders softened. "Are you okay?"

I waved away her concern. "Perfectly fine. Better than fine. I feel like I'm on top of the world. Plus, my editor sent me a new cover that isn't entirely dreadful. Do you want to see?"

"Sure."

I opened my laptop. "Giles, I got a new cover. Do you want to see?" He was used to me communicating between our connecting door and answered in the affirmative. Though he hadn't seen the first covers, I'd told him all about them. I wanted him to see the progress I'd made.

"Hello, Claudia," he said when he entered. Both of them stood behind me as I opened the file, but I could smell his aftershave. It was old-fashioned and light. If I had to describe the smell of the English Department in two words, it would be Giles's aftershave and Pine-Sol.

I leaned back in my chair. "Here it is."

After a moment, Claudia said, "Wonderful!"

Giles said, "Very nice."

I turned to them with a smile. It was good to have friends who celebrated your successes, no matter how big or small. I could have hugged them both. "My editor said the book would come out in January of next year. I'll be officially published."

"I'll mention it at the celebration, if you don't mind," said Giles. "We'll celebrate Ms. Prather *and* Mr. Shakespeare tomorrow."

"Those are two names I never thought I'd hear in the same sentence," chuckled Claudia.

"That reminds me," I said, "is Andy feeling better? Will he be there?"

"Much better," said Giles. "He and Felix will both be at the party but are leaving immediately afterwards. I have to drive them to the airport."

"I would offer, but my car—" I stopped myself. No way was I telling Giles about last night. I didn't want him to worry for my safety. He had enough concerns, including getting our visiting scholars back home in one piece. "Anyway, I'm glad they're able to attend, though I'm sorry they had so much trouble."

"Trouble, for sure," said Giles, the lines on his forehead deepening. "Do you know he's thinking of suing the school?"

"For what?" said Claudia. "He was poisoned with antifreeze. It had nothing to do with Bluff View Restaurant or the university."

"Someone from the university tried to kill him, though," said Giles. "According to Felix, that's grounds for a personal lawsuit against the school."

"I'm calling Gene," said Claudia, grabbing her cellphone from her pocket. "He'll be able to tell me if Andy has a case." She checked the time. "After class. I have to go." She turned to me. "Call me if you need anything."

I nodded. "Thanks, Claudia."

Giles followed her out the door.

Chapter Thirty

—

A FTER LENNY WAS finished with his student conference, he took me to lunch downtown. We had chili-cheese dogs and crinkly fries at Harry's. He said he was glad the carbon monoxide hadn't affected my appetite. It hadn't. Like everything else, I just appreciated it more. The food tasted better, especially while I was sitting across from Lenny, and we ate and talked for two hours. Then we walked back to his car, enjoying the sunny day and warm afternoon air. Some of the stores had their front doors open to catch the fresh spring breeze. The Book Barn had two racks of discount books outside that we perused before moving on. The entrance to Petal's Place was adorned with trays of petunias. They looked like colorful window boxes framing the cute store.

Petal was inside, talking to a customer. Her love for her profession was written on her face, and I wondered if I looked that happy correcting comma splices. I kind of doubted it. She was as cheerful as the flowers that surrounded her. Roses, carnations, sunflowers … wait. *There was the plant.* It was identical to the one in Mia's living room window.

"Lenny," I said. "Look, it's Mia's plant."

He put his face closer to the window. "You're right. It has the same weird leaves."

"Let's go inside." I pulled open the door and walked over to the house plants. Their glossy foliage filled the corner. I inspected the tag on the plant identical to Mia's.

"That's an umbrella plant," said Petal, who'd finished with her customer. She was wearing the same heavy canvas apron, but today her pixie cut was disarranged. It reminded me of one of her spiky plants. "Super easy to care for and nice-sized. You won't find another one in Copper Bluff as big."

That got me thinking. It was big—big enough to disguise a small pot of pansies. What if whoever bought the plant stole the pansies at the same time? That way, no one would be able to trace the purchase to the person. We knew the pansies came from Petal's Place. Hers was the only store in Copper Bluff selling them. No way was someone walking out of the store with this plant, though. It was too big. "This is important, Petal. Have you sold any of these recently?"

"Yes," she said. "I saw the sale when I was typing up my reorder form."

"It's a big plant," said Lenny. "Do you remember who bought it?"

Petal thought for a moment. "I wish I could help you, but I can't. I didn't sell it." She tapped her pencil on the counter. "Let me get your number. When the girl who works for me comes in, I'll ask her if she knows."

"Any description might help," I said. "Even male or female."

I gave her my phone number, and she promised she'd let me know.

"What did you mean by 'male or female'?" said Lenny as we got into his car. "The plant's in Mia's house. Can't we assume one of them bought it?"

"Not necessarily," I said. "Jacob could have bought Mia the plant. You saw how uncomfortable he was the other night when you mentioned antifreeze. Denton could have, too, but

I have a harder time imagining him bringing them a gift. A plant might be his style, though. A touch awkward, if you know what I mean."

Lenny started the car. "Plus, it had to take some muscle to move Tanner's body into the garden. A guy would have an easier time."

Maybe or maybe not. Hailey and Mackenzie played sports for the university. I didn't doubt their ability to move a body, especially when the body couldn't fight back.

"It's easy enough to find out," said Lenny. "We can ask them who bought the plant."

"I don't want to spook the killer when we're this close," I said. "Even if Mia bought the plant, stole the pansies, and placed them on my porch, it doesn't prove she killed Tanner. We need proof. Then everything else will fall into place."

A group of students ran out of Harry's, laughing. We followed them with our eyes as the car idled. Oh, to be an undergraduate again, when drinking beer at three o'clock on a Thursday always seemed like a good idea.

"Giles said Andy was feeling better," I said. "We should be able to talk to him now about the night he was poisoned. Maybe he'll remember a detail that will point us to the murderer. Whoever attempted to kill him probably killed Tanner. The poison is the same."

"The hospital?" he said, putting his car in reverse.

I shook my head. "Giles said he was released. He'll be at Happy Rest Motel."

Happy Rest was the small motel on Birch Street where Andy was staying. Recently, a larger chain hotel had opened in Copper Bluff, but the lot was usually empty. The university liked to give visitors the *local* experience, I guessed, because most of them stayed here, in the blue rectangle perched on the corner.

The entrance was marked by a sign emblazoned with HAPPY REST, the words swinging in a hammock, and as we walked in, we were greeted with a hearty welcome by the desk clerk, who was a whirl of energy. We explained we were with the university and would like to talk to Andy, one of our guests. We asked for his room number.

"Sorry! I can't give that out, but if you hang on one teeny-weeny second, I'll give his room a ring and tell him you're here." Her plump cheeks were deeply dimpled, and her round face kept its smile as she punched the numbers on her phone. She pointed to the side table. "Help yourself to a cookie. I just put them out."

"Thank you," I said, meandering toward the sweets.

"We just ate," Lenny whispered.

"It's dessert," I said, selecting a chocolate chip cookie. "Life's too short to pass up free cookies."

"You have a point," said Lenny, grabbing an M&M cookie.

"He's coming!" said the desk clerk. "Be patient. The poor dear just got out of the hospital. Something he ate, I believe."

When Andy walked into the lobby, I was taken aback by his appearance. He was still well-groomed and smartly dressed. But the clothes hung off his frame, a size too big, and his skin was ashen against his blue-black hair.

"You're staring," Lenny murmured.

I blinked and threw my napkin in the garbage. "Hey, Andy. How are you feeling?"

"How do you think I feel?" he said, sitting down on one of the four chairs in the lobby. "Terrible. I can't wait to get out of here."

"I'm sorry," I said. We sat down. "I'm just glad we figured out what made you sick."

"*Em* figured it out," said Lenny.

Andy looked at me for a moment. "Thanks. I didn't realize."

"You're welcome." I folded my hands in my lap. "I know you don't feel well, so I'll be brief. Do you know how you ingested the antifreeze that night? Did anything at the banquet taste unusual?"

"The police asked me that, too," said Andy. "I had those rum and sodas. I started to feel sick after I drank them—and not from overindulging." He narrowed his eyes, perhaps remembering how Lenny and I assumed he'd drank too much.

"Did they taste normal?" asked Lenny.

"I think so," said Andy. "They came in a big glass. That was different. They're usually served in cocktail glasses."

"If the poison was poured in your drink, it would explain why no one else got sick," I said. "Plus, antifreeze is sweet, like rum and soda. You wouldn't be able to detect it."

"Why would anyone want to kill me?" said Andy.

I could name a couple reasons but kept them to myself. "Think back to that night. Did you recognize anyone? See anyone suspicious hanging around the bar?"

"I don't know anyone in town, except Tanner, and he's dead," said Andy.

"Maybe you know something about his death," said Lenny. "Something that could help us catch his killer."

"I don't know anything." Andy shook his head in exasperation. "I swear."

We needed to try a different tactic. I backed up the timeline. "By the time you reached Bluff View Restaurant, someone had already decided to kill you. Think about it. You ordered your drinks right away. Did you fight with anyone before Felix's keynote speech?"

He thought a moment. "No."

"How about during the speech?" I prodded.

"Just you two," he muttered.

"What do you mean?" said Lenny. "We didn't argue with you."

"You were mad at me, remember?" Andy said. "For dismissing Tanner as a hack."

I thought back to the conversation in the auditorium. It wasn't an argument. We had our opinions; Andy had his. Andy considered Tanner's research bogus. He said even undergraduates agreed. That gave me an idea. "You mentioned an undergraduate arguing with Tanner at the symposium the morning of his presentation. Did you get a good look at the person?"

"She had long dark hair, almost as dark as mine," said Andy. "She was cute."

Dark hair again! The problem was none of the suspects had dark hair.

"How do you know she was an undergrad?" said Lenny.

"I guess I don't," said Andy. "She just looked young."

"Was she tall, short, muscular?" Anything might help narrow down the person's identity.

"Average, I guess," said Andy. "I can't remember. I only remember her hair."

I pressed my fingertips to my temples. My head was starting to hurt. Every step forward brought with it a step backwards.

"You saw her, Emmeline," said Andy. "You should remember."

Black hair was on the skull left in the bathroom and on the flowers in Jacob's costume. If I'd seen anyone with moderately dark hair this week, besides Andy, I'd remember. "When?"

"She was the person who asked a question after your presentation," said Andy. "About murder."

"About murder …" I repeated. Now I remembered. She'd asked me why people committed murder. At the time, I thought it was a good question. We assumed only disturbed people committed murder, but from my experience, anyone was capable of the dark deed if they or someone they loved were threatened.

I closed my eyes, trying to remember her face. Like Andy, I recalled her hair. It was dark, coarse, and a bit frizzy. Most of her face was covered by her hair. She was seated, so I couldn't determine her stature. Plus, she was in the back row. I wouldn't have been able to see her well. She wasn't familiar to me. "I recall she had dark hair. Do you remember her, Lenny?"

He shook his head. "I remember the question. That's all."

I turned to Andy. "What about her argument with Tanner? What did she say? What did he say? Anything might be helpful."

Andy unbuttoned his jacket and leaned back. There was no concealing the discomfort he still felt from the antifreeze poisoning. Even the brush of his clothes seemed to bother him. "She called him a hack. He called her a psycho. Then he pulled at her hair." He tapped his knee, underscoring his last statement. "Pulling her hair—that was over the top. I wondered if Tanner had a violent temper. He could be pushy with girls."

"Em and I have wondered that too," said Lenny.

But I'd stopped listening when I heard the word *psycho*. It was the same word Tanner had used when he left Mia's house. Whoever killed him was inside the house that day. I'd bet my tulip bulbs on it. I needed to find a way into the house.

Chapter Thirty-One

———

"No way," was Lenny's answer when I told him about my plan to sneak into Mia's house that night. We were sitting at my kitchen table, eating the soup Mrs. Gunderson had brought me. Filled with chicken, vegetables, and homemade pasta, it was delicious.

I dunked a piece of French bread. "They'll be at the All-Star volleyball game. Remember? Hailey's receiving an award."

"Since when do you follow sports?"

"Since two of the suspects play them," I said, putting down my bread. "All I want to do is get in there and take a quick look around. I might be able to spot something that tells me who the killer is, handwriting, for instance."

From their separate chairs, Lenny and Dickinson stared. It felt like they were ganging up on me.

"We're professors," said Lenny. "We can't go sneaking into a student's house."

I knew what he said was true. But I also knew I had a duty to protect students from the killer. Life was precious and could be taken in an instant. I wasn't going to allow it to happen to one of them. "The murderer tried to kill me and Andy. I'm not going to let anyone else get hurt."

"Which is exactly why you should leave this to the police," said Lenny. "You just got out of the hospital. You promised Beamer you'd take care of yourself."

"We have to take care of the students, too. There has to be a way to do both." I stirred my soup, thinking of legal ways to get into the house—without the roommates watching my every move. Then it came to me. It was the end of the semester; the house was for rent. We could ask to see it tonight while they were at the game. I told Lenny, "Say you're the one looking to rent—so that you can be closer to me," I said. "Everyone knows I live down the street."

Lenny paused, his spoon in the air. "I'm not sure I'd want to be your neighbor."

"Very funny," I said, grabbing my purse. "I'm a great neighbor. Just ask Mrs. Gunderson." On my cellphone was a missed call and voicemail. I didn't recognize the number. I put the phone on the table and pressed the speaker button.

"Hi, Emmeline. This is Petal Petersen. Just talked to my employee, and she said a girl with black hair bought the plant. Probably college aged. Anyway, that's all I know. I hope it helps. Take care."

"Black hair, again!" I shut the phone app and opened the Internet, searching for the rental agency. "I'm putting it out of my mind, Lenny. I'm focusing on this agency, that house, and the facts." I pressed the number for the office. "Black hair doesn't fit."

"The fact is someone with black hair is involved in Tanner's murder," said Lenny. "You'd better get used to the idea, whether you like it or not."

I put my finger to my lips to quiet him. When the listing agent got on the line, I told him the situation. Lenny and I needed to see the house tonight. Could we meet at half-past seven? He agreed, and I clicked off the line.

"So, what if I end up liking the house?" said Lenny. "Do I have your permission to rent it? I like the idea of being closer to you."

"Believe me, you won't," I said, gathering our soup bowls, "like the house, I mean. I don't pass by that place without getting a chill. It's creepy." I gave him a smile. "But closer would be nice."

He pulled me onto his lap. "This close?"

I set down the bowls on the table. "That's pretty close."

He brushed my lips with his. I could feel the stubble of his five o'clock shadow.

"I like being here," he said.

"I like you being here."

Offended by the lack of attention, Dickinson jumped up on the table and meowed in our faces.

"I guess someone else likes your being here, too," I said with a laugh.

WHEN SEVEN THIRTY came, we were ready. I wore a hat to disguise my curls and limit neighborhood gossip. I didn't want it getting back to the students that I'd snooped in their house, even if it was for their own good, and I knew very well how neighbors talked. Especially with the nice weather, they were bound to be outside, soaking up the last warm rays of the day. If they didn't recognize me, it would mean one less chance for word to get back to the students. I was convinced one of them was the killer. Until I figured out who, I needed to be careful. I didn't want to draw attention to any of the other girls. I could take care of myself, but the girls weren't aware of the danger of their situation. As long as they remained ignorant, they were safe from retaliation.

The students across the street were playing Frisbee, but to my delight, they were also listening to music and drinking beer. They didn't notice Lenny and me walk up the front steps to meet the man from the rental agency, or if they did, they paid scant attention and went right back to their game.

"Hi, I'm Emmeline. We spoke on the phone." I stuck out my hand, and the agent shook it. "And this is Lenny. He's the one looking to rent."

"To be closer to my loved one," added Lenny, shaking the agent's hand.

I bit my lip to keep from laughing. Still, it was nice being called his loved one, even comically.

"Good to meet you both," said the agent, but all his attention was on his prospective renter. "I'm Roger." He opened the door with his key. "This beauty hasn't been available for three years. Grad students have been renting it, but a couple of them graduate in May. It'll go fast, so look carefully."

I glanced around the foyer. Were we looking at the same house? Even in the last hour of sunlight, the rooms were dark. The heavily curtained windows didn't help, nor did the fringed shades, which added another layer of darkness. The woodwork was dark walnut. Had the windows been open, it would have been tolerable. As it was, however, the air was stifling.

"A little messy," said Roger, "but what can you expect? They're college students, and they weren't expecting me to bring someone through tonight."

"Not a problem," I said, looking past the rumpled pillows and blankets on the floor. "We understand. The kitchen is this way?"

"Yep, straight through the dining area there," said Roger.

I hadn't realized it was a dining area. It was stuffed with a green reclining sofa and flat-screen TV. I squeezed through the doorway to the kitchen. I thought I might find a snippet of handwriting or something else that would confirm the killer lived in the house. Cereal boxes, noodle packages, paper plates—but no writing. I checked for a bulletin board, anywhere I might see uppercase writing. I shook my head at Lenny. It was time to head upstairs to the bedrooms.

"Would you mind showing me the furnace, water heater—

the electrical room?" Lenny asked Roger. "I'd like to check out the bones of the place."

"No problem," said Roger. "It's in the basement."

"I'm going to look upstairs," I said.

The wood on the staircase was beautiful, but the steps were covered in blue shag carpet that reached all four bedrooms. The doors were shut. I hesitated to open them. These were their private sanctuaries. I took a breath and opened the first door. What I was doing could save a life. If that meant seeing someone's underpants, so be it.

I didn't know enough about the students to identify whose room I was in. A twin mattress was on the floor, covered with a raggedy quilt. I peeked in the tiny closet and saw a picture of the volleyball team. It had to be Hailey's room. She also had a baseball bat. The Riverside Edition of Shakespeare was in there, too. That was interesting. From what she'd told me, she was into set design. I supposed anyone with a love of theater studied Shakespeare, though. I thumbed through the book, wondering if maybe I'd find a torn page like the one left in the garden. Nothing.

The next room was Mia's. I could tell from the posters on the wall, drawings of elaborate costumes labeled with their characters—Marie Antoinette, Lady Macbeth, and others. On her desk was a sketch pad and colored pencils. I opened the drawer. A worn leather journal was tucked inside. I paused, struggling with the ethics of reading someone else's private thoughts. I valued journaling too much to expose a writer, but these were extraordinary circumstances. I checked over my shoulder. Lenny and Roger were still downstairs. I opened it up.

What I found were pages and pages of Mia dealing with Tanner's death. The sadness, the guilt. At times, she said, she'd wished him dead. But why? I thumbed backwards. "That's why," I said out loud. Tanner had been abusive, mentally and—recently—physically. Small instances at first—tugging her hand, grabbing her arm—and then squeezing her shoulder and leaving a bruise. Every time he hurt her, she believed he was sorry. That their relationship would go back to normal after his research was finished and his part in *Hamlet* was over. She excused it as stress. He'd never treated Mackenzie this way when they'd dated. Why did he do it to her? Had she done something to provoke the behavior? She blamed herself.

I put the journal away. It was heartbreaking. It also gave her a motive for killing Tanner. But the writing was in cursive, not all-caps. Thomas said whoever wrote the sonnet habitually used all caps. He could be wrong. "I could be too," I said as I shut the door quietly behind me.

In the hallway, I opened the closet. Towels, toilet paper, flat irons, curling irons—I pushed them aside. I looked for anything with flowers on the labels: perfume, lotion, shampoo. If one of them had an affinity for flowers, I couldn't tell from their hygiene products.

Next to the closet was a laundry chute with an ornately carved door. At one time, the house might have been grand, maybe even the envy of the neighborhood. Laundry chutes were nifty ways to get clothes from one level to another. Theoretically, I could send something down to the basement right now, and Lenny would catch it. I probably shouldn't try. From the force required to yank open the door, the chute hadn't been used for some time.

I looked into the void in the wall. No metal, no plastic, just a dark wooden tunnel. I stuck my head in, tempted to call down to Lenny just for the fun of it. That's when I saw something dark in a crevice. I squinted, getting a closer look. Was it a dead animal? I reached out to touch it and jerked back, hitting my head. It was fuzzy, like an animal. I took a deep breath and tried again. It wasn't fur. It was … hair. I turned the black mass over in my hands. Of course, a wig! What an idiot I'd been. The woman with black hair was wearing a wig. That's why she didn't fit with my suspects. But which one of them wore it? I thought back to my presentation. It was impossible to know.

I took off my hat and slipped on the wig, stuffing my ponytail under the elastic cap. I wasn't completely successful, and it took several tries. I turned to the full-length hallway mirror. The transformation was startling. No wonder I didn't recognize any of them. I didn't recognize myself. The long black hair and blunt bangs disguised every feature. My skin looked pale, my eyes appeared darker, and my face seemed smaller, engulfed by hair.

"What are you doing in Mia's wig?"

I saw Alice reflected in the mirror. Dread coursed through my veins. I felt vulnerable, exposed, and embarrassed. There was no way other than the truth to explain what I was doing.

I pulled the wig off my head. "Is this Mia's? It's a fun way to try a new look."

"She needs it for the theater," said Alice. "You shouldn't have it on."

It made sense. The same hair was found in the skull and on the bouquet of flowers—both in the theater. I turned around and gave it to her.

"What are you doing here? What's going on?" She was trying to be polite. I was a professor and she was a good student. But she knew something was very wrong.

"Professor Jenkins is thinking about renting this house next year," I said. "We're here with the realtor. They're in the basement."

"So you decided to come up here and go through our things?" Alice said.

The confusion in her voice was clear, and I didn't know how to respond. Here was a student I liked, who'd enrolled in my class next semester, and she'd found me upstairs in her house with her friend's wig on. I had to tell her why. I couldn't allow her to think I was a creep. "Look, Alice, I'm going to be frank with you. I think you're in danger. I think Mia might have done something to Tanner, and she might do something to one of you. You need to be careful."

"Mia?" Alice shook her head. "No, Tanner was the one who hurt her. She would never hurt one of us."

"I understand how you feel, but you have to believe me," I said. "If she was being abused, it's all the more reason for her to strike out again."

"Why should I believe you?" Her brown eyes narrowed on me. "I've known Mia for almost three years."

She was smart and would listen to reason. I tried explaining. "I'm a good teacher. I care about my students. Ask anyone. I didn't mean any harm—just the opposite. I'm trying to protect you and your roommates."

She shifted her weight. "I know that's true. I just can't believe Mia would do anything to one of us."

"Maybe she wouldn't," I rushed to say. "But she's in a very dark place right now and has done some very disturbing things."

"You think she's disturbed?"

"I'm not a medical doctor," I said. "But if that's her wig, I think it's possible that she's struggling with mental illness and needs help. Did she ever see a counselor?"

She thought for a moment before answering. "I don't know."

I could hear Lenny and the agent discussing rental terms downstairs. They must have returned from the basement. I took a step toward the stairwell. "Please don't tell anyone I was here."

After wrestling with the request for a minute, she nodded, and I started down the steps.

"Professor Prather?"

I turned back.

"If he was abusing her, though, don't you think he had it coming?"

"Sorry, Alice. That's one question I can't answer."

Chapter Thirty-Two

—

W HEN WE GOT back to my house, I decided to call Sophie Barnes. She needed to know what I'd found. She'd told me before that she didn't have enough evidence for a search warrant. Tanner was found in Shakespeare's Garden, and nothing linked him back to the house. Now something did— the black wig.

"I can't believe Alice saw you with the wig on," said Lenny as he poured us each a cup of decaf. "You know that's going to get back to Giles, right?"

I dug my cellphone out of my purse. "I felt terrible. She didn't want to believe those things about her friend. I wouldn't either." I dialed Sophie's cell number; it was after eight, so she wouldn't be at the station. She answered right away.

"Hi, Sophie. It's Emmeline."

"Oh my gosh," said Sophie. "Are you okay? Beamer said you were in the hospital?"

"I'm fine," I assured her. "They kept me overnight for observation. That's all."

"I would've called if I'd known you'd been released," said Sophie. "What an ordeal."

"For sure," I said. "Listen, Sophie, I've been in Mia's house, and I found something."

"Please tell me you didn't break in."

"I didn't break in," I said.

"Thank goodness. I would have had to arrest you."

That gave me pause. Sophie used to be my student, but that didn't mean she would bend the rules—or the law—for me. "The house is for rent, and Lenny wanted to check it out."

"Mrs. Gunderson said you guys were getting close," said Sophie. "When I talked to her about the antifreeze, she said Lenny's at your house nearly every day. She thinks it's a good sign."

I glanced at Lenny, who was on the couch sipping his coffee and petting the cat. It was nice to know Mrs. Gunderson thought we were in a good place. "While we were at Mia's house, I found a black wig. Alice said it's Mia's. I think Mia killed Tanner."

"That would explain why we haven't been able to find this woman with black hair we keep hearing about, but why would Mia kill him? She seemed to really love him."

"I know, but I found a journal of hers that said he'd been abusive lately," I said. "She might have struck back."

"Striking back I could see," said Sophie. "That happens a lot in abusive relationships, a confrontation turning physical. But poisoning takes forethought, planning. Did you recognize the handwriting in the journal?"

I let out a breath, feeling a bit defeated. I'd told her Thomas's theory about the sonnet. We both thought the killer had sent a warning. "The entries were written in cursive, not all-caps."

"So anyone might have worn Mia's wig."

"I suppose. It came from the theater. Technically, it's not even Mia's." I was back at square one. Not exactly square one, because the wig belonged to someone in the house.

"Well, I'll run it by Beamer," said Sophie. "I don't know if it's enough, and I don't know if he'll like that you were poking around Mia's house. If she's the killer, you're in more danger than ever."

"Alice said she wouldn't mention I was there."

"And you trust her?" said Sophie.

"I guess," I said. "She's getting her TESOL degree."

"Boy, things have changed since I was a student."

Spoken like a true graduate. "Let me know," I said.

She promised she would before she ended the call.

I joined Lenny on the couch, and he handed me my cup of coffee. I was glad he was here. If Alice did tell Mia or anyone else, we could be in for a long night. Though I didn't mind being alone, it was nice having help close by if I needed it.

"So, I've decided not to rent the house on the corner," said Lenny.

I took a sip. "What was it? The shag carpet or the killer living upstairs?"

"Neither," said Lenny. "There are termites in the basement. The agent tried dismissing it as old wood."

"Gross," I said. "You know I love old houses, but that's one house that should be condemned. It's just spooky."

"Normally I wouldn't agree with you, but I do." He tapped his cup. "There's just something about that place that bugs me, and it's not the bugs."

"Do you think Mia poisoned him there, then dragged him to the garden?"

"No," said Lenny. "If his symptoms were the same as Andy's, he was probably poisoned earlier, at the bar." Lenny was quiet for a moment "Get this: both Andy and Tanner might have been poisoned at a bar."

"What are you saying?" I said, feeling excited. "Our killer is a bartender?"

"I don't know," said Lenny. "It could be the connection we're looking for."

"I wish I knew more about Mia and her roommates. I

have no idea where or if they work. You would think if they bartended at Harry's, though, we would have seen them. We eat there all the time."

"You know how it is. The place is a revolving door for grad students. And we eat Italian—a lot."

"True," I said. "Harry's doesn't open until eleven, but Bluff View serves breakfast." I grabbed my phone and opened my Clock app. "I'm setting my alarm. Let's grab breakfast before class. We can ask questions then."

Lenny blinked. "But I don't teach in the morning."

I gave him a grin. "The sacrifices we make for love."

THE NEXT DAY, we were out the door early. Bluff View was a short drive from town, and I wanted plenty of time to ask questions before my classes. Lenny wanted plenty of coffee. Dickinson had harassed him during the night, and he was dragging. I could tell by the shadows under his eyes. But I felt freshly motivated by having a new avenue to explore, and it was a gorgeous morning for a drive.

The sun shone over the prairie grass like a lamp over a book, revealing its secrets to the reader. After the long winter, the sun was a spectacle, a yellow star in the cornflower-blue day. It warmed the fields that would soon be filled with soybeans and corn. With Lenny at my side and the semester almost over, I couldn't think of a better way to start the spring day. Minus the murder investigation, of course. But even that was almost resolved. I'd narrowed down the suspects. Now I needed proof that my suspicions were correct.

Without the twinkling white lights, Bluff View Restaurant wasn't as pretty as it was in the evening. It looked older but sturdy, clinging to the rocky edge of the bluff—a testament to the staying power I associated with the Great Plains. Even when times were hard, as they often were, pioneers dug in their heels, making the once-barren fields provide sustenance. As I got out of the car, I looked around at the empty fields, sprinkled with stubble. If the pioneers could do all that, surely I could catch one little killer.

"Let me order first," said Lenny, holding open the restaurant door. "Once they bring the coffee, you're free to start your interrogation. Promise?"

"Promise," I said. The hostess greeted us with a smile, and I told her two for breakfast. She led us to a beautiful spot overlooking the bluff, handing out menus before she left.

I opened to the daily specials. "I was thinking about the wig last night and—"

Lenny glanced up from his menu. "Remember our deal."

Our deal was not questioning the staff. He didn't say anything about not discussing the wig or how tight it was on my head. After the Marie Antoinette fiasco, I was starting to worry about the size of my melon. It had to be my hair.

I focused on the menu, deciding on the Pioneer Pancakes. Topped with pecans and real maple syrup, they sounded delicious. I shut the menu, and Lenny did the same. I smiled at him, and he returned the smile.

"How did you sleep?" I asked. Though I knew the answer, I wanted to show him I could talk about something else besides murder.

"Like I was in the center ring of a three-ring circus," he muttered. "How about you?"

"Same," I said, "but I'm used to it."

When Hailey walked up to our table, I could have fainted. I was that surprised. Dressed in black pants and a white button-up dress shirt, she was obviously our waitress, which meant Lenny's theory could be right. Andy might have been poisoned by someone who worked here. Much to Lenny's delight, Hailey was carrying a coffee thermos. We both turned over our cups as she approached.

"Good morning," Hailey said. "Coffee?"

"Good morning, Hailey. Yes, thank you." I waited for her to pour Lenny's coffee before I asked my first question. Despite my excitement, I was determined to act normal—and allow Lenny another cup of coffee. "This is a beautiful view. Have you been working here a long time?"

"A couple of years," Hailey said. A customer signaled for assistance. "I'll be right back to take your order."

Staring out the window, Lenny took a long sip of his coffee. "It *is* a beautiful view. We should come here more often."

"Don't you know who that is?" I whispered.

"Of course I do." He glanced at me then back at the bluff. "If you pulled a gun out of your backpack right now, and said, 'This is a stickup,' I wouldn't be surprised. You look that suspicious."

I threw him a look, which he didn't catch, and turned to the window. Taking a deep breath, I relaxed my shoulders. I tried focusing on the rolling hills, greened by the rain and warmer temperatures of spring, and it started working. From this vantage point, I could see better, think better. It gave me the clarity I needed to solve Tanner's murder and maybe a little pioneer perseverance, too.

Hailey returned to our table, and I calmly ordered the pancakes. Lenny ordered the Big Bluff Breakfast, which included eggs, sausage, bacon, pancakes, and hash browns. Either he was really hungry or not as anxious as I was to solve this case.

"How was the volleyball game last night?" I asked as she tucked her pen in her order pad.

"Good," she said. "Were you there?"

I was relieved Alice hadn't told her I was in their house. I knew I could trust her. "No, I wanted to go but couldn't."

"How's Mia?" Lenny asked, refilling his coffee mug.

"As good as can be expected," said Hailey. Her tone was no-nonsense like her hair, pulled into a simple ponytail. "It'll be better once we graduate and move out."

"Did she ever talk to the counselor?" I asked. "I know you mentioned a brochure."

"That brochure wasn't for her." Her voice was harsher.

"Sorry," I said. "I didn't mean to upset you." Maybe the brochure was for Hailey, herself. She was a strong athlete and student. She might have a hard time admitting she needed help coping.

She shook her head. "No, I'm sorry. I just think people expect too much of Mia. She needs time, you know?"

"Exactly," said Lenny. "She's going to be fine. Anyway, can I ask you a question about something else? Some gossip I heard?"

Hailey grinned. "As long as it's not about me."

"Nah," said Lenny. "It's about one of the visiting professors on campus. Andy Wells?"

Lenny was getting good at this—too good. I felt envious of how easily he played it cool.

"That guy who got sick?" Hailey asked.

Lenny nodded. "I heard he was pretty drunk the night of the banquet. Was he?"

Two could play at this game. If he was bad cop, I could be good cop. "I heard it was tainted food. He had to go to the hospital."

"The guy can't hold his liquor," said Lenny. "That's all."

"Can you settle it for us?" I asked Hailey. "Were you working?"

"No, I only work early mornings, because of theater, but I heard about it." She lowered her voice. "Between you and me, management was freaking out. They called everyone into a meeting to make sure no one had violated any food-safety standards. They said the guy was drunk. I guess that was the case because we never heard anymore."

"I knew I was right," said Lenny. "I think she should buy breakfast. Don't you?"

She put up her hands. "I'll leave that for you two to decide."

Hailey disappeared to place our order.

"Well, this was a huge waste of time," I said. "She wasn't even working the night Andy was poisoned."

"Gee, thanks," said Lenny.

I grabbed his hand across the table. "I'm sorry. I didn't mean that. It's been a great morning. I could get used to having breakfast with you."

"Could you?" He studied my face.

"Of course. It's the most important meal of the day." Leave it to me to say something stupid like that, but Lenny just laughed and squeezed my hand tighter.

Chapter Thirty-Three

———

AN HOUR LATER, Lenny dropped me off at campus. He needed to grab a change of clothes before Shakespeare's birthday party, and I needed to teach class. I weaved my way through students rushing out of one building and piling into another. Like the air, their chatter was crisp. The end of the semester was near, and the energy was almost palpable. Soon the campus would be a ghost town, a dream at the center of Copper Bluff. The students would disappear, and the days would grow humid and sleepy. I loved those days; they were perfect for reading.

I was thinking about my growing to-read pile when I noticed Mia bent down at the gate of Shakespeare's Garden. She was placing a red rose on the heap of gifts and mementos outside the garden. I slowed my pace, watching her read some of the notes. A single tear fell from her face onto a slip of paper.

"Hi, Mia," I said.

She started at the sound of my voice.

"I'm sorry," I said. "I didn't mean to interrupt you."

She brushed away the tear. "You didn't."

"How are you doing?"

"I'm okay." She stood slowly. "They say it gets easier, but I don't see how. I can't believe I'll never see him again."

"Tanner was full of life," I said. "Nothing will fill that void, but time will ease the pain."

"Have you ever lost someone close to you?" she said.

"I lost a student two years ago," I said. "It was hard to go into the classroom for a while. I kept seeing his face."

A student whizzed by on a bike, and we stepped off the path.

"I wished I could have done something to prevent it." I shook my head. "I still blame myself."

"It's good to hear you say that," said Mia, brushing back a piece of her long blonde hair. "I mean, it's not *good*, but I thought I was the only one. I blame myself, too."

"Alice said Tanner was abusive." I wondered how much I could or should say. I knew victims often blamed themselves instead of the abusers. I wanted Mia to know she wasn't at fault, but I didn't want to tell her I'd read her journal.

"I love Alice, I really do, but that's her own history talking. She was abused by her father. That's how she got the scar on her face."

No wonder Alice recognized the red flags. She'd suffered abuse herself.

Mia cleared her throat and continued, "Tanner had become physical lately, that's true, but he never hit me. He'd hit the wall or throw a book. He was under a lot of stress."

"He never hurt you?" I clarified.

"He squeezed my arm once, left a bruise."

That sounded like abuse to me.

"I know what you're thinking," she said, glancing at me. "But he was passionate—like lots of people in the theater. They have a hard time dealing with their emotions."

I had friends in the arts, and none of them were abusive. That was simply an excuse for Tanner's growing anger issues. But I didn't want to argue with her. For the first time, it felt as if she was opening up. If she wouldn't talk to a counselor, at least she would talk to me. I didn't want to scare her away now by pushing. "At one o'clock, there's a party for Shakespeare's birthday at Harmony Music Museum. Are you coming?"

She shook her head.

"Why not?" I prodded. "There will be snacks."

She smiled. "It's not that I don't want to go. I have to work. Professor Schwartz has me on the schedule until finals."

"You've been working at the theater all semester?"

"Every afternoon, no exceptions," she said, in a startling accurate imitation of Schwartz's voice.

My heartbeat quickened at the revelation. She had access to the skull from Hamlet, Jacob's Hamlet costume, and the black wig. She was in the theater every afternoon, which provided her access. But it also provided her with something else: an alibi. Mia couldn't have been home the afternoon Tanner called her "psycho." That meant the psycho he was talking about wasn't Mia. It was someone else in the house, and I'd bet it was the woman in the wig. That's why he grabbed her hair at the symposium; he was trying to tear off the wig and expose her. "Luckily for you, Schwartz will be at the celebration, so he won't be working," I said. "It's the last chance to see Shakespeare's First Folio. You won't want to miss it."

"If you're sure it'll be okay …."

"Positive," I said. "I'll tell him I gave you permission, if you want."

"I guess I'll see you there, then."

"I'm looking forward to it." I continued briskly toward Stanton Hall so I wouldn't be late for class. Distracted, I nearly ran into a student as I pulled open the door. I mumbled an apology, but I couldn't keep my mind off the new information: Mia wasn't the psycho, which meant she wasn't the killer. So, who was?

As I began class, my mind was still whirring with possibilities, and none of them had to do with my composition course. Actually, one of them did relate, but not directly. Our final essay was the research paper, and today we were going over logical fallacies—faulty logic. We were completing a worksheet as a class, and a student was reading over relevance fallacies when a line tripped the thought.

"Wait," I said. "Could you read that again, please?"

The student nodded and read the line slowly. "Absence of evidence is not evidence of absence."

"Absence of evidence is not evidence of absence," I repeated. I thought back to the banquet. Though I didn't have evidence, one person was not absent. One person, and one person alone had a very good reason for being there. She also had a reason for killing Tanner and poisoning Andy.

The class responded to my enthusiasm with deadpan stares. I checked the clock. "Finish the worksheet at home and return it on Monday. Shakespeare's birthday party starts in fifteen minutes. I hope to see you there."

As they packed up early, their moods improved greatly. So did mine. I knew who the killer was, and I was about to prove it. I pulled out my phone and called Sophie, describing my plan as I hurried down the stairs. She promised to meet me at Harmony. I wanted to test my theory, and if there was anything I was good at, it was tests. This one would prove once and for all who killed Tanner, poisoned Andy, and tried to kill me.

Racing into the museum, I paused briefly at the folio. Shakespeare was at the center of the story. Tanner had been determined to expose him as a fake. Tanner also attempted to reveal the identity of the woman in the wig, but she deftly dodged him. She wouldn't dodge me, for I knew how cunning she was, how crafty, and how dangerous. She'd managed to deceive me more than anyone, and I felt a trickle of what Tanner felt as he revealed the identity of Shakespeare. Betrayed and angry, I was determined to put her in jail.

A sign pointed the way to the location of Shakespeare's birthday party, the large lecture hall on the first floor. Instead of auditorium seating, there were benches—rows and rows of them. Felix, Andy, Reed, and Giles were at a table near the podium. On the table was a huge cake topped with a bust of Shakespeare, and behind it, a white board with markers. *Perfect.*

I made my way toward the group, excusing myself as I zigzagged through the crowd just starting to form. "Andy, glad to see you're feeling better. Hi, Felix. Giles, I need to talk to you."

"Of course." Giles turned to Felix, Andy, and Reed. "Excuse me."

When we were a few steps away, I told him my plan. For it to work, I needed to make a slight room alteration and introduce our guests. Sophie would be here soon, so no one would be in danger.

"I don't see what that would hurt," said Giles. "I'll have Reed cut the cake instead of introduce our guests."

Never mind protocol, did he realize I'd found the killer? I asked him.

"Of course you did," said Giles. "I have the utmost confidence in your abilities. I can't tell you how much it means to me, personally." Bowing slightly, he added, "Thank you."

Leaving me humbled and proud, he returned to the table. While the crowd gathered, I put the suspect to the test. She didn't disappoint. Then I joined the four men behind the table.

Chapter Thirty-Four

GILES THANKED EVERYONE for coming to the celebration. "April twenty-third," he said, "is an important day for Shakespeare scholars. It's the day we celebrate the life and the death of the author whose work is on exhibit downstairs. Regardless of the mysteries that remain concerning the author himself, the work he left behind has stood the test of time. His sonnets are still read, his plays still produced, and his life still celebrated, because audiences connect with his words even today. Scholars pass stories from one generation to the next. We are stewards of information and must do our jobs with care."

He glanced at me. I was ready.

"I know Professor Prather will take good care to introduce our distinguished guests, who are sadly leaving today," he said. "Please give her your full attention."

I stood and walked to the podium, glad I'd worn my red heels. I didn't have to adjust the microphone. "Thank you, Professor Giles, and thanks to all of you for coming." Seated on the third bench, Lenny gave me a thumbs-up. In front of him were Mia and her roommates. Next to Mia was Jacob, and a few rows back was Denton. Sophie and Beamer stood at the double doors.

"Professor Giles said it best," I continued. "We're stewards of knowledge, and when it comes to Shakespeare, no one is more knowledgeable than Felix Lewis. He's dedicated his life to the author's work—studying at Oxford, writing books, mentoring new scholars." I motioned to his understudy, Andy. "With his stellar reputation, it might be hard to understand why I thought he was capable of killing Tanner Sparks." A murmur rippled through the room, and I moved closer to the microphone. "It was these very reasons that made me believe it was possible. He has dedicated his life to an author Tanner Sparks dismissed as a phony. Many of you were angry. Imagine being Felix Lewis."

"Rubbish," said Felix. "I was angry at Reed, here, for allowing it. He didn't give the boy good advice."

I ignored the interruption. "Andy, also, devoted a book to the great bard. With its release pending this fall, he had to dismiss Tanner's scholarship as slipshod or suffer a worse fate himself: seeing his book poorly received."

"My book's already been well received," huffed Andy. "Read the reviews!"

I quelled his fears with a wave of my hand. "It was *possible* they killed Tanner. They submitted sonnets, they argued with Tanner—Andy even studied with him as an undergrad. But they didn't kill him. How do I know this?"

"Let me guess," said Jane Lemort, seated in the front row. "You're going to tell us."

"The woman in the wig told me," I said.

"I've read that!" said Kat, a student from my Crimes and Passions course last semester.

"You're thinking of *The Woman in the Window*," I whispered. "But let us continue. Several times in the course of the investigation, black hair has been mentioned or left behind. Andy himself noticed a woman with black hair—which is why she tried to eliminate him. Tanner, too, knew her identity. He tried to expose her at the symposium by pulling off her wig."

"Who was she?" asked Mia.

"For a long time, I thought it was you."

"What?" said Mia. "Why?"

I motioned to Alexander Schwartz, who was leaning against the wall. "It was Professor Schwartz who told me the person who'd left the skull in the bathroom had intimate knowledge of the theater. He or she was familiar with the tunnel that ran under the stage. You yourself mentioned working at the theater every afternoon, and I knew the killer and the woman were one in the same."

"I don't know what you're talking about," said Mia. "I didn't kill Tanner!"

"I know you didn't," I said. "I know Jacob and Denton didn't either." Jacob was slumped low in his chair, trying to look casual. Denton adjusted his glasses, interested in what I had to say. "While Jacob had access to and knowledge of the theater, he himself was a victim. I knew by his dismal performance Friday night he hadn't left the flowers for himself."

"Gee, thanks," Jacob said.

"You're welcome." I nodded at Denton. "And while Mr. Smart is smart enough to get away with murder, he, too, was a victim. His acceptance into the summer research program was put on hold, which was enough for him to put away the de Vere theory for good. He took no further interest in it."

"So then who?" said Claudia. Sitting next to Lenny, she was growing impatient.

"I was left with the girls down the street: Mia, Hailey, Alice, and Mackenzie."

"Wait," said Mia. "You said it wasn't me."

I shook my head. "You had motive to kill Tanner. Plus, you were closest to him. Poisoning him would have been easy for you. But you're right. You didn't do it. One of your friends wanted me to think you did, though."

Mia leaned back from the group.

"I saw Tanner as he was leaving your house one day," I continued. "He said 'That girl is psycho.' I assumed he meant you, but later I realized that couldn't have been. You were working for Professor Schwartz that afternoon. So it must have been one of your roommates, the same one he tried to expose at the symposium."

Mia blinked back tears, shaking her head. "No, they didn't. They couldn't have."

"They could, and one did." I ticked off the possibilities from my mental list. "Hailey is the strongest and the most familiar with the theater. Plus, she works at Bluff View, the restaurant where Andy was poisoned. Mackenzie dated Tanner and knew him better than the others. As a musician, she also had unlimited access to the theater. Alice was the youngest, but smartest, and had her own reasons for hating Tanner."

"Which one was it?" said Mia.

I stepped to the side, directing everyone's attention to the whiteboard. "See for yourself." In black, all-capital letters, it read HAPPY BIRTHDAY, SHAKESPEARE!

"It's the writing," gasped Claudia. "The uppercase writing from the sonnet."

"I was right," said Thomas Cook, who was at Lenny's other side.

"Correct and correct again," I said. "Minutes before we began, I asked one of the girls to write the message on the board. She quickly obliged, revealing her identity as the sonnet writer with the stroke of her hurried hand."

Slowly, like raindrops, the clapping began. It became stronger and stronger until everyone was staring at Alice, who was applauding me. She stood and tipped a pretend hat. Her hair might be a beautiful shade, but it was also very short, short enough to wear the wig and cover her scar.

"I think you should sit down," I said.

"And not defend myself?" Alice shook her head. "You tricked me, Professor."

"No, Alice, you tricked me." I could hear the anger in my own voice. "At every turn. you left clues pointing to Mia: the bouquet, the skull, the wig. *She* was the victim. How could you do that to your friend?"

"I needed to teach her a lesson," said Alice. "She wouldn't listen to me. I told her that Tanner was abusive. One day he'd go too far, and she'd be left with a face like mine. What theater would take her then?"

"I knew that scar bothered you!" said Hailey. "That's why I left the health services brochure on the table. I wanted you to talk to someone about it."

"It doesn't bother me," said Alice. "It's proof of what I've been through, a boot spur to the face." She turned to Mia. "You should be grateful."

"For your attempts to send me to jail?" said Mia.

"A jail cell is better than a casket, isn't it?" said Alice. "That's what happened to my mother. She was a funeral director. My dad made sure she got to try one out for herself."

"*That's* how you know so much about flowers," I said.

"Yes, my mom knew the perfect flower for every occasion," said Alice. "Hers was the most beautiful funeral of all, and she never got to see it. Isn't that ironic, Professor Prather? I bet I used the term correctly. You're not the only smart person in the English Department."

"Yes, Alice, you're very smart." I knew what she wanted to hear, and I was about to tell her. "Share with me how you did it."

Alice smiled at the compliment. "Hailey or Mackenzie might have done it."

"No, they're not nearly as clever as you," I said, continuing with the charade. "This murder was a work of art."

She let out a hiss of air. "I knew you'd think so, and I wanted to impress you. I hoped we'd talk about it in class next semester."

"And we will," I said. "But I need to know how. You've stumped me."

She stared at me like I was the only person in the room, the crowd fading into the pale-green walls. The look sent me off-kilter, and I glanced at Lenny to steady myself before turning my attention back to Alice.

"I put the antifreeze in his bottle of soda after the performance," explained Alice. "He drank it down in a few swigs. When he started getting sick, I knew it was working and followed him home. He only made it halfway across campus before he had to stop in the garden, which was open for Friday's event. He passed out on the bench."

It made sense now. No one carried him to the bench; he walked there himself.

"I wasn't going to miss *that* opportunity," said Alice. "So later, when I knew he was dead, I brought back the liquid and poured it in his ear. The disgusting pig had fallen over, and I had to touch him, but it was worth it. I knew you'd pick up on the scene from *Hamlet* right away."

"Bravo," I said. "A-plus work."

"It would have been—if Andy hadn't recognized me from the conference." She shoved her hands in her pockets. "When he told you about me at Felix's keynote speech, I knew I had to act, but there wasn't much time. I was rushed. I didn't put enough antifreeze in his drinks." She took her hands out of her pockets and pounded her fists into her thighs. "Stupid, stupid. I ruined all my plans."

"Don't blame yourself." I tried to calm her down as Beamer approached with handcuffs. "It was the alcohol that lessened its efficacy. Besides, I knew it was you already."

"You did?" Alice looked almost relieved.

"First, there was the sonnet, written in perfect iambic pentameter," I said. "Not easily done outside the English Department. Then there were my missing keys. Who else but someone in the department would know my penchant for late-night walks? Finally, if Andy was poisoned at the English banquet, which I surmised, you were the only one on the guest list." I shook my head. "I felt foolish for not thinking of that earlier."

"What about the plant?" said Lenny. "Don't forget that."

"Right," I said. "I also knew you purchased the plant. Your roommates are graduating; you're not. They wouldn't purchase a giant houseplant before moving. You did it for one reason: to cover up another purchase you made—a pot of pansies."

She dug in her heels as Beamer put on the cuffs. Her sneakers squeaked on the floor as he tried to move her. "I wish you'd died there in your garage. If it wasn't for that crazy neighbor of yours, you'd be dead right now, and I'd be free."

A woman wearing pink lipstick stood up in the back row. "I'd mind my manners if I were you, missy. You're the one in handcuffs."

I squinted. "Mrs. Gunderson, is that you?"

"Of course it is, dear," she said. "At my age, I don't miss a chance for free cake."

Epilogue

━━

Back at my house, I started tidying up. Alice was going to jail, and I was safe. That meant Lenny would be collecting his things, the remnants of our last few days together. I sighed as I picked up a sweatshirt he'd left on the couch. I brought it to my face and inhaled. If the wind had a scent, this was it. I'd miss having him around. His voice, his laughter, his kindness. Dickinson jumped on the back of the couch. She'd miss him too.

Hearing a knock at the screen door, I turned around. Like magic, it was Lenny. In a poof, he'd arrived just as I was thinking of him. I tossed the sweatshirt over my shoulder, and it landed on Dickinson. I knew because she uttered a meow.

I opened the door.

"Come in," I said.

Once inside the porch, he produced a single red rose from behind his back. "I know how much you like flowers. I didn't want Tanner's death to change that."

"It's beautiful," I said. "Thank you." I brought the flower to my nose, closed my eyes, and inhaled. When I opened my eyes, I noticed something gold in the middle of the petals. My eyes flew to Lenny's.

"Go ahead," he said. "Look."

Inside the rose was a diamond ring. My hand trembled as I retrieved it from the petals. A thin gold band, a bright white diamond—it could only mean one thing. My breath caught in my throat.

"I'm going to say this before I lose my nerve," said Lenny. "I wish I could be like those guys you read about in your romance novels, but I'm not. I'm just a guy who loves you." He took the ring and slid it on my fourth finger. "I've loved you for a long time, and I have to know, do you love me?"

Tears flooded my eyes. "Yes, I love you."

He took a breath. "Will you marry me?"

He was my best friend, my soul mate, my partner-in-crime. No matter what we did or where we went, if I said yes, we would always be together. "Yes."

"Thank god." He tipped my chin and kissed me tenderly. Then we embraced, the tears from my eyes wetting his shirt. When we parted, I still had the rose in my hand, and he had something else in his.

"What's that?"

Smiling, he handed me the paper. "Our honeymoon reservation."

I squinted to read the small font. "Wait, this can't be right. Saint Émilion." I looked up. "That's in France."

"Happy wedding day, Em. You're going to France."

Julie Prairie Photography

MARY ANGELA IS the author of the Professor Prather academic mystery series, which has been called "enjoyable" and "clever" by *Publishers Weekly*. She is also an educator and has taught English and humanities at South Dakota's public and private universities for over ten years. When Mary isn't writing or teaching, she enjoys reading, traveling, and spending time with her family.

For more information about Mary or the series, go to MaryAngelaBooks.com.

CPSIA information can be obtained
at www.ICGtesting.com
Printed in the USA
FSHW010548051119
63774FS